DAWN OF LEGACY

THE MONSTERS AND MEN TRILOGY
BOOK THREE

LAWRENCE DAVIS

DAWN OF LEGACY published by:

WILDBLUE PRESS
P.O. Box 102440
Denver, Colorado 80250

Publisher Disclaimer: Any opinions, statements of fact or fiction, descriptions, dialogue, and citations found in this book were provided by the author and are solely those of the author. The publisher makes no claim as to their veracity or accuracy and assumes no liability for the content.

Copyright 2023 by Lawrence Davis

All rights reserved. No part of this book may be reproduced in any form or by any means without the prior written consent of the Publisher, excepting brief quotes used in reviews.

WILDBLUE PRESS is registered at the U.S. Patent and Trademark Offices.

ISBN 978-1-960332-11-0 Trade Paperback
ISBN 978-1-960332-13-4 eBook
ISBN 978-1-960332-12-7 Hardback

Cover design © 2023 WildBlue Press. All rights reserved.
Interior Formatting and Cover Design by Elijah Toten
www.totencreative.com

This Book is dedicated to my son, Cash Patrick Davis.

They do not make words impactful enough to describe my love for you, but I'll spend a lifetime trying to write them. Thank you for bringing such joy to your mother and me.

"Fuck the Balance."

It was hard to pretend that that didn't tickle me, though I did try to keep up appearances. All of us still looked like we'd been put through a meat grinder, and I was happy to hear that I would walk mostly right again and was even eyeballing a full recovery. After getting a few pictures of Max and some more home-cooked food, I actually felt pretty good.

I was at peace with what had happened, what we as a group had taken on and defeated. I knew I could survive another few months of this, but even more than getting out, what I looked forward to most was getting back to work.

I was so preoccupied that I didn't think anything of the chill that settled over the visitor block of the jail. Instead, I gave each person a goodbye hug and sat down again, quietly eating my cookies and falling out of touch with the present. I'm big on daydreaming, especially when I'm relaxed, and with a bellyful of cookies fresh off a shot of morphine from the med-bay, I was feeling pretty zen.

Suddenly, my spine stiffened, and my heart sped up, and I was instantly upright. There was a suffocating presence of pure awful, and something across the room caught my eye; my sixth sense was howling an inaudible warning, sending every hair on my body to attention.

It was Her.

CHAPTER 1

Imprison the Body—Free the Mind

... Her.

    I tried to grab onto any semblance of reality that I could, but it slipped through my fingertips as I tumbled into a multi-dimensional freefall. The landscape shifted in an instant, and I had a vague recollection of making eye contact with a portly, nervous guy with thinning black hair and dodgy eyes. And then he was gone.
    I had been transported.
    I was staring at *Her*, the living darkness that had been at the center of the hellscape that had been my life for the last two years. The scene was a place that I did not recognize. It was surreal and served as the backdrop for what I could only assume was either a figment of my addled imagination or an unthinkable trip to another dimension. The terrain was alive with violence and motion, and in the blurring myriad were thousands of faces, emblems, weapons, and exchanges. Each of them setting off a spark of memory: a quick and abrupt eruption of recollection that fizzled out as quickly as it came. It was daunting to try to hold on to any of these images, and by the time the totality of it felt ready to blanket me, I found that I couldn't settle on a single one.
    But I did remember Her.
    When I looked at this iteration of her, it was different. She was more human somehow. Maybe human wasn't the right word exactly, but human-esque? I guess in order to understand the

difference in seeing her now, I would have to describe what the experience was like during past encounters, which was impossible really. It was like trying to define an *anti*-frequency or the pull of a black hole. When this dark creature from the Abyss locked eyes on you, you felt a dread in the deepest parts of your mind. That dread dug deeper into an even deeper, primordial place like your soul.

This time I could still identify that powerful, alien evil but it didn't actively take from me as it had before. The image she presented in this form had something familiar, and even relatable to it. I watched as her fist twisted in contempt with a palpable, taunting rage that hinted at the darkness I knew as her trademark. What shocked me this time was that I could see beneath the rage to the pain that drove it: a void of sadness and inconsolable loss.

Not only was it written all over her, but I abruptly realized … It was aimed at me.

A version of me.

I occupied a body I didn't identify with, and I was surrounded by things that felt familiar, but I couldn't place any of it. Like trying to grab smoke, true understanding danced just outside my reach. She and I were at odds, and it felt as if we were fighting over something powerful; powerful, and deeply personal. Whatever this was, it had the stink of the kind of conflict that inevitably turned into a vendetta. Something as personal as it was powerful.

The kind of thing that begets disaster and tragedy with equal regularity.

The still-frame stirred back into motion, and those fire-wrought, visceral eyes narrowed and turned on me. They hit me like a battering ram to the chest, and all at once the swell of a storming battle was a savage soundtrack fully immersing me in the scene I'd been transported to. Her scream was piercing, and it had a physical impact on me. I distantly felt myself recoil in terror and then lurch into a fighting stance.

I gulped down a mouthful of air as my awareness abruptly returned to the present.

My wide-eyed expression normally won a lot of people over, but it seemed that during my little excursion into that other dimension my body had remained here, and I must have created quite a spectacle of myself. I was still in the visitor's lounge, and both the guards and my friends were looking at me with fear and worry dripping all over their faces. Whatever had happened here in this room during my "absence" obviously freaked everyone out—which was an easy read judging by their confused worried expressions. My friends were refusing to leave until they knew I was ok, but they were being ushered out by the guards and were torn with the awareness that any resistance might harm my standing here, but their concern was as visible as their hesitance.

I felt like I was coming down off of a tornado, and the fact that I'd been thrown into movements that I could only vaguely recall brought me to an easy surrender as the guards got within arm's reach. I was surprised at how kind and gentle they behaved; in fact, the one who looked like he'd shared some kind of lineage with a golden retriever even had the decency to shoot me a reassuring smile as he ushered me away from my friends.

To say I was shaken would have been an understatement. When you danced between two worlds like I did, you not only had to immediately assume a worst case scenario, but you had the proverbial two sides of the coin to pick from.

Meaning that since I was such a stellar custodian of my own well-being, both my professional and personal life were currently in shambles. Either I was starting to show even more severe consequences from the regular concussions I managed to acquire (outside of the near constant ringing in my ears) or I just had a genuine vision. It felt like my already questionable grasp on this rollercoaster of madness which had been my life of late was starting to slip. An idea that I found particularly perplexing given that my current understanding of all that was happening already felt bizarre and disjointed on its best day.

I gritted my teeth, assured the guards that I was just having a minor episode of epilepsy that hadn't been diagnosed, and shuffled back into the line that housed the rest of the inmates being herded out of the visitor's lounge. I tried to convey some sense of confidence to my group of uneasy friends in the form of a fast smile, even mockingly shaking my head and firing off a slightly embarrassed expression at what had happened. Most of them bought it without much of a second thought, though Kaycee hit me with a withering stare while gnawing thoughtfully on the edge of one of the cookies I'd left sitting on the table. I knew that look well enough to know that it was going to be the subject of a talk the next time we met, and I was happy to avoid it for now.

I had a lot to think about, and luckily …

I had nothing but time.

***

There's something quietly comforting about the repetitive existence that comes with incarceration. Routine as rigorous as this tapers the decision-making matrix down to almost nothing, so you basically get to spend the day just thinking—syrup-slow molasses type thinking.

And I did have a lot to think about.

With good behavior, my nine month sentence had the potential to be kicked down to six, and with prison overpopulation being such a big thing, which was a real possibility. These long spells of thoughtfulness helped me keep my mouth shut, which in turn kept me out of trouble, which could also help get me literally out.

Seemed like the possibility of an early release was looking pretty good, even if the threat of death by boredom was an equally distinct possibility.

My mind wandered to the problems with the prison-industrial complex as I eyed the steely bars that kept me caged. I wasn't the guy to take on the monumental task of fixing the prison-for-profit industry, I had my own evil organization hellbent on the enslavement of mankind to contend with. Plus, even with a gun to my head I couldn't tell you the difference between Congress and the Senate, so I probably wasn't the guy to tackle this kind of thing. There was also the fact that a guy like me had to keep it a special kind of simple. Where I came from, being concise and the farthest thing from cryptic was the only way you could communicate effectively. Even a notorious blabbermouth like me was full of straightforwardness and candor when compared to the political landscape.

Cleveland was a tough city; its people had a code and even the worst of them were principled in their own way. I suspected that this code was born from the grit of the town itself. Anyone in this city worth their salt worked for a living; it was an ethic that people were proud of—even if it lacked glitz and glam.

I took to prison life better than I'd care to admit and by month five I had the lay of the land down cold. Counting down the days until I could get out of here became a daily obsession and reminded me why I needed to keep my shit together and not mess up in the final stretch. I doubled down on my studies so that I could actually understand the stuff I kept scribbling on every tool, weapon, and accessory I could get my hands on. I'd been enhancing the equipment outside of my time with Zachariah with what could be called Shotgun Artificer. It was effective work but still left a lot to be desired and lacked the finesse and nuisance of the higher tiered stuff I'd seen my mentor fashion so seamlessly. Volunteering for details got me out of my cell often enough, but the best work went to the old timers or people better connected.

Prison isn't how you think it is either: my cell door was usually open and fed into a large space connecting all of our individual units that served as a common area. Our red jumpsuits were a constant reminder of where we were (not that we needed it) ... of course everything in the place was designed to do that. There was a litany of alliances here that kept the whole thing running smoothly.

Like all chaos, it can't help but fall into some order on a long enough timeline; prisoners, guards, gangs and the like connected with each other, creating a streamlined hierarchy that even included a type of currency that ultimately dictates what happens. The masters of those systems are the real players in this place. The behavioral patterns are easy enough to catch on to if you realize it's no different from a school yard or an office.

This is America after all.

My grin was cut short when my eyes caught activity in the main hallway. I'm not overly magical myself which is why I'm an Artificer and not something sexy and much more useful like a Warlock, but I can feel when something bad is nearby. You swim in these waters long enough you get a feel for the current. Magic of any kind has an atmosphere about it. Put that together with my background and you've got someone with dead-on intuition and a sixth sense refined by hard-won trial-and-error. I sensed something I didn't like in the air, and that stopped my inner contemplation cold.

Three new people rolled in, and I immediately knew there was going to be a problem. To the average human eye, they wouldn't have seemed out of place; wouldn't even have warranted a second thought.

But I knew better.

Ghouls had a kind of ashen quality to their skin, and while it isn't so alien as to be alarming to a casual observer, there's definitely a sickly tone to it. That's not the tell though. It's their eyes: beady and alive with a kind of static, rabid energy. See, they profiled like addicts but lacked that glossed over, dead-eyed look. Sure, you could argue that somebody needing a fix had a fidgety, higher-octane quality to them but the fixation, the compulsion driving it was much different than the predatorial-edge in the eyes of an undead.

They're gangly, which helps sell their unassuming stature and none of them are particularly tall—nothing remarkable or even noteworthy about any of them individually.

It's the slightly stilted gait and the pack mentality that's the tip-off. That wretched feeling that took hold in the pit of my stomach was all the confirmation I needed. Most would think that it's just three junkies with some kind of hepatitis that's turned into a kind of off-brand jaundice, but I knew better. They cackled like the hyenas they are, and moved with the confidence you'd expect out of an apex predator. An assuredness not normally seen from people who profiled like them, and especially not here. Most of all, they seemed happy to be here. None of that boded well for any of us...and I had the sinking suspicion it was especially not good for me.

Now I don't want to sound blasé about awful things that go bump in the night, but like anything else in life, there is an order to just how frightening these things could be. A ghoul was problematic because they tended to be stronger and much more durable than a big-bodied fighter, but they were sluggish too, and couldn't be credited with an overabundance of intelligence. Sharks were scarier until you drug one on land, then they were just another fish out of water.

But jump in the ocean, watch the way they swim, and suddenly you'll see why they predated humankind by a few million millennia.

Usually in an alleyway with all my gear on I could handle all three of them: space to move would buy me time for a little improvising and then I could hit them with some firepower before shooting off a catch phrase and striking a pose. I'm not saying I would get cocky, but it could be done, and I certainly would feel good about my odds. Here in this cell? With very little room to maneuver, none of my gear, and even just one of these vicious single-minded killers coming at me—I was toast. Three of them were just the kind of overkill that belonged in one of those gore-porn horror flicks that were so wildly popular a few years back.

Another excellent glimpse into our psyche as a people...but I digress.

The "maybe they aren't here for me" idea didn't even bother trying to make a purchase in my mind, I was too seasoned for that kind of shit. Optimism isn't really my cup of tea anyway and given how idyllic my whole prison sentence had been up to this point I should have seen something like this coming. In my head I try to do the math on how this could go down, and while I was no mathematician, I could tell you that my rough estimate told me that it didn't look good.

How long could I avoid them…and just how stupid were they? I mean, as much as I liked to believe I could stay ahead of this trifecta of award-winning scholars who were currently huddled together trying to make sense of the numbers above each cell, I knew that even they couldn't mess up if they asked for me by name.

Until now I had mostly stayed off the map, which was a feat for me given that I would talk to a duck if it stood still and quacked. It was safe to say that even with a toned-down version of my personality I was still a fairly well-known quantity. As I said, I spent a lot of time thinking … And that thoughtfulness turned to mindfulness which turned into can't-mind-my-own-business…ness.

On the other hand, some of my time here has indeed been well spent.

Kaycee secretly slipped some textbooks to me on one of our visits, and I had caught up on some of the finer points of the Artificery study that I had willfully neglected. Between that and being able to do nothing other than workout with no access to midnight McDonalds runs, I had thinned down quite a bit and was in pretty good shape if I do say so myself. Still, I could see no scenario in which this scene came out in my favor.

I had to think.

"… walked over your grave."

It's funny how consuming an internal dialog can be, and how it can hold your attention so strongly that you don't even notice what's going on around you. Suddenly I heard the tail end of something someone aimed my way, followed by a rush of noise from the common room. It's actually loud as hell in prison, almost like a high school cafeteria, just with less cursing and more metal toilets.

"Huh?" I queried.

"I said," replied a very mock-annoyed Beau, who wasn't surprised at my inattention and having to repeat himself. Even irritated, there was an almost jovial tenor about the guy.

He gets it. I zone out. A lot.

"You looked like someone just walked over your grave."

"Thanks for the comforting thought, man, you really know how to brighten a guy's day."

"Well, I mean ... this is prison, and you did destroy that Jim Brown statu—"

"Stop."

Being the famous punk who defaced the statue of the city of Cleveland's favorite son was a lot worse than I thought. Sure, I knew I wasn't going to be popular, but there was only one class of imprisoned citizen lower on the totem pole than me, and that was a child molester.

And I'm pretty sure there were some diehard Brownies that didn't agree with that pecking order either.

Luckily in this day and age, news ran twenty-four hours a day sensationalizing anything and everything, so for the most part the contempt had died down to a murmur. Beau, the man beside me, was exceedingly pleased with himself for having found a seemingly innocuous reason to speak my crime aloud, and thereby remind me that he could make it the talk of the yard again. Inmates call all guards Boss to butter them up, and guards eat that shit up, but Beau didn't like it, to what I think was his credit.

Beau's alright. Truthfully, he's above that kind of thing and the fact that nobody ever used the moniker when talking to him was more of a compliment than a reflection of his authority. He's the cousin of one of the witches I knew, and she'd called him on my behalf. He didn't really have much in the way of pull, being just another low man on the totem pole, but he was someone to pass the time with who could have an eye on my back whenever the job allowed the man to spare it. I hesitate to call him a friend, but we understood one another, got along, and our principles seem to stay in step for the most part. He's taller than me but only just, and he's thicker too. I wouldn't call him an outcast or a loner but there was something decidedly him which didn't quite fit any traditional mold or template. Mostly though he's got common sense smarts that are a lot more useful (and rare) than people realize. He's a corn-fed midwestern type, but just because Beau talked slow didn't mean he was.

"Friends of yours?"

The guard's intense gaze moved to the three cohorts circling one another, twitching intermittently as they hurriedly discussed something serious. I caught the disapproving frown, as he made a game out of guessing where I came from and who I ran with and got the impression that the prospect of me being associated with that lot would have been a disappointment to him.

When his estranged cousin called him, despite them getting along well enough, he was shocked. She was something of a family pariah—even though Beau had never treated her like one. Jamie was a well-meaning witch with a background in botany and an affinity for plant life, and despite being the proud owner of the black sheep title she always stayed inside the lines of the law and never made any trouble for anybody really, and the guard knew she was as kindhearted and well-intentioned as anyone alive.

So when she phoned in on behalf of an inmate, he was floored. Apparently, the green thumb didn't usually run in circles with friends who were incarcerated, so ever since I had arrived and we'd gotten past our first couple of verbal sparring sessions, the man had made a game of guessing where it was I came from, who I ran with, and how I ranked this high with his cousin. This bunch didn't have his approval, and I could see it had him rethinking how okay it was that his favorite cousin and I seemed to be in the same proverbial circle.

"No, but they're from my block." Lying to a friend was tough, especially one that was a cop when you were an inmate. Friends know your tells, and more often than not when you're lying to them, they have a sense of it. Coupling that with the fact that the man was in Law Enforcement, and trained to sniff out deception, making trying to get an absolute lie past him all but impossible without some of the stink escaping.

Using a kernel of truth helps though, and it was the half-truth in my lie that seemed to make him buy it.

"They're trouble. Used to raise hell up and down the street either looking for a fix, robbing for a fix, or celebrating having found a fix." It's not that the man didn't believe me, but the measured look he gave me was delivered by someone who thought he deserved a little more respect than that.

"And we may have crossed paths a few times," I relented, weirdly chipping away at his very spot-on skepticism with more lies.

"And because you only have two and a half more weeks," "I want to avoid them altogether."

I held both my breath and my tongue, watching as he took a spell of silence to deliberate on what could be done about it.

Beau had a tell when he was thinking, and you didn't have to be a prized detective to sniff it out.

He would just start rolling this old gold coin over his knuckles as he eyeballed the thing he was contemplating. I had seen enough of these things to know it was some kind of military coin, but instead of having the insignia of a high-ranking officer, it simply had some letters and numbers. I suspected it was an identifier for the unit he served with when he was in the Army. I really wanted to make fun of it being a cliché, but he had a way about him—like he was above that kind of noise, so I held my tongue and kept my Bond-like villain quip to myself.

I heard the murmur of the word "right," and though that didn't say much, the small salute he provided while moving over to the three baddies gave my mounting dread a solid reason to pause. Positioned so that I could see them while remaining unseen, I watched as he corralled the trio and moved them through the common room and into another wing.

I couldn't be absolutely sure that they were here for me, but the fact that the mongrels came together at the entrance of my cell didn't bode well. There really aren't any coincidences in my world, and I've learned the hard way that it's best not to believe in them.

Looked like it was gonna be another sleepless night for me.

***

It was about midnight when the next rotation of guards came through. This isn't a max security type place (though we've had our fair share of undesirables) so the guards weren't as abrasive as TV shows might lead you to believe. It's not like we're exactly friendly with each other, but when people are forced to live and work together, they tend to reach a level of civility you wouldn't expect in this type of environment. All ecosystems came into balance, even if this wasn't exactly a harmonious one.

Wiping some of the sleep out of my eyes, I slid out of bed and over to my little handheld mirror. We've got a small faucet in our room, and even if it's prone to giving out a long whine whenever you turn it on there was nothing about the sound that was out of the ordinary or cause for alarm.

Making quick work out of the sigils with my dry erase marker until the entire face of the square mirror was outlined with them, I reached for the water. Water is a conduit which helps a thing pass from one place to another: energy, magic, or literally any object was all well served by a conduit. I wet my hand until some of the calloused started to soften, before flicking water over the mirror.

The steady sound of running water masks my quiet, ritualistic utterances, a kind of phrase I use to center my focus when trying to call on magic. I'm an artificer, so ... It's different. Usually, people like me stick to the shadows, a behind the curtain kind of act and not a center stage type. We have enough natural talent to imbue a relic, sigil or rune with power, but that's about it. Wizards, Mages, Sorcerers, and about a dozen other magical practitioners were much more effective and impressive than me.

Basically, I was at the bottom of the lowest rung of casters. Still, I could capture a dollop of magic given enough time and practice, which is precisely what I did – with the help of my mantra.

My mantra is Shakira's "Hips Don't Lie" song, so that's why I church-up the explanation a bit. It isn't meant to be as funny as it is. When Zachariah first explained the practice to me, I poked fun at it in practice by using the song's chorus as my phrase of choice for centering: which was actually an attempt to grate at my mentor's nerves, which it did.

The joke's on me though because it stuck—in my head. Now whenever I try to deploy the lesson learned so long ago about essentially capturing these small grasps of magic the only time I have even an iota of success is when I use the song.

Now? It works, every time. When the Stalker first locked its attention on me that song was the only thing that came to my mind and sure enough, it beat back the suffocating fear long enough to allow me to focus: to fixate on what tools I had on me and how to use them cleverly enough to stay alive for another night. Since that fateful day in that alley, it's the most effective thing I do to bring myself back to that state of mind … so, to say it's become a staple is not an exaggeration.

So here I am, in prison, singing Shakira's "Hips Don't Lie" a little after midnight.

I'll let that joke write itself.

With my middle and pointer fingers pressed to my forehead, I experienced images swirling to the rhythm of the song I had picked as my collecting mantra. When I moved my joined fingers and pressed them to the mirror, it brought the runes I had drawn earlier to life.

The drops of water flattened and the corner symbols I had drawn into the mirror momentarily flashed before the flattened water began to steadily vibrate. There's a shimmer, and I angle the mirror up to my own face and take a look. The memory I pulled was superimposed onto my face, which normally is really bizarre, but this time it wasn't all that strange.

It was me a little over two years ago. Crazy to think how much had changed since then, even if that time was something of a rock bottom for me.

I mean, I know it's a weird thing to be in a jail cell, casting low level glamor spells on a prison-approved vanity mirror at midnight two feet from a soundly snoring car thief and calling another time in my life the lowest point, but it is what it is. I had been lost, and depression mixed with a lack of purpose made me feel useless and I acted accordingly.

Snapping back to the present, I reminded myself that time is on a budget, so I got back to work. I was thirty, maybe forty pounds heavier back then and had a goatee thing going on, with short, cropped hair. My guess is that that's the last time they saw me.

I repeat the gesture of touching my forehead then mirror and show what I would look like in my current state, completely shaved, head and face. My hope was to get out of here before this escalated into a conflict. This wasn't paranoia; ghouls don't get caught by regular cops, they're the horror stories you hear about when somebody tells you what seems to be an exaggerated story about a random nobody on PCP breaking out of handcuffs and smashing through reinforced panel windows. They're here for me—and if not for me, they're probably going to call it a bonus. This was a losing fight before it began.

If it took them half a week to get the lay of the land, it'll take them another half a week to get eyes on me for the first time. If I can slip them once or twice, it might buy me another day or two but that probably won't be enough. I know it sounds looney toons, but what these guys lacked in intelligence they made up for in ferocity.

Effectively, I had just entered into a maze where the dead ends were aptly named.

Wiping away the mirror, I remind myself that even as a kid with half-cocked schemes, I could avoid a ghoul without any issue. I'd spent the last few months studying and memorizing ancient writings, learning to meditate, and taking the equivalent of three full semesters of advanced schoolwork. I repeat all of this to myself, and the fact that I am not some scruffy kid anymore that's gonna be caught flatfooted and unaware.

I also reminded myself, pretty pointedly, that they're stuck in here with me too.

***

"Motherf—"

The edge of the cafeteria table clipped my knee, interrupting the momentum of my flight into it and sending me heel over head into the table behind it. Every bit of my body hurt, but the lack of blurry vision told me I may have avoided another concussion.

I duck, and if I lived long enough to be asked why I ducked at that moment, I would swear it was because I realized I hadn't yet had my skull caved in. I always imagined that was the very thing somebody who was about to have their skull caved thought. They may call me crazy, but when I ducked, the ghoul behind me missed with the big chunk of table he'd ripped clean off its hinges and swung at me like a baseball bat.

For half a second, I thought about kicking his feet from under him, but the truth is that that would give him a better opportunity to get his hands on me, and once that happened, I was as good as dead.

This was all getting out of control, and it had happened so damn fast. I swore after a night of tossing and turning that I would stop panicking so much and remember that there was no way I couldn't stay a step ahead of these idiots. Then, not halfway into the breakfast line, this one started throwing aside white-collar criminals and gang bangers with equal ease while making a beeline right for my unfortunate ass.

All the gusto and bravado I worked up when reciting tough-guy affirmations to myself burnt away, eviscerated at the realization of how out of my depth I was without my team. That thing broke two bodies getting to me and managed to hurl me over a table before I could even muster an idea of what to do, let alone break into any action.

It knew who I was, there was no ducking behind a fake name tag or trying to dupe them with some cockamamie story I pulled out of my ass. This ghoul wasn't just after me, he was rabid. Some poor inmate turned himself into a Trekkie redshirt by going after the seemingly slightly built inmate with a full throttle tackle. He'd lost his meal when the bean pole turned me into a projectile and I landed on their collective table, the unforgiving wood having the decency to break my fall.

The tackles' impact drags the ghoul back a few feet, but doesn't drop him, and the offending inmate is still furiously driving forward with his feet against the standstill. It viciously slammed those mangling arms into the back of the inmate like a silverback gorilla, nearly breaking the man in half in the process. I'm dragging myself backward, trying to scramble to my feet when the alarm sounds; its shriek cry was enough to momentarily startle the dead set ghoul that was gunning for me.

Life in a prison was rough, rough for everyone, because once this one-man riot broke out so did the gear to deal with this kind of thing. The first guard had about as much luck as the gangster who had tried to spear the monster, but unlike him there was a second and a third guy just on his heel. Eventually the numbers game had the thing succumbing, and even as a dozen of them mercilessly beat and wrestled this thing to the ground it kept clawing its way after me.

The thing's chattering, fractured teeth gnashed at the air, and its mangled fingers reached out from beneath a dozen or so guards that had crashed on top of it, like a prehistoric nightmare trying to struggle out of a tar pit. The fact that it took a couple of prideful locals and a dozen cops with clubs to take one of these ghouls down is a vivid reminder of just how outmatched I am without having anyone or anything to back me up.

Well ... that's one down, I thought as I wiped a mouthful of blood off my lip. I was surprised at how calm I felt staring at the pile of bodies ruthlessly working the ghoul over.

Even if that took one out of the equation, I couldn't really celebrate. They not only came in here with me in mind, but they had been properly motivated. Somebody had made sure these single-minded murder machines not only knew me but had my scent as well. I'm still dabbing at the blood on my jaw when I look up from my prone position on the cafeteria floor and see the other two.

One looked downright rabid, his desperate grip wrenching the steel bars and actually making them whine a bit at the pressure. The other? The other seemed fixated, and that concentration was troubling to see on what was usually a mindless monster.

It's an intelligence in the eyes that didn't belong there, and it wasn't the first time I'd seen it. Cursing luck, and nursing the newly busted lip, I just kept my head down while the rest of the riot squad sorted out the whole of this mess. All of us involved in the altercation would get some kind of consequence, but I had guessed it would be a day or two in the hole. Solitary is for punishment, and for once I was actually happy to see it go that way. Hell, at one point this morning I had entertained starting a fight to get into solitary, but I was in the only penitentiary that didn't mind doubling a sentence if you got out of hand, so I shitcanned that idea. Elongating my sentence was no different than tightening my own noose.

I knew it would be easy enough to prove that I wasn't either the aggressor or instigator, so I took that as a win even as some of the guardsmen started to circle me.

The last thing I see while being escorted off are the cold, staring eyes of the intelligent one.

***

"Helix, Robinson, you're out." A nondescript guard with a low-rent shiner called out to me while signaling for my room to be opened.

Helix, that's such a cool name. Not such a cool guy.

Helix is the poster child for the system; he's been in and out of it since he was an early teenager. He's my age and spent more years locked up than free. Still, like a lot of people raised in a system, the man had a code, and I could identify with that.

"Janzen," We'd barely been led back into the yard proper, and the only reason Helix paused as long as he did to continue speaking to me was to cast the guard a sneering send off.

"Yo, what the hell was that about? That crackhead wanted your dumbass legit dead."

What he lacked in eloquence he made up in being able to articulate sentiment.

"Yeah, uh, an old ... beef from the block." I felt stupid the second I said it.

"Talk like *you*, I'm not an idiot an' you sound like one when you do that."

"Right. That guy works for people who don't like me."

I had a thought, and it wasn't an entirely pure one.

"He's just amped up on drugs, probably got a bad score from the outside."

"They holdin'?" With the bait taken, now it was only a matter of setting the hook.

"Usually." Pausing for effect. "They used to push junk in my neighborhood. That's how we ended up crossing paths."

"Ah... you one of those do-gooding type Janzen? I wouldn't have guessed that, I don't know... you're to -"

"Selfish?"

"I was gonna say rude." Quipped the man I had just interrupted...and not for the first time.

Helix took my measure for a few seconds, and knowing the unwritten rules of the jungle we lived in I held fast, it's only when the man gave me a terse nod that I took my leave. There's a part of me that felt bad, manipulating him into believing there was a pair of new, disrespectful crackheads who just happened to have drugs on them inside the prison.

But this was war, and war didn't have any rules.

CHAPTER 2

Blurred Lines

"Out." The guard at my cell seemed to have just appeared. Conditioning worked wonders, and after almost six months I felt my body going into motion before my brain could make any sense of it.

"Not you." Beau stopped me with a look, and that look gave me time to acclimate myself a bit more. My innate mindset was reactionary at this point, and my personal motto of 'do my time' quietly helped this place shape me into what it wanted me to be. The guard and I were almost friends, and I think in a different set of circumstances we would have been pretty close. I knew I looked like hell, and the look he gave me confirmed as much. Not sleeping for the second night in a row was catching up to me, and the busted nose from the ambush in the breakfast line wasn't doing me any kind of favor either.

"What the hell happened yesterday?"

I knew the fight brought a lot of unwanted attention; that kind of commotion stood out. This was a sleepy prison as far as prisons go (or so I was told, not like I could tell the difference).

To say that it warranted asking me about the day was a little suspicious, but Beau and I were almost friends as stated and if anybody was going to see this behavior as out of character for me, it would be a guard that actually knew me and didn't just associate me with the series of numbers scrolled across my back.

"It was a fight, I told you, me and those guys don't get along."

"Yeah yeah, okay, you can piss on my face but don't tell me it's raining."

I really like this guy and chortled helplessly a bit at the rejoinder.

"My cousin calls about you daily,"

It had been brought up in about every iteration and variation that it could be brought up that his cousin seemed particularly invested in me. To tell you the truth I was surprised, but apparently the idea that Cleveland now had a resident protector was getting around town: and nothing that went bump in the night could trespass without having to pay for it with their own pound of flesh. Honestly, it was embarrassing, but that didn't keep me from using the tools, trinkets, and study material they snuck in, or eating the hell out of the bakery stuff they sent. The support was nice, but most importantly it was a network we could start to use as a resource—not only for our wild ass investigations and adventures, but to build community and help one another.

"I tell her about the fight and try to calm her down by telling her you're fine – that this kind of stuff happens here, but she won't hear any of it."

He interrupted my attempt to interrupt him to emphasize his point.

"Any of it."

God, I like this dude, he even punctuated his points dramatically and interrupted people intermittently with nonsensical add-ons and tidbits. I noticed his frown and realized he's been talking, and I hadn't heard any of it.

"Like I said, she asked me a dozen questions about the whole thing and after I told her about that maniac who put a pair of inmates and guards in the hospital. Then she begged me to rewatch the tape—closely."

Beau is interrupted by somebody trying to turn and walk straight into my cell. I immediately realized it was Helix, and just when I thought I was going to get a mouthful he stopped. If looks could kill Beau would be dead, and I wasn't too keen on the one Helix aimed at me either before he started moving down the walkway and leaving us to our private, discreet conversation.

Crap, that couldn't have looked good.

"So what was that? I know my cousin is wonky, she likes all that hocus pocus devil stuff."

"Pagan."

"Huh?"

"Pagan. Your cousin is a specific kind of pagan witch, some kind of Irish sect if I remember. A pretty good one, too. It's the reason she's a kindergarten teacher and a vegetarian—they like to nurture things. It's a part of their way and belief."

The seemingly simple, detached guard used some of that astuteness to measure how serious I was about the amount of respect I had just given to something he obviously thought was ridiculous.

"Right, I know she's a witch, but I also know she isn't really all that weird. I've seen her do some stuff," The dodgy eyes made sure nobody was in earshot, and it was easy to see how spooked he was.

"And that guy yesterday...that wasn't natural. Everybody else is just chalking it up to some bad luck and potent uppers but that dude wasn't strung out. That dude was on a mission."

Wheels turning, it wouldn't be long now until he's figured it all out. Honestly, I think it helped growing up in the cusp of the late eighties/early nineties. Don't ask me why, maybe something about being a middling generation that grew up on wild stories and cut their teeth in the boom of the fantasy genre. Not that the seventies didn't have Star Wars and their own wild adventurers, but something about the Gremlins movie made you believe it could happen.

Personally, I've always been more of a Goonies guy.

"So how can I help you, Beau?"

"What's going on in my prison?"

"Noth-"

"Bullshit." The finger to the chest wasn't winning him any awards in my book, but what he said next struck a chord in me that even my stubborn ass couldn't ignore.

"I am responsible for the people in this prison, including their safety."

Now when I tell you we shared a silence, it's easy to assume it's just a few seconds. Like that cinematic pause they always show in a movie when a pair of oppositional characters finally give a nod of respect to one another. This wasn't that. We sat in silence for a while, an easy two minutes, before I couldn't do anything else but shrug. There was something companionable about the quiet, and by the end of it ...

Beau Barth was my friend.

"They're ghouls." I said almost helplessly.

Now, I should have waited more than two minutes before spilling one of the greatest secrets of the modern age but if you've been with me this long you know how impatient I am .... Plus, what the hell else was I gonna do?

His incredulous face was surprising, but not for the expected reasons and I'll tell you why.

I've gotten laughter. Doubt is usually the other staple for people who've seen a thing or two. There's classic outrage and then my personal favorite, the scoff. From Beau, I got incredulous, which was strange because he was normally skeptical, but that wasn't the charging emotion behind the expression. Cautious entertainment was the muse of that dubiousness, and for some reason the prospect wasn't immediately, and completely, discarded.

"Ghouls? Like uh, zombies?"

"I mean, kinda? I don't know ... are you like a Romero zombie guy, or one of those wrong people that think zombies should run because they miss the point of using zombies as a -"

The man went to interrupt me, and I trumped him with a steady look that demanded I be heard.

"- plot device."

This time the silence is more Hollywood style.

"So," watching a headache come to life was something I had experience with—it's kind of a gift. "Ghouls?" the guard asked while pinching the bridge of his nose.

The taste of his annoyance is enough to sate my sarcastic side, at least long enough for me to check the hallway and make sure we were alone and sit him down. I had about an hour to give him the ugly version of it all, a basic rundown of the stuff that I thought he could hold onto while treading out in these deep, uncharted waters. Waters I myself was barely more than a novice in, but we all had to start somewhere. Normally people can relate to stuff they've never seen before in whatever type of medium they consume their entertainment in. Keep it to vampires, werewolves—those types of creatures—and it's not so hard. I usually use the whole bit that all myths come from some truth and expand on it from there.

The point is that I gave him enough to consider without turning his whole world upside down. I couldn't tell what he thought by the time he left, but I was confident he'd watch that security footage about a hundred more times. Calling his cousin would help too, and I'm sure that once they got to the point where she heard it was me that clued him into all the happenings in our world, she would know she kind of had a green light to speak a little more openly on the subject.

Not that I was an authority mind you, but the heat would be on me, and it wasn't like I had a stellar reputation anyway. I usually wasn't keen on being the person that had to pull the wool off somebody's eyes; it was a messy prospect for them and could ruffle feathers in the community. If it ruffled enough feathers there used to be a governing body that took care of those 'crimes.' Now that the House of Unet and the Masarou Tribe had been dealt such a crippling blow it was hard to say with any certainty what would be next in terms of enforcement. Still, even with the prospect of avoiding any repercussions for letting our dirty little secret out, I didn't like doing it. It invited them to begin looking into the Abyss, and as anybody who has watched a shitty, B quality horror flick undoubtedly knows, if you stare into the Abyss long enough …

It stares back.

I should know, given how much Abyss staring I have done (literally).

The enjoyment of my word play fell short because I had become living proof that the adage was true. By just thinking about the Abyss for as long as I had there was a cold that had seeped into my bones, and whenever the word passed the threshold of my conscious mind it seemed to set off a blizzard in my body. The churning in my stomach was new, but when I tried to blink it away the image of that awful, ichor covered, fang baring Bitch flashed in my mind's eye, and it took more concentration than I care to admit to turning it off. It's easy to be snarky as a way to avoid the gravity of it all, but there's no way to shake off the darkness forever. It's an insidious thing that doesn't sleep and is always pressing in on you. No matter how vigilant you are, it'll eventually slip past your exhausted guard.

Maybe that was our burden to bear – in order for there to be light, some of us had to hold back the dark....

CHAPTER 3

When Good Men Do Something

There's a weird thing when you walk in the worlds that I do, where you have to partition your mind so securely that you almost start to compartmentalize every single emotion through a different lens. Take something like fear; the human side of me knew to be afraid of Helix, to be mindful of his connections, the man himself, and the gang he seemed to be a considerable figurehead of.

Watching him walk into the laundry room it's evident he had a kind of clout, especially since bruiser One and Two stayed close to him as if he was a planetary object that they revolved around. I'm not really sure how else to describe the guys other than muscle.

The other side of me feared what would happen if this idiot pushed me too far, and I had to force feed him every one of his teeth. I never pretended not to love what I did, even the ugly part of it. I can't say why I am not entirely shocked to see him in the laundry room; I'm not even shocked to see the reinforcements he brought in the thick bodied, tattooed gang-banger types standing on either side of him.

Hell, even Shawn—the most corrupt guard in the place—standing at the front entrance to the laundry room didn't surprise me; that guy was shady as hell, and even if he wasn't taking a cut from the criminal element here in the prison, I was pretty sure the sicko was the kind of sadist who would help arrange these kind of beatdowns just to make sure he had a front row seat.

Shawn looks so much like a cop it's ridiculous. His eighties buzz cut is complemented by a seventy's porn-stache, and the aviators the man wore seemed absurdly exaggerated. Even the way he chomped rather than chewed his gum was irritating. Honestly if somebody showed me a caricature of what they thought a corrupt police officer looked like, it would be a dead ringer for Shawn.

I'd respect him more if he was doing this just for the bribes, but I could tell that that was secondary to him. Shawn just wanted to see people tortured and exert a modicum of authority over them so that he could feel like some kind of big timer lording it over those beneath him.

"You ain't got that guard buddy to back you up now," It wasn't much in the way of a secret that Beau and I got along, and despite what some dramatizations might tell you, there's some... agreeableness isn't quite the right word, but it wasn't uncommon to have some kind of understanding between guards and inmates that allowed them to coexist.

"Maybe I can borrow yours," The uneasy shift from the crew made me smile. An ass whooping looked inevitable, so if I could land a couple of quips at least I could get my metaphorical pound of flesh. I abandoned the white linens I was working on; I wasn't any good at handling linen, but I did enjoy the mindless work as a way of mentally checking out. Folding sheets was quite a bit better than getting the shit kicked out of you.

"This isn't about the block man; this is between you and him. I'm just here to facilitate."

All at once I felt the shred of smugness, I was holding on to leave me. A dread entered my blood, and I turned just as a lengthy, body-rattling vessel lumbered through the back entrance. Everyone here kept thinking that this was just some kind of tweaker, but of course I knew better.

"Helix, you idiot," Immediately backtracking, the sharpness in the eyes of the ghoul was too intelligent. It's not that the undead were incapable of thought (God, I wish I had time for a zombie pun), but they had a rabidness that made them more monster than man. The stalking should have been done by now; he should have crossed the threshold.

There was a stretch of two long narrow tables that broke up the laundry room, and the walls had massive machines made to handle industrial size loads. Only the doors were unimpeded, and even the steel-woven glass that prisons used actually had caging on both sides of it. This was basically a cage match between men, and a mind-raped, super strong, flesh-eating freak.

Talking to the man piloting the mind-broken monster might be my only hope.

"The Balance ain't gonna be happy with you dropping a pair of great white sharks in a tank made for goldfish."

There's something human about the smile on the face of the emaciated ghoul, but a snap of the jowls wiped it away; the steady stalking was just to torment me, like a cat playing with a mouse... and it was working.

"This doesn't stop with me," It seemed the most toothless of my threats, but that's the one that made the thing pause. All of this sounded completely insane to anybody in earshot, and the dumb look on the faces of Helix and his cohorts was fitting, seeing as how they were being played so easily. I felt a little responsible for setting them up like that.

I am responsible for the people in this prison, and their safety.

Me and you both buddy.

Shit.

Shawn interrupted the suspension of action by banging his baton against the doorframe.

"Let's get to the dance ladies. Daddy's got a hot date tonight and I don't want to be late."

This guy was so bad it was like sitcom level lazy, which made it even more absurd that he's a real person. Should have known though, even Beau warned me he's more moron than he is any kind of ringmaster.

Just then the thing shifted, and the waifish ghoul swayed thoughtfully while considering something unseen. Its voice strained and its jaw worked in a stilted fashion, but the damn thing managed to answer me.

"It ends with you."

Ghouls are strong, durable as hell, immune to pain and are actually deceptively fast for about twenty to thirty feet – which meant in this setting, I was fucked.

Proper fucked.

I had been timing my retreat so that I was at the head of one of the tables when the thing lunged to close the distance between us. Given that I wasn't only expecting it but had wound my legs up beneath me to the best of my ability while staying inconspicuous about it, I was also prepared for it.

Don't ask me why, but for some reason I thought that if I could take the corners quickly enough it might slow him down. I guess somewhere in my mind I imagined the ghoul was like an alligator and only fast in short, straight distances.

Come to think of it, I don't even know if that's true. I mean it sounds true, but what the hell do I know about those prehistoric Disneyland Dinosaurs?

It didn't slow him down.

The fingers I felt sink into my shoulders felt like blades; their grip cut into sinew and killed my circulation. The pencil-thin abomination ripped me off my feet and threw me all the way back into one of the washers.

The body has a couple of amazing defense systems against pain, and the engineering brilliance that is the brain knew to let loose a flood of chemicals to conceal the agony of my crash into the steel industrial box behind me. I heard more than felt it, and the lucky slab of concrete beneath me gave me a cold embrace.

Those bony, bruising, body-breaking fingers seized the back of my shirt and hoisted me up like a rag doll, and the maestro got a face full of laundry detergent for his trouble because I wasn't so good with gratitude. Lucky for me, I was an absolute slob and forgetful as hell, so when I had first been assigned this job detail, I had forgotten to get a cup for the powdered laundry detergent… so I had a bunch in my pocket.

Sometimes being lazy can be lucky, and this was one of those times.

While the organ functions of the ghoul (really any undead) were minimal, they still needed things like eyes … And in fact, the sense of sight tended to be so important that overwhelming it was a great way to disorient the thing.

At least that's what I told Grove when we rigged an under-construction building with explosives and amplifiers so I could play trashy hair-rock while we fought the Stalker.

After all, who wouldn't want their own real-life soundtrack?

But the grip didn't relent, and the things second hand secured its hold on me. Fortunately, before he could shove me back into the washer that he'd indented with my body an instant earlier, I actually managed to slip completely out of my shirt. Unbuttoned, and about to be washed, this had given me a second lucky escape in as many minutes, and I was beginning to think that I was wasting what I had left of my nine lives pretty fast.

The stumble to get back to my feet was also fortuitous because it gave me the window of time I needed to look at the ground and without thinking, grab up the big shard of glass I was staring at. The jagged edges did a number on my hand, but the spire was big enough to use as a poor man's shank. The fact that he'd rag-dolled me hard enough into the machine to break pieces loose and shatter glass was concerning, but I could sort out the internal bleeding later.

Plus, if it's internal is it really even bleeding?

I was running between tables, and the gangster trio seemed to start to take on some kind of realization that this wasn't exactly a normal beating. Watching a guy who looked like he couldn't be over a buck-twenty soaking wet throw me across a room with ease had to be quite a shock.

People here knew me well enough. I was known as the guy who tried to keep it light and had a penchant for avoiding any kind of unnecessary conflict (if you ain't like a gangly undead or magic-cast demon born it ain't my business), but I had made it a point of pride to never be punked.

Ever.

I turned in time to catch the brunt of the thing in full sprint—it had managed to make up the space between us in a few strides, and the hit caught me with enough force to catapult me again, this time into the three stooges.

Somewhere during my pinball experience I had lost the glass-knife I was trying to use, which had been the only thing that had given me any kind of hope.

"Hey man, we can just hold him," Helix said, acting as the peacemaker. He was still under the delusion that this guy was just trying to make a point out of me and that after he got his beatdown this would all be over. I was willing to bet that whoever was inhabiting these trade-in assassins turned the drug-connection seed I planted in Helix's head against me, promising to deliver some goods in return for a little bit of help.

Never underestimate an active drug addict's mind or the general predictability of stupid.

I was doubtful he had any real drug connection (whoever was driving this thing) but it wasn't like that mattered. I mean, after they killed me, it was likely they were just going to untether this one, and the other ghoul they still had loaded in the chamber of their ghoul-aimed guns.

Still, unlike this interloper, Helix and I belonged to this community—whether we liked it or not—and within this community we had rules, a system, and we acknowledged and respected them ... Insomuch as a group of criminals were capable of doing. This was outside the way we operated, and even as they caged each of my respective arms and Helix himself wrapped my flailing head up in a sloppy headlock, I could feel his comfort and conviction starting to wane.

The alien gaze returned, and the eyes seemed to consider all of us for a second, before it resumed its awkward walk toward me. Why was it so goddamn rigid?

They are fighting against the possession, I distantly realized, and then I nearly blacked out because the punch this thing landed damn near tore my fucking head off. I spit a molar out, my second since I had gotten back to work, and I quietly congratulated myself on my thriftiness for how much money I must be saving at the dentist.

Managing pithy while being punched wasn't easy, but I managed.

I vaguely heard shouting, and I saw the boots of the guard join the sneakers of the other inmates. I couldn't hold my head up, and their voices sounded like that garbled mess from Peanuts whenever an adult talked.

So that part was normal.

It's possessed.

For the life of me I couldn't figure out why that was important, but luckily my damaged brain was not only repeating that fact for me but was also making this cool whish noise anytime I moved my head, so I had a theme music going to cue me into my eventual demise.

The corrupt guard put something beneath my chin, and the guy who held my left arm seemed to be hoisting up the majority of my weight by himself. Helix had moved to put himself between the scrawny and highly agitated ghoul and me while also trying to speak over it with the guard.

"If he doesn't get his beat down, I don't get my product and you don't get paid."

"He's already out on his fe-"

I didn't so much as swing at Shawn as kind of just throw my fist at him. It was enough though, because the guy who was supposed to be keeping me caged had gone from holding the limb to using it to keep me upright. I'd made sure to play dead, mostly because when I attempted to get my legs under me, they just kind of…buckled anyway.

I had enough for that, and if this guy was gonna end up eating my face, I was going to make sure to rearrange his mother fucking face at least once. It was a good shot too. All desperation with the kind of recklessness you'd expect from a dead man walking.

I put him on the floor, and in the resulting surprise I managed to free my other arm by dropping it low and then wrenching it back upward. My elbow came careening back after breaking free and slammed right into the face of the other inmate who'd come in with Helix.

I had enough sense to cover up, not with any real clarity or design, and it was enough to absorb the wild haymaker from Helix and the follow-up kicks from his cohort, but it was something. I don't know when I ended up on the ground, but that isn't what actually got my attention.

What got my attention while curled up in a ball absorbing kicks from three pissed off gangsters who looked like the reject cast of a modern-day Scarface was the guard.

Shawn always had a kind of haughtiness about him; the shitty kind of superiority that small men get when given even just a modicum, a parcel of power. In these walls he was a kind of king, ruling over anybody who found themselves in his domain ... So when I saw his face devoid of that confidence, that smarmy kind of shit-eating-grin that I wanted to feed him every day, there was a flash of ugly satisfaction.

Then the reality of the situation caught up with me, and I realized why my mind was trying so hard to push the fact that the Ghoul was possessed to the forefront.

It was possessed...and that was why it was moving so awkwardly. It was struggling with stilted limbs preventing it from erupting with the primal energy it usually expressed when on the offensive. That's when I started to piece together the rest of this. There were six sneakers working me over in a classic beatdown, and another pair was at the feet of the fallen prison guard who was trying to scurry away.

Somebody stopped, and then a second person, and then there was that muffled, distorted talking that was starting to become dangerously familiar.

It was too late though.

One of Helix's two men tried to calm the ghoul down and had been a little too physical in his intervention. Luckily for Shawn, the Ghoul that was clawing up the column of his prone body found the interrupting inmate enough of a nuisance to violently turn on him. With bared teeth, bloodshot eyes, and a vice-like, bone-twisting grip, it set after Helix's crony for disturbing what was about to be an easy meal.

In an instant they were down in a tornado of flailing limbs, and the ghoul was rabidly attacking and tearing into him. Those harrowing screams, the ones of nightmares, filled the laundry room and probably reached into every corridor of the prison. Helix and his remaining partner in crime—knowing that this was fast going from a beatdown to a murder charge—bolted over to try and stop the ghoul.

Helix misunderstood my weak bid to grab his ankle, and sadly my attempt to yell stop was cut short by him giving me one departing kick to the midsection. Still, never underestimate an old man in a profession where men die young, and at thirty-ish, Helix was an old man in his profession. He had lived as unforgiving a life as I did—minus the supernatural brutality—until now. Stalling long enough to see the macabre portrait of his dying compatriot having his innards torn clean out of him, Helix cast a frightened look at me as a slow-burning realization started to spread across his face like wildfire; he couldn't tell why I had tried to stop him initially but could see now that I hadn't been interested in retaliation. This was a thing spinning out of control and we were running out of time.

They did a good job of getting the ghoul off their screeching friend, though he died in the process. Seems the damn thing had been holding onto a still working organ, and that it was torn out of him during their attempted rescue.

I'm too concussed to point out the irony—at least out loud.

Still, the thin-yet-inhumanly-strong-bodied beast was even more frenzied now, and I was too head-rocked to tell them to just let the damn thing go. Our best chance would have been to let it have the kill but pulling it off their friend turned it from just fixated to angry, which was definitely worse.

Ghouls aren't terribly complicated, and while that could make them easy to fight when you were prepared and equipped for it, that simplicity also made them extremely effective if they ever caught you off guard.

Not only were we way off guard, we were trapped with this thing in a window-barred room.

I never got the names of the two men Helix brought with him, but the dead one had lasted just under half a minute with the thing. Ghouls relied on their strength and ferocity, and after he got his hand on the other one it was only a matter of time. Like I said, they aren't terribly complicated but they're effective. It would just wrestle you down, and scrap, bite and beat you until you went limp and made something of a more agreeable meal.

I grimaced as a rather thoughtless Star Trek reference passed my head, though the poor red shirt did buy me enough time to kind of get the last semblance of my scrambled wits about me. I was locked in on the thought-loop of fuck, fuck, fuck as I staggered upright.

That is really what panic is ultimately. Something big, traumatic, ugly, or violent knocks you out of your normal thought patterns and then the dread and anxiety of that starts to create a kind of mental molasses. That molasses insidiously evolves into something even more suffocating, a tar-like stranglehold over your ability to think and make sense of what is happening. The solution is what my military buddy used to call his OODA-loop; you observe, you orient, you decide and then you act.

Whenever I am at a loss, I run through a version of my own OODA-loop; it'll either get me back on track or be the last series of thoughts going through my head when fate's hangman finally manages to get my ever-elusive neck in its endgame noose.

But hey…death is the price of admission after all.

Sadly, we didn't have enough time to turn the tide on this one-sided ass kicking, and we didn't have enough time to escape either. I was still reeling. Helix was so badly paralyzed by fear that he'd become immobile, and with pinpoint focus the ghoul turned from his fresh kill to us.

It was about to attack when a wrecking ball of blurring black crashed into it, sending the thing off its feet and sliding it back across the floor in a mess of uncoordinated limbs and blood. It was soaked from the two bodies it had torn to ribbons—though Shawn was still alive somehow after the ghouls' brutal offensive and had managed to claw his way to the hallway entrance he had been serving as a barricade for five minutes earlier. He reminded me of a rat, and I hated how often those types tended to get off the sinking ship; especially when they were the ones that set the sinking in motion.

When the dazed thing managed to find its feet and turn on us with a feral hiss it made quite the striking image.

Beau didn't even slow down long enough to let the thing finish that horrid sound before sending a heavy hand nightstick into its face. My body moved before my mind could make sense of it and I hurled my entire self at the thing's retaliating arm to keep it from capturing our newfound ally in the throes of that death-grip it was so reliant upon. Beau was a big enough guy, little over average height and heavy, but once a warrior always a warrior—and Beau hailed from a fraternity of truly legendary warriors. I didn't know a lot about Army Rangers, but if what Grove had told me was true, it was no wonder that the good-natured guard didn't hesitate in the face of horrendous brutality, even on this scale.

"Don't let it get a hold of you," I heard myself scream, and the officer who didn't seem to understand exactly what was happening kept on, and he thrashed it with a vicious shot right above the brow. Weapons training is important, and while I've belabored this point to death, there's two types of combatants ultimately: trained and untrained.

Beau was trained. The thing was untrained and lacked finesse, but what it lacked in discipline it made up for in enough strength to actually whip me forward and then back, discarding me like a wet shirt stuck to his arm. Luckily it was an easy couple of tumbles on the tile.

I'm up in time to see Beau (quite skillfully if I must say) use his baton to actually intercept each attempted grab by the ghoul. It's a smart counterattack by the guard, and he's mangling those grabbing fingers which purchased the aforementioned death-grip.

I didn't have time to outline the plot of this bloodbath with my new friend, but ever since his cousin introduced us, he'd admittedly taken a shine to me. My hope was that, given her background as a low-level witch who'd gotten support in our little makeshift network, she'd advocated strongly enough for me to warrant him having my back... but this was a step above and beyond. This was a commentary on his character, and for a moment I remembered something he said to me when first suspecting that something bad could be on the loose inside the jail.

These people are my responsibility.
Including me.

I rounded the table back to the original entrance that the now bleeding Shawn and company had blockaded earlier. On my way there I almost crashed into Helix, who was frozen in the kind of fear that told me there would be little hope of him being any real help to us. Still, I got a fistful of his bloodied shirt, tore him around, and pulled his face into mine.

"Get the guards."

Normally I would get some bullshit about being a snitch or him posturing about his status as some kind of Made Man in this hell hole, but Helix had just had a seat in the front row of a real-life massacre. Not some Hollywood depiction.

He was close enough to watch life leave his compatriots' eyes; to see the minute the body went from being a working vessel of consciousness to just an inanimate bag of bones and flesh. To see it, to hear what they wrote about in languages now dead, about what it was to be feasted upon by a wild, unruly monster was totally different.

Helix would never be the same.

I'm sure he'd seen people die, but even people gunned down in the street die cleaner than this nightmare.

"GO!" I screamed with such intensity that it jump-started his budding panic and sent him into action.

Turning back to the wounded guard, I sprinted to the crumpled over Shawn and ended with a sliding knee that actually carried me the full length of the room, which should tell you just how much blood was on the floor.

I immediately started to slap at the utility belt that's cinched around his waist and screamed "where's your baton!"

Shawn weakly handed it over, which given that I expected him to be one of those 'take it from my cold, dead hands' types, was a comment on how quickly the situation had deteriorated. With his shaky help I managed to disengage the canister of this super-mace they had an affinity for using on us. Luckily the thing had a handle because my hands had a nice coat of blood all over them. It's not just that it's gross, but it also compromises my damn grip. I didn't have time to worry about that right now, I could clean up later.

Beau was losing ground, and even though the ghoul had been deterred brutally and often, the body-hijacked, still rabid fiend was starting to show more restraint in its incessant approaches. With mindful consideration it was making the lunges less frequent, but more dangerous. Beau couldn't back-peddle much more without being pinned between three feet of rebar reinforced concrete and this wild-eyed ghoul turned street shark.

Normally, this would be where I threw myself headlong into the fight; the signature recklessness that's put a few more decades on what some might consider a still young body. Most of what I tangled with could have an issue with a strong, prepared, competent human. Add in a magic gizmo and a trick, and that made us as big a threat to them, as they are to us.

This wasn't the case here, and with that reality came a shift in tactics. Now, the undead worked off magic born from the Abyss. All those types could heal considerably faster than us, but it still took time. How much time was dependent upon how high up the food chain you sat. A stalker that took a hummer hit at sixty miles per hour dead on, shrugged it off in the matter of an evening. Some older vampires could really take some damage and be after you for revenge in the span of a week.

Ghouls were significantly down the food chain, and since this rat-faced fuck looked to be from my generation of lowlifes it wasn't like he was going to be bouncing back from any real damage all that quickly.

So instead I go low, but not before catching the notice of the guard. Beau was in the military, so I lifted my hand up and made an L, then mouth ambush over and over. Luckily, he understood immediately.

Beau gave a loud roar and came out swinging. To the ghoul, it probably seemed like the last desperate effort from an exhausted man. The truth was that it was designed to seize the monster's whole attention and make sure that with the promise of a fresh meal looming so close he wouldn't look anywhere else.

In our ambush he was the base of fire, supplying the action that would keep our target in place.

Me? I was the flanking part, and while I wasn't taking my time, I was also keenly aware that we had precisely one chance at this, so I didn't do my usual leap before looking shit. It was less a rush and more a prowl, and my lungs felt like they were sucking down mouthfuls of fire, but I didn't let that steal any of my concentration.

I cracked the thing with a downward chop, coming in at a sharp angle and making sure I sent a surge of strength behind my arm so that when it hit the thing's right knee it didn't just buckle it, it broke and bent it at a horrific angle. Don't strike at a thing, strike through it.

Ghouls aren't outright immune to pain, but they're tough, so normally it takes a lot to put them down but if you're in a jam, kneecapping one isn't a bad strategy.

This thing had torn apart two men in as many minutes, and there was no way I was going to spare it from my own considerable mean-streak.

The hissing expression got a mouthful of iron, then a second and a third.

It's about the ninth hit when Beau gets his hands on me and is actually restraining me. Honestly, it's good that he did because my instinct was to shrug him off and get back to work on the things already mangled face.

In the distance I could hear somebody screaming my name, and it took me a full minute to realize that it was the guard holding on to me for everything he was worth.

"It's down, Janzen, JANZEN–"

I can't see with any real clarity between the blood loss, injuries and adrenaline; my vision has tunneled to this broken thing, and I'm laboring for breath in sickly, wheezing gasps.

Only then am I painfully aware of how gruesome this is. One dead, one literally torn open and feasted upon, the pale, still dumbstruck Shawn propped up by the door was fast fading but still here. Helix was gone but given the bloody handprint by the door I assume he left on his way out my guess was he was still searching for help. My brain struggled to piece even that much together, but the steadiness of Guard Bartch helps.

"– Fuck man, you can't just ..." Beau was looking from the baton, to Shawn, and back at me.

Inspecting Shawn with a look, the former Ranger announced more than aimed the next bit. "We gotta get our story straight right now –"

Beau was smart, and even in the brief exchange between himself and the other guard I could tell that both of them had their proverbial wheels turning, even if Shawn was worse for the wear. It was Shawn that clued me into how wrong this thing was about to go.

Sluggishly struggling to his feet and eventually propped against the doorframe, the weak guard shifted from battle-weary and dumbstruck to wide-eyed and terrified.

I turned just in time to see the thing club Beau on his leg, and before either of us could respond, the beast was clawing up the length of his body – all of this is easy to explain, but hard to stop, because it was one fluid motion as if long rehearsed. It's straddling the guard before I can even fully turn back around ...

... And it sank those cruel, stunted, once human teeth into his throat before I could cross the length of the laundry room. It's the eyes, the bloody grin it aimed at me, before the gaze went back to something feral: it let me know that whoever was behind this attack had recognized a near unconscious ghoul would be easier to control, and jumped back in to control so they could take this ally from my side.

To kill my friend.

It's a crazed collection of rabidness by the time I get there. The fact that it's just a mindless monster doesn't take away from any of the dark thrill I get in hearing the way the baton cracks the bones in its nose, and the hit had enough behind it to peel the thing off my friend.

Wherever the head goes, the body follows.

That hit took the last vestige of fight from the thing, and it mewled pathetically on the floor rolling left to right as if so disoriented it couldn't even figure out that it was only halfway conscious.

The rumbling of the riot-geared guards isn't far off now, and even the steady hum of the laundry machines can't cover the noise; the noise that let me know that the last ghoul was still with us on the opposite side of the rebar-fitted wall. I saw its profile through the glass, the double-sided caging did little to disrupt the condescending look on the things face.

I make sure to keep hold of its eyes as I trudge over to the last accomplice it had used to ambush me. I let it watch as I dropped a knee on either side of its hips. Shawn and I lock eyes, and even if I hated the man with every fiber of my being, I watch him check down the hallway to see how close the reinforcements are, and back at me.

He nodded.

I smashed the spire of the baton down the throat of the dying ghoul, and I kept a firm hold of the other one with my eyes as I wrenched the grip up, breaking its neck in the process.

Last thing I remember is being dragged off by a host of guards as I stared death into the eyes of the last ghoul, holding court with the thieving consciousness of the mastermind behind this assault for as long as I could.

CHAPTER 4

Penance Thru Pain

"Good behavior is off the table." My normally irritated lawyer (Grove's sister Amie) was a lot softer today. Maybe it was the mile-long stare I knew was housed in my tired eyes. Most likely it was the still mourning witch sitting beside her. Ignoring people is rude, and when you're as situationally aware as I am you only do it to be rude—so instead of that, I acknowledged her with a look. Being able to read between the lines was a family trait both Grove and his sister had, and she respectfully fell silent.

"How was the ceremony?" I'd been in solitary for the last month, so the sound of my own voice was a bit odd for me. The added baritone from the rawness of being unused for so long was disconcerting.

"It was nice. Matt wanted it to be a party not a funeral, so we obliged. A lot of his old Ranger buddies showed up too."

That made a lot of sense and said even more about the pedigree of my departed friend.

"Did you bring everything I asked for?"

The normally diminutive witch was far from meek today, and with the brazenness of a lion walking her savannah she smacked a blanket full of stuff on the table. The concern written all over my lawyer's face was short-lived, turning to shock soon after, because the notoriously dick-ish guard that monitors these private visits abruptly turned around, and instead checked the hallway as if more concerned about the goings-on outside the room than in it. Shawn and I wouldn't ever be drinking buddies, but we would walk side-by-side for now, in the name of revenge.

The still injured guard wasn't a good man, but that didn't mean he didn't love and respect Beau. It didn't mean that these men didn't operate with a code, and when it's a code born of brotherhood it's usually regarded with a kind of respect that arrogance and wretchedness could never truly take from them.

"I need another month here," surprising the lawyer but not the witch. "So don't bother lobbying for good behavior."

I had work to do.

"It's probably for the best, I mean you got out of that ..." chewing on how best to address the elephant in the room, she instead just relied on tact. "Incident without additional time, but they aren't crazy about you on the judicial side of things. If not for all the guards vouching for you that Helix was the main instigator this would have been so much worse."

"It's what happened," I lied with the practice ease of a career criminal.

That much she didn't believe, and it was outlined on her face; usually it would be plain as day, but she was holding on to diplomacy for the sake of the still-sad witch beside her. She could tell there were several discussions happening in this one conversation.

There's something that should be said here, and yet I don't know what it is. Struggling to find the perfect thing to say wasn't my forte even on a good day, but the realization that anybody who comes into my orbit may end up dead wasn't exactly a fun one. That, and I really liked Beau; solid oak fell because he fell into my mess.

"You're going to find out who did this?"

The witch was asking, but it was really more than that.

"Yes."

Plausible deniability was still a thing, and it's why she didn't follow up with a *why*. I didn't need to elaborate, my reputation spoke for itself, but she wasn't done. She stood and gave a dutiful nod of thanks to my lawyer. She laid a single gold coin on the blanket-wrapped pile of stuff I had asked for.

It was easy to recognize, and it would take me a month to even balance it on my knuckles well enough to try and walk it down my fingers like Beau did so easily, but that wasn't the point.

"He didn't deserve this Janzen. He had done his time in hell, and he did it without losing the goodness in him. All he ever wanted to do is protect decent people and live a good life."

The feel of the coin in my hand reignited some of the fire in my soul; fire I used to forge an iron-clad plan. The decent people part struck me because I never realized that Beau still thought of himself as a protector of decent people, even here.

These people are my responsibility to keep safe.

"I'm so sorr-"

"Are you glad to be alive?"

That hit me like a slap, and it was jarring because the change in her voice was so abrupt that it almost seemed like it came from a different person altogether.

"Yes."

"Then you're not sorry."

I had an argument to make over that, but grief was a hell of a thing. You mix that with high octane emotions and things you said didn't have to make sense to anyone but you. She wasn't right. I am sorry, human enough to admit that I prefer staying alive and terrified of dying on some of my darker days.

She was just lashing out.

"I don't need you to be sorry. I need you to make it right."

The use of the word "need" didn't escape me, and despite the newfound fire she had in her own belly I could see it wavering in the face of the unyielding realization that one of her oldest, closest people had been savagely taken from her and the rest of the world. She was utterly heartbroken, and worse yet she felt responsible.

I know she did, because I did too.

"I seem like the type not to square a debt?" There was a sharp, almost immediate scathingness to my tone and I felt more than saw the way each of the respective women reacted.

It was the kind of answer that didn't bear any further discussion. The witch and I didn't have to get any further into it, she knew enough about me to know that I would take this to the mat, and that if I couldn't get my pound of flesh I would die trying. She gave us all one last look before leaving, even stopping to have a quiet word with Shawn who—to my surprise—walked her out.

Perspective is a funny thing, and I tried to remind myself that I've only seen one facet of Shawn, and only at one time in his life, which launched me into one of my daydreaming episodes.

I came back to the living, and saw my lawyer steadily side-eyeing me and waiting.

"Anything else?"

The weight of interacting is heavier than it usually is; my introvertedness is stronger than people might think for somebody who likes the sound of their own voice as much as I do. I'm aware of the contradiction but what's true is true. It's the showman in me half the time, and right now I was so bankrupt and emotionally exhausted I couldn't even fake it.

"How can I help?"

This was the first time I've ever really looked at Groves' sister. Mostly because all she had for me was practiced scowls and sharp quips, not that I could blame her, but when someone is so obviously turned off by you, it doesn't make much sense to try and force any kind of relationship with them.

Something about the authenticity in her voice stuck with me. It reminded me that she's made of the same stuff as my partner, which is why I immediately respected her. She's really pretty, but such a consummate professional that the realization comes late to anyone who's dealing with her. She's my height, in good shape, smartly dressed and usually has a very severe expression on her face. I'd heard some call it a resting bitch face, but I didn't pretend to understand the struggles a woman faced in a professional setting. I think pretending to get it is a form of mansplaining.

I suspected that toughness came from the Grove household; they had a thing about just not taking shit from anybody. It's why our relationship felt so perpetually oppositional – she had no tolerance for sarcasm, and it was the only dialect I spoke competently.

"Keep me in jail for another six weeks and tell my people that I'm good. Not fine, good."

The reflective look ended with a kind of resigned sigh, her eyes having something akin to sympathy in them. When she stood, I followed, and in her heels, she had a solid two or three inches on me. Short-cropped hair framed her face; fiercer and more stylish than the classic I-want-a-manager middle-aged-mom look.

"I can't tell if you're the unluckiest good guy in the world, or just some schmuck who tries to do the right thing more often than not."

Despite myself I smiled, and when I grabbed the bundled-up blanket in front of me, only then realized how long and tightly I had been holding onto the coin Jamie had given me. The one Beau used to roll over his fingers thoughtfully when deciding whether or not he was going to buy the line of shit I had just sold him.

I'm really going to miss that guy. He was solid oak.

"So I have six more weeks to convince my brother you're a lost cause. After that, you're out of here. And don't forget, these little meetings aren't free, at least not for you."

This time there aren't any real teeth to the remark, and the hand she offered me was cordial. It was also the first time she'd taken the time to do so. I shook it while keeping my eyes on hers, a show of respect to a woman who deserved it.

"Put it on my tab?"

Given she'd done all of our work pro bono because her wayward sibling was knee-deep in this shit with me didn't escape her or me, and that softening look soured a bit as she walked out. Not seriously, mind you, but just enough to remind me that she still thinks that I am something of an asshole.

Of course that was the desired result, and she would hopefully be able to update my people on the happenings and do so with news that while wounded, I was good.

Even if this hurt felt like it was changing more than just my mood and outlook.

Shawn met me at the door so he could escort me back to the common area. He's about ten pounds lighter now, his frame swimming in the once well-kept lines of his uniform, but that didn't take from the somber determination written over every inch of his fast-aging face.

***

Another two weeks in solitary helped me get completely right. When Shawn found me pacing my cell, it wasn't because of anxiety—I had latent energy, a restlessness born of ugly eagerness. The sour-faced guard was without the mustache now, and judging from the faint stench of whiskey I got off of him he wasn't doing any better than the last time I saw him.

"It's set up," he said. Dead eyes dropped to a watch he wore on the inside of his wrist rather than the outside; it was an old sniper trick to make sure the face of the watch didn't accidentally catch sunlight and reflect it back, consequentially giving away your position. On another day I would have thought that curious, but today it was just a thing to acknowledge.

"You got about twenty minutes."

I swallowed the urge to say something, mostly because I wanted to make sure I used every single minute of the time productively. We walk in silence, though there's nothing companionable about it; I don't like Shawn, and he's of no mind to be a friend either; but mutual goals make strange bedfellows.

"Twenty minutes," The reminder is curt and somber as he deposits me at the door of the communal bathroom, and I head inside. The way he checked his watch seemed to both confirm the fact as well as illustrate the point.

Showtime.

CHAPTER 5

The Forging Of A Protector

The acoustics inside the latrine allow me to hear them in the back of the shower area. Shawn is projecting his voice to clue me in that they're here. "After this, we're done."

Shawn's thirst for revenge coupled with his drive for self-preservation were the two reasons I trusted him now. I had fed him a version of what happened that he could make sense of, and I could see that he was ready to have it all behind him. He knew better than to allow something that had almost eaten him and had killed a friend to be here. There's probably more to it than that, but neither of us cared to get into it.

The bathroom is a purely functional space. When you walk in, you see a wide opening on the far wall with sinks and mirrors lined up on both sides of the opening. The flanking walls were lined with urinals and bathroom stalls. That opening on the far wall is the entrance to a wide space that serves as the common shower area.

I stepped into a stall, sat, pulled up my feet, and waited. Running showers muffle noise and create steam which confuses the senses. The headphones I had put on had a steady single beat to them: a soothing song that helped keep me focused. Their conversation was easy enough to hear, and when the thing ambled past my stall, I untucked my folded feet from the toilet seat and stood.

It was a strange thing to realize how calm and at ease I felt when on the precipice of violence. Funny how being the one aiming the attack makes you feel in more control, even if that's something of an illusion too.

I pushed the thought out of my head with an exhale, and slowly remove each earbud.

The creature was thrown by the distractions of water and steam, but eventually it keyed in on something elemental, something reliable. Following my scent led it to the last bathroom stall, and the barbaric strength of the fiend was on full display as clubbing limbs sent the stall door erupting in shards. The surprise when faced with what was inside the stall was priceless.

The possessing consciousness who held firm to the ghouls' body was shocked; and the vessel itself momentarily stupefied. What they found inside was a red jumpsuit, a well-worn undershirt, and a pair of boots set up perfectly. By the time the thing could have thought to turn around, I was on it.

The hit I scored to the back of its neck was enough to stun it. Not only that, it was enough force that whoever was riding shotgun in this damned thing was rocked too. I've done this myself, and you don't just feel everything the host body does, it somehow sticks with you long after. Paradoxically, your body is good at adapting and moving on; it's the mind that struggles with it.

The hit to the back of its neck was more than just an overhand right fueled by anger; the brass knuckles I wore actually had a three-pronged, knotted head, with a coin shaped frame in the middle of them. Those three prongs dug an inch or so deep into the still malleable flesh of the hijacked ghoul.

Not resting on the small win, I grabbed the doorframe of the stall and hoisted myself up so that I could propel both my legs forward and mule-kick him into the wall. I heard the thing violently thrashing around in there, desperate to try and claw out the three-prong thing I had just embedded into its neck at the base of its skull—so much so that it was momentarily uninterested in me.

Of course I already knew why, and actually took the time to walk across the room, giving the ghoul and its possessor time to try and orient itself, and understand its new situation.

The thing looked absolutely hostile when it exploded out the bathroom stall entryway, but despite the violence reverberating off of it, I stood my ground, which I am sure only made it even more enraged and vexed. The confused face matched the fact that it hadn't charged me, occasionally slapping at the back of its neck as if agitated by some unseen annoyance.

I could tell it wanted to talk but couldn't, which told me more about it than it may have realized.

"You're trapped." I answered the first of the two questions it undoubtedly had. The other? Well, I was standing across from it completely naked, and I am sure that if it wasn't dealing with a searing trapping sigil stabbed into its neck the thing might have a mind to ask me about that too. The mind and the body have a link, an irrevocable one. The center prong of the device drove home a golden coin and the fire sigil inscribed within is what fused it to the flesh. Flanking the coin were two circular pods of silver, the still hot-from-being-heated pods were burning into its undead flesh, dissolving traces of silver into the thing and sapping it of its strength as the metalloid blended with the ichor-like blood.

"See, I was confused at first. Inhabiting one ghoul, sure, a low-level nobody could manage that with some help or the right tool," My mind momentarily flashes to the *goo* we'd caught Nicholas Greene using that ended up being a magical narcotic that sapped the user. "- even though it would be a struggle."

A struggle I watched this one have time and time again whenever the ghoul would start to get a little rabid.

"But you had three, and for the life of me I couldn't figure it out… it's why at first I thought you were struggling with them, that juggling all three was taxing you."

It's teetering between attacking and listening, usually monologuing was something only a movie could get right but occasionally if you had somebody dead-to-rights they had a mind to listen. This was an absolute pin, a phrase in chess that essentially meant no matter where you moved it was going to hurt. Plus, the searing distraction was a struggle not only because of the agony, but the panic setting in for the body-snatcher, fearing they'd been ensnared in the host and were now trapped in the vile beast forever.

According to the behavioral patterns reported to me by Shawn, this mysterious possessor often slipped out of the body whenever it was confined to solitary. Exhaustion was forcing the occasional, careful break, though the culprit behind this couldn't risk letting this thing off the leash for too long.

Like any trapped coward, it was willing to listen now that an easy meal wasn't on the table.

That's when even bad guys get a bit keener on the idea of options.

"Then I realized when you were down to two it was still difficult for you, and the only time you ever looked to be in any kind of control was when you only had one of them left to command."

I walked down the aisle of stalls, and as expected the thing reluctantly mirrored me until we got into the wide open expanse of the still running showers, standing just outside the splashing water.

"See, I think you're some nobody that's trying to win favor with the black-hearted bitch we sent packing back to the Abyss, and this –"

I slapped the back of my own neck to signal it.

"– confirmed my suspicion. You got your hand on some of the gunk I used to go stomping around downtown last year in that Jim Brown Statue, except you put it in ink and tattooed it onto three ghouls. Points on ingenuity by the way ..."

That snarl told me in no certain terms that I was right, and the fact that the noise was the catalyst of it catapulting itself forward let me know what a big nerve I hit. Just as the thing got to me my left hand shot out, an open palm strike used like a football stiff-arm to keep some distance. It was a move that the monster could take advantage of, because the first thing it did was reach with those filthy fingers out and take hold of my arm.

An arm slick with Vaseline.

An arm it couldn't get a hold of even though it desperately wanted to. I used the now straight-fixed limb to line up another right, and this one came with the full force of my condensed, fiercely concentrated hatred behind it. A brass-knuckle shielded fist went flying across the space between us and the caustic hit I scored on its face was so fucking gratifying that I found myself smiling in the middle of the fight.

I couldn't sneak anything truly destructive into the prison, even with Shawn, but with a little cleverness I was able to put enough stuff together to do real damage. The seal was done by the witch Jamie and was infused with a magic that—in the utmost of irony—was used to sustain and keep life.

Infusing it into this undead thing would normally have had little effect but stamping it onto the tattooed sigil on the back of its neck was enough to trap the consciousness of the pilot inside this body that I was about to systematically break down. It anchored the thing to the body, so there was not only no chance of escaping, but it pulled more of their mind into it.

They felt everything I did including that punch. A ghoul, even a silver-sickened weakened one, could take a lot more punishment than a human—a fact I wouldn't be quick to forget, and one that had sustained my contempt like the last bit of mythical oil which would ward off the night for those who kept faith.

"So when you're down to one you couldn't just let it stomp around unchecked," a broken nose is easy enough for a ghoul to take, but for a human being who wasn't brought up in the thick of violence this was a painful and distracting problem. I watched as the thing worked its jaw and tried to center itself, suddenly conscious and cautious, its hands even touching at the gaunt face.

"You figured correctly that you couldn't let me get out of here alive so that I could track you down."

That's when it launched at me... except now, when the unnaturally strong limbs flexed to push it forward, those once trusted feet slipped completely out from beneath it. The wet tile was slick because of all the dish soap I had spread over the floor before turning the water on. It's gratifying to see how something that was once so terrifying was reduced to looking like a drunken idiot that couldn't find its footing. Undead flesh didn't have good sensory systems anyway, and the more complex experiences were already diminished when tied up in the whole possession thing.

"So I waited until you were exhausted, and I sat in solitary for another month and had the guard check in on you every night. Every restless night you had trying to keep a hold of this thing so that it didn't kill its new bunkmate and get sent away to a supermax. You didn't think it through very well, because even if you did kill me, the amount of noise your bunch of apex predators made when you dropped them into a buffet like this would undoubtedly get you noticed."

It had made it almost to the edge of the soapy floor, but I sent it slip-sliding all the way back with another bone crunching, knuckle-breaking right cross. Its jaw came unhinged, the mandible absolutely shattered, and the son-of-a-bitch inside it was feeling every iota of that agony.

Ghouls didn't wail like this, and it was music to my ears. I watched it flail in futility, those harrowing cries drowned out the minute I pressed play on the big ass radio I brought with me. It echoed harshly, but it also smothered the crying.

"Get up."

Scared eyes search for an exit, any exit, and all that does is provoke my wrath even more. Still, I had to play this smart, and so I didn't charge, I just waited. I even walked across to the sinks so it could try and crawl off the showered tiles and onto the steadier ones. Because it's undead flesh there's no swelling or bruising, so its sunken features are made even more macabre by how clearly I can see the broken nose and fractured jaw. That fear touched on whatever resentment brought this thing here, and that resentment moved on to antipathy.

But the one inside of it knew that it could wait me out, that if it just exhibited some uncharacteristic patience eventually this setting could work in its favor.

So I walked to the bathroom, murmured a prayer and dropped something inside the toilet I had been sitting on at the beginning of this. It took a moment but wasn't long before the piggy-backed ghoul realized what I had just done.

The water spitting out of the shower spout was suddenly poisonous to the touch for anything undead. The religious talisman I had used as a keepsake to remember Bhalore by was more than enough to bless the water when I added the right words. The invocation bolstered my resolve, and the effect as well. This move was outside my normal wheelhouse, so I had Jamie stop by Justin's church and ask the annoyingly aloof priest if something like this would work.

He would have made me figure it out for myself, but I figured Jamie would have better luck than I usually had with the cryptic creature. Fortunately, he confirmed our suspicion to her and here we were.

The holy water was scalding the creature, and like a wet cat, it shot up and then fell over itself several times trying to claw its way out of the shower area on all fours. I greet it with a raised knee to the face, the painful bite of it coursing through the beast and into the pilot itself.

If you can't win a fair fight, don't fight fair. Truthfully, if you enter into a fair fight, you're a shit planner anyway and obviously haven't fully grasped the concept of what a fight is supposed to be. A fight is something you should avoid at all costs because there is no winner, and it involves the direst of circumstances; and if somebody brings one to you?

Make them pay, and then make them an example.

As it writhed on its back it gave me a great angle to fire off a soccer kick to the groin—I do believe in being methodical after all. I peeled its left arm off the body, thwarting its incessant desire to curl into the fetal position, and with a specific hurt-lock I had learned from Grove I broke the thing's wrist. The right gets the same treatment, but with that one I took a bit more time so as to be thorough.

Methodical.

The undead tended not to be as gushy with blood, mostly because of the coagulation. I took hold of the broken jaw and turned the thing to face me.

This human body was so badly broken that I couldn't even imagine the kind of pain it must have caused whoever was behind it all, and so I wait until they've collected themselves to make any meaningful eye contact.

"I don't know who you are, and I don't care. You killed a good friend, and an even better man." There's something ugly in me watching this all go down, and it's not just the thrill of the violence, it's something deeper.

Something much more wicked.

I let it hold a place in my heart: let that vile voice fill my head, and honestly, I relished it.

"This is over." The truth is I wasn't sure killing the ghoul would translate to a dead wielder as well, and I didn't want to risk a loose end on a coin toss.

When my hand rolled to the back of its neck, fingernails catching the lip of the caging token I put over the tattoo there, we were virtually face to face. I know better than to play with odds, so my other arm's forearm was pressed against the throat of the thing and crushing a bit —a ghoul wouldn't care about the loss of oxygen, but a human would.

"We're done," I said, answered by a gurgling sound, one I suspected was something that was agreeable to what it is I was saying. I let the moment linger, as if considering crushing its skull with this entity still inside, but I don't. "I want your word."

A weak nod was all the thing could manage in the state it was in, and without another word I ripped the coin out of its neck.

There's an immediate shift in the entirety of the body before it curled into itself and fixated on the pain it could no longer tolerate as it thrashed beneath me.

I made quick work of killing the ghoul's body and collecting all the stuff that could lead this back to me. As agreed, Shawn is at the bathroom entrance waiting for me beneath the doorway that served as the entrance.

From that vantage point he could see most of what had happened. I traded my discarded jumpsuit from the obliterated stall with a brand new one and left the rest of the warzone for him to clean up. By the end of it the seasoned prison guard knew how to orchestrate the scene to make it look like retaliation, or some kind of organized crime thing.

They would chalk it up as revenge for what happened to Helix and his people. Of course, Helix was glad to bolster the insinuation for social credit not thinking through the potential consequences. I later heard it actually got the gang banger another decade attached to his existing sentence, and truthfully, I lost exactly zero sleep over it.

I was sad to see a token from Bhalore lost against such an unworthy adversary, but the old Muslim warrior would laugh at that and probably talk about the importance of making it to tomorrow so that you had one more glorious day of fighting in the never-ending battle. I thought about the interesting symmetry between Beau and Bhalore while ritualistically running my thumb over the golden coin keepsake I'd possessed from the prison guard.

Token for a token, maybe? I'd stylized the coin a little, carving a trapping emblem into the side I'd sanded down so I could carve the complex sigil into the face of it. I kept the side which carried the insignia of his unit, the side I saw him use for the favorable outcome of a coin flip, intact though.

That night, for the first time since seeing the three stilted, horrific ghouls, I slept.

I slept like the dead.

CHAPTER 6

The More Things Change

The out processing took longer than expected. Of course, most of the experience broke my sitcom-level understanding of how the whole legal system actually worked. When I was finally out it reminded me a little bit of The Blues Brothers (the original version), except as Grove pulled up, I realized we had traded out the Everyman sedan with a handsome new pick-up.

Nice Ride Soldier-Boy I sign, more seamlessly than he's used to seeing, and the face I wore when eyeballing the truck was mirrored by Groves' own expression at my marked improvement. *Prison library* I finish, before tossing my bag in the admirably spacious back seat and stepping up, into the vehicle. The high-five/embrace combination is good, and after Grove gave a testing and complimentary slap to my chest – nodding a little at the improved physique to accompany the crisper signing.

"Yeah, it really is a tried-and-true method. Want a better body? Commit a mid-level felony."

It only dawned on me how stupid it is to impersonate the voice of a generic infomercial guy (or any of the other voices I had a proclivity of imitating) with Grove, but that didn't stop me. There's an approving glint in the once over my partner gave me, before he shifted the truck into drive. I spend a significant amount of time making a show of pressing at a few screens, toying with some buttons and flipping at the gadgets and gizmos on my seat.

Grove has the all-American, good natured farm boy look down to a T. The former soldier was in as good a shape as you could be in, taking the superhero good look thing to a totally new level. With matching blue eyes he was guaranteed to make it so that any girl at a bar was talking to you second. The kind of classic good looks that superseded a lot of the noise. Grove was the type of guy that showed you being as righteous, good, and badass as Superman was possible—and it made me hate them both a little bit more for it. As usual, he was in his unofficial uniform: a strong colored V-neck shirt (today was dark red) and khaki pants with all terrain shoes.

"*So...?*" The finger-spin indicated the inside of the ride.

"The agency has been doing well," Grove explained (his ability to speak had not been affected by the explosion that took his hearing), after uncharacteristically deliberating for a moment. "Really well actually. We started a community tithe, so on top of taking cases, we managed not only to get up on our feet, but we've actually been getting ahead. It works."

"Tithing? Geez Grove, you're only about one more Medieval throwback act away from literally being a knight in shining armor—you know that, right?" Our hybrid method of signing and lip-reading speaking was back on track without either of us having to even try. I usually maintained some semblance of signing as an aid to the soldier.

I smiled, even though the edge came off a little inauthentic as I mulled over the surface of what I was seeing and hearing.

"Sounds like you guys just needed to get me out of the way." I doubt my attempt to sound pithy veils the little sting I felt underneath it. Honestly, I'm not even sure where that came from; it's unlike me to not be happy with my people finding success.

Grove waited for me as I came out of the reflection, a smug half-knowing look written all over his face. He's sporting a light, cultivated beard now. Personally, I hate it. I was hoping the not chubby version of me would be the show-stealer, but bearded Grove was a much bigger attention grabber than my new svelte self.

My ego is a small, petty thing, and I reward it accordingly. "We used your cut for this surprise party that you explicitly didn't ask for—and don't worry, the whole city beneath the city is under the impression that the neighborhood watch network thing is your doing."

I don't know what's worse, the fact that he's basically catching me with a wounded ego, or the fact that the medicine he's giving it is working. Despite all the attention-seeking behavior, anytime I got genuine praise or was put in the spotlight I spiraled down with anything from full on self-sabotage to a good old fashion shutdown.

"So this ... tithing thing?" Grove regarded me and then turned his eyes forward, indicating that the conversation was over, or even more one-way than usual. I thought he was going to shrug off the question but after an exit or two he spelled it out.

"Everyone in the community who has any kind of talent is more in sync and sensitive than ever, and a lot of latent talent has started to blossom. Ever since things started to happen with our stuff, it's had a ripple effect. A lot of people worry that it's the beginning of something. So, it became kind of natural for everyone to start to congregate on our block. Between Kaycee and us, it was a focal point...and ever since the Last Love joined the block -"

"The Last Love moved?" I blurted out, so shocked you could have knocked me over with a feather.

"Well... it was kind of destroyed."

"Oh, yeah... guess that does make sense."

I'd forgotten we'd basically picked a broken-in-half Xander out of the rubble, and only now did I have the bandwidth to consider the cost and impact it might have had on Gale and her entire organization. Moving the whole operation after the underground staple was home of a couple brutal battle-royals wasn't the craziest thing I'd ever heard. Which explained the move from downtown to our little industrial corner of the world. It also reminded me that we'd pretty much been a wrecking ball through the place twice in as many years.

It probably wasn't the worst idea for it to get a fresh start.

Scoffing a little, the realization doubled down on the amount of change that had happened since I was away, and made it feel a lot more real...more important somehow. Apparently, there was something of a citizen's brigade that had started up, and our stretch of sidewalk had become the unofficial center of this World of Weird. Thrown in that Grove was in a brand-new truck, and this ragtag idea we'd spun up started to resemble a respectable company.

All while I was away.

I guess control settles in a little better with the absence of chaos, but it was hard not to notice the sense of a theme starting to crop up that maybe I might have been gunking up the works.

"... and so everyone just does a collection at the events. Kaycee is running an unofficial kind of school to help shape those with enough talent. Pooling resources makes sense and offers ways for people to connect and help one another." I had zoned out a little and missed the first part, but it sounded like they'd forged bonds within the community and created a meaningful way for people to get stronger and find ways to ward off the dark themselves.

"So we're headed to the Last Love then?" Knowing that if they were going to go against the grain and insist on some kind of welcome home shindig, they would at least have the decency to put it in a place where I could get a proper cocktail, preferably one that hadn't spent time fermenting in a toilet.

"Ever the detective," he quipped.

"You're basically a cop now from the sounds of it." My disdain for authority helped charge my counter quip.

Grove, not rising to the bait, just rolled his eyes to the road, signaling our repartee was over as he pulled into the parking lot of the freshly relocated Last Love. Despite how natural it felt to get back into such an easy rhythm with my old friend, I couldn't help but think it might not be so easy with everything else.

The new face of the Last Love Bar was very, very on point. An industrial corner building fashioned with a descending stairwell, which left the eye level facade part looking almost abandoned except for a small clearing at the base that had an awesome aesthetic. It was a marriage of burnished, rustic, and industrial, and produced an amazing signature. I didn't have any gear that would get weighed down or altered by a magical barrier, but as I pushed open the first door, I was confident that there was one. The outside glyph work was subtle and magnificent, and though it had a similarity to what I did, it went several steps beyond that. If not for my recent tenure in jail forcing me to become a lot more studious, I would not have appreciated it and probably only caught half of it.

After the entry there was a landing: to the left was an elevator, to the right a double door entrance into the bar proper, and in between, a familiar smirking face. Verrak in human form, just shy of six feet and built like a champion fighter. Her compact muscle was shapely in a beautifully threatening fashion, and when I saw the lazy way she shrugged off the wall she was leaning against I was reminded of a jungle cat.

Just as I thought about what a fitting choice she was to replace Xander, a wave of sadness washed over me. Xander Lawson, the former Doorman (among other things), was a collection of juxtaposing energies. Bigger than most professional football players, his intimidating presence was counterbalanced by an undeniably warm undertone. He was extremely well-liked, and I suspected the flannel she wore was an homage to the late guardian. Xander was a Rougarou, in the simplest of terms, a purebred lupine—essentially a massive werewolf. Xander was an outcast from his native tribe, which was how he ended up with Gale who'd a well-documented affinity for adopting strays. There was magic about him in the metaphoric sense and a kind of wild purity that was addicting to be around. You were as likely to see the man we had affectionately known as the Regulator with an ear-to-ear grin as you were to see him serving as a menacing vanguard whilst standing over the old bar's entrance, stoneface tucked beneath the brim of his cowboy hat.

Truthfully, Verrak was the only person I could think of who had any chance of filling his shoes. It was a feather in the cap of the Lost Love and the menagerie of weirdness that called this place home that she chose to be here.

Her grunt was met with a clasping of forearms, dropping our heads softly into one another and exchanging an *Un - Khai*. It was a greeting in her old clan; a clan that had been all but eradicated by the Woman of the Abyss before enslaving the few remaining survivors, turning them from warriors to slaves. Verrak taught it to me on her weekly visit, which became a surprising constant that I looked forward to. The Cura'Sha were incredibly driven, whether in hunting you down or navigating Cleveland public transit, and because of that had a reliability about them.

The outfit still had very much of a rocker influence, and she wore it extremely well. The top of her hair was cropped in a low, menacing mohawk, and each shaved side was now inked with a tribal design running the length of the cut. The smatterings of piercings and ink all had a thoughtfulness to them, and despite being very obviously capable in her role as bouncer there was still a very dangerous but decidedly feminine energy about the newly anointed guardian. The role of Doorman at the Last Love was a lot more than just ceremony.

"You look well."

"Yeah, imagine what kind of life I live when prison is the reprieve."

"Men do better when they don't have to think." It felt like she smirked, but she was tough to read.

"I guess incarceration does kind of take the whole decision-making thing out of the equation. Truthfully, that was nicer than I care to admit."

"Don't feel bad, that was my favorite thing about the Army," Grove added.

"There's a joke in there about how identical the experiences are that I'm just not gonna touch."

Grove had the same cheeky look I did as Verrak managed to push open the very heavy door with embarrassing ease. The thick panel and steel framework of the thing clued me in to just *how* heavy it must have been, but I just stepped inside at the behest of her nod. The breath I sucked in turned to a bit of shock as I rounded the spiral staircase that bled into the establishment. The first thing I noticed was that the place was basically empty.

I was grateful for it, honestly.

The second was the new layout. It was perfect... at least to me it was. The first section was green with wood trim and brass accents. There were short-legged, wide tables, and a pair of booths on each of the flanking walls. That area led to a large rectangular space, with a bar-top-height divider straight down the middle and stools on both sides. On the right were restrooms, and walls full of an assortment of eclectic memories, memorabilia and eccentricities, as well as a killer looking jukebox. The left held a full bar that spanned the whole of the wall.

That's where Gale Houdini, would-be Queen of this ragtag community of ours, held court and served drinks. The spot was achingly vacant for the moment, and as I continued to look around, I followed the line of the bar to the back of the room where I saw a stage. It wouldn't be the Last Love Bar without music and a place to showcase it after all.

Gale was like a breath of fresh air, and I actually caught my breath when she came cat-walking around to position herself across from me with only the bar between us. It'd been a while since I'd seen the fierce redhead in person, let alone in action. Gale was a strikingly gorgeous thing, with an alien quality that gave her a signature that felt perfectly aligned with the aesthetic of the bar. Freckles, and an olive complexion, green eyes that shimmered with a preternatural quality from time to time (almost as if on command). It was like every piece of the map had a say in her configuration, all with a modern-day Stevie Nicks influenced exterior. Rumor had it she'd been stealing the show since the age of prohibition though I hadn't done the leg work to confirm that.

Grove gave me a shoulder-nudge while passing by, signing to me that the party wasn't for another hour and a half, cluing me into the time I had to catch up with the legendary bartender and decompress. As I said, it was a relief—not that I didn't want to see everyone but getting to take it in stride was a blessing. My partner in crime knew me well. I surveyed the backdrop more mindfully as I sat on the stool closest to her. She curbed the normal indifference that her haughty air usually projected and flashed a smile of gratitude for our last endeavor. The kerfuffle we'd found ourselves in was the main reason I had spent the much of my last year behind bars ... But I'd do it again without having to be asked, because Gale had proven with action above all else that when push came to shove, she had my back. That went a long way for anyone, I don't care where you come from or what you've been through.

Gale engaged first, just as I started to settle in.

"As I live and breathe." The swooning element in her voice is a heavy-handed exaggeration.

Gale never gave undivided attention in the traditional sense, but having been on the other end of one of her more pointed looks I wondered if that was for our benefit rather than a byproduct of unconscious rudeness. There was something percolating just beneath the surface of those fetching eyes that drove home the other-worldly quality of the woman, especially as they settled on you. The smile is as real as the stout she'd uncorked and plopped in front of me, but it wasn't exactly human.

"...I like the new digs," With the practiced ease of a once heavy drinker I manage to scope, sip and swivel the beer around to pinpoint a few pieces of decor I was particularly keen on. "It's as if designers were trying to create a dive-bar."

"Manufactured authenticity," Gale groaned, "and just spare me the joke about paying for ripped jeans please."

I chuckled, knocking off my normal always-abrasive routine with a surrendering lift of my hand as I took another swig. "So you're chipping in on this newfound neighborhood watch?"

Something in the way Gale blinked told me she was inclined to outright ignore the question, yet as she leaned back on the opposite side of the bar, I kept my rare streak of quiet going to see if she would say anything. "It felt ... I don't know...right somehow? Plus, I considered it my debt to you." Turning away, she paused the motion to flick a glance back over at me.

"We're square, by the way."

"Nine months behind bars, concussions number thirteen and fourteen - thirteen I'm calling Steve, and fourteen I'm calling Fourteen to have some fun with it - and a throw down with a Blind Judge and you think we're square because you let everyone with a decoder ring get in on the business discount?" Skepticism traveled from my tone to my eyes, which traveled to the bottle in my hand. "Oh, and let's not forget the free warm beer."

"The beer isn't free." Gale said serenely in the face of my rather sarcastic diatribe, her brief nod punctuating how unphased she was. "You're welcome."

My mouth opened to debate the entire premise of Gales' failed logic, but somebody interjected, somebody who said my name in a frighteningly familiar fashion—hoity-toity accent notwithstanding.

"Janzen Robinson."

I felt my resistance to let the debate at hand get shelved: one, because it felt absolutely ridiculous, and two, because the way Gale conveyed the finality of it told me she really had somehow done something meaningful enough to qualify as squaring our debt to one another. Her type took this kind of stuff deadly seriously, like some kind of weird mentalist trap with a Grimm-lore answer key.

Still, somebody just used my full name. I had a rule: nobody using your full name was about to tell you something you'd like hearing…ever.

The English had a way of saying your full name with an authority that usurped any of your own. Distantly, it reminded me of my old mentor. "I have been waiting to have this talk with you for some time," she said. This woman was probably in her late fifties, fashionably dressed in a suit that somehow made white on white not seem tacky or even out of place. Lean hands folded together on themselves at the head of an elegant walking stick. She was accompanied by a tall, youngish, exceptionally good-looking man. It wasn't lost on me that this duo had managed to get the drop on me, and while some might credit that to rust, I would be quick to remind them that I'd just spent my off time surviving in jail.

They occupied the mouth of the space at the entrance to the bar area. Judging by the lack of surprise on the proprietor's face it was easy to guess that she knew who this was, a suspicion validated as the redhead sinuously swayed a hand in the general direction of the duo and began introductions.

"Janzen," Gale was a voice that could impart a lot with a tone, and the way she uttered my name cautioned me to have patience and to mind myself. That was a lot to convey in a single utterance, which made it all the more impressive. Honestly, Gale could divulge an entire sermon with a turn of phrase if she'd ever the mind too. "This is Helena Muranti. Sorceress, Master Artificer of the Iandor Institute, and widow of your former teacher, Zachariah."

Whatever snarky thing had been dancing on the tip of my tongue died as quickly as it had been formulated when I heard that last tidbit. I was so surprised that I hadn't even realized I'd come out of my stool in an unconscious response.

CHAPTER 7

Legacy

"You're late."

Chastised, I barely looked up from the weird workbook Zachariah had designed for me a few years before. It was a little childish on the surface, but as I went through it for the hundredth time there was an appreciation I was starting to grow for it; the way it got me so intimately familiar with the basics, the real bones of this craft I was taking on.

Zachariah Evans Thomas, a name he assured me to be deeply English by pedigree, was a fit man probably on the back nine of his fourth decade, at least in looks but I knew him to be a few years over fifty. A little above average height, and always in some muted color suit that was both tailored and impeccable. Some of the accoutrements would have seemed a little silly and antiquated to the casual observer, but over time I'd come to learn that every eccentric trinket or dated pocket watch was a serviceable tool of the trade disguised to appear ordinary. The routine of detaching and systematically laying those very things out was undertaken after walking into his workshop.

We didn't talk about personal stuff which was still mutual despite how much time had come to pass in our makeshift partnership. I'd actually gleaned a lot about him just by being within earshot when he met with various customers who knew him. "Why do you keep assuming we're on some kind of joint schedule over which you have any say?"

Grumpy pants.

That was becoming something of a factory setting with him but given his version of being a jerk didn't wade anywhere near the deep waters in which I swam, it never really bothered me. Zachariah was strict but the guy was a good dude and the thin veneer of asshole he'd tried to layer on top didn't deter most of us from being able to see right through it.

"If you were a wizard, you'd at least make the crankiness pithy."

"If I was a wizard, I'd be one of the first thousand families of the Lake, who were among the first emissaries of real Magic brought over from the Veil."

I mouthed along as he spoke and to his credit he kept going unperturbed until he realized I was pantomiming along with the practiced and scripted monologue. Here, most of the actual awful teacher types would blow a gasket but all Zachariah did was deflate a little bit as his regimented, intense nature became the butt of the joke.

"Bhalore and I were investigating some of those anomalies we've been tracking, and I just lost track of time." He offered despite the earlier bit of sarcasm. "How's the workbook coming?"

How's the workbook coming was a commonplace deflection.

"Same this hundredth time as it was the last hundredth time, though a little more gamey than the hundredth time before that." My riposte was as familiar as the deflection. I closed the workbook.

"These 'anomalies' are really digging at you, aren't they?" The air quotes around anomalies was my none-to-subtle way of pointing out he'd yet to tell me what these were precisely.

"Maybe," he paused, "though it could simply be old habits dying hard." It was a pleasant surprise to watch my teacher toss that dapper coat over the opposite chair rather than place it neatly on the wall hook. As he sat down, he reached out and turned the workbook toward himself, peeling back the first few pages absently, more thumbing over them than really reviewing anything.

Zachariah checked me with a glance, and I held my inclination to ask about … stuff. Stuff about his past and about these weird cases he and Bhalore had been investigating. Cases that led to a revolving door of outsiders and foreigners, most with more juice than a city like Cleveland should warrant, and each of them acting painfully secretive about whatever assistance they were giving. The glance suspended my half-opened mouth, and the approving smirk clapped it shut. Zachariah had a way of making people talk by looking at them with unblinking silence, a tactic that had a way of getting people to open up.

I leaned back, mirrored the smirk, and waved my hand inviting him to talk, instead of asking him anything. Letting people find their way to a thing could oftentimes be even more revealing than digging after it, and so I waited.

"I was a member of a magical Magistrate."

"The Iandor Institute?"

"Yes. The Iandor Institute. We're less enforcers, more Vanguards. Well, I suppose it rather depends on the division and rank and so forth, but quite simply we're a governing agency for interactions with Humankind and well, all this stuff I've been teaching you about." A glance at the counter in the makeshift office stirred him out of the seat he'd just dropped into, and he trudged over to the tea the way an American might to coffee. "The Iandor Institute is a very, very old institute. It has had some other names in fact, but this iteration will probably stand the longest test of time."

"Who's older, the Queen of England or you guys?" I asked, sounding like an idiot.

It hurt him sometimes that I was so painfully *American*. There was a lamenting sigh that excused my barbaric inquiry, though he did have the decency to answer it. "Us. I would love to tell you that the monarchy sustained itself as neatly as some of the history would have you believe, but it didn't."

"Is Merlin real?" I fastballed in, interrupting another attempt to get back on track but feeling like the ask was worth the risk.

"Somewhat. Merlin was actually a collection of people. The thousand families of the lake would be a good starting point for you to research all of that when we get to that time in your tutelage." The reprimand came with a reminder, as if making sure I made note of the suggestion. A lifted mug of tea was the only question…whether I wanted one or not. I nodded. "That is in fact where the myth originated."

"Kind of like Billy Shakespeare?"

"You live to wound."

By the time he'd poured my cup of tea and sat down again, I had fallen into the practiced quiet he'd taught me earlier, a reminder of how to get someone to continue talking. There's another flash of approval in those dark blue eyes, eyes that held me while pushing the mug made for me over to my end of the table. "It's an old institute, and big. Those things have a way of being cumbersome, and I worked for the division that tried to see to loose ends: Watchers, investigators, and the like."

"Cops?"

My disdain for cops is not much of a secret, and Zachariah chortles a little at that.

"No. We divide things a little differently in our duties. We have something of a warrior group too, but I wasn't a part of that."

That was a touch surprising. Outside of maybe two people, I couldn't think of anyone who'd want to go toe-to-toe with Zachariah and his menagerie of magically enhanced weaponry. To think that he wasn't in the enforcement arm of the organization was a little perplexing.

"More MacGyver, less Magnum?"

"Astute and erudite as always, Janzen." The sip of tea had a calming effect on the man, one that was visible. "Whenever I see something strange, I have an almost obsessive need to investigate it. That's why I ended up in Cleveland."

"Yeah, I don't know how people keep believing this is the Browns year either, but here we are."

Zachariah chuckle tempered into a tight, amused smile.

This not asking thing was already bearing fruit, given that I was now getting my first hint as to how he'd picked our quaint little nothingburger of a city to decamp to in the apparent trivialness of retirement. I half wondered if the information he shared was awarded as a way to reinforce the lesson. I wouldn't put it past him; the four-layered mind frame of the man wasn't to be underestimated. If the Englishman was exhausted or half-distracted it was impossible to get a read on him. The urge to dig was written all over my face, but I did an admirable job of deflecting the eagerness by exaggerating an air of patience.

Zachariah sighed but continued.

"There are a few places around the world where magic and the energies associated with it act a little off script. Not only that, but these places seem to have an enhancing effect on those with any kind of magical talent. Cases bleed over from the other worlds with a regularity and an almost magnetic pull that makes them places of unusual saturation. Cleveland is the least exotic or attractive of these places. It is also the least known." A half-shrug confirmed what I had suspected: Cleveland hadn't been a beacon until recently, and this was the reason it had caught the interest of my teacher. "Although it most certainly is known now."

"So you opted for early retirement to do some work here?"

"Sort of." He responded, making his signature double tongue tap sound to punctuate the pause. I could tell Zachariah was about to either taper off or elaborate.

"So you're still working, off book and off payroll, and I'm guessing the Iandor Institute isn't a big believer in your theory?" I asked with the absolute worst English accent you'd ever heard.

"Unfortunately, we have a difference of opinion, yes."

"Evidence weak, or you couldn't get the point across?"

"Maybe a degree of both? Maybe a touch of neither. As I said, it's an old agency that comes with biases, prejudices, ignorance and so forth; very set in their ways. Cleveland may not have the appeal of some of the seven wonders—home to miracles and the impossible—but there's definitely something here. The average number of gifted people is ten times that of anywhere else, and it just doesn't get noticed because of their bloodline, or the fact that they're merely gifted and not up to the standards of an Iandor Academy-type threshold."

"More magic-ability per capita?" I joked, though he captured the comment and surged on.

"Yes. Something that would be a lot more evident if this place had any kind of footprint, or documentation or even formal teachers. As it stands, it just comes across as an inordinate number of clairvoyants and empaths. It's also home to an abnormal number of happenings ... Again, it just reads as dog attacks and missing people reports, but it's there." That last thought was stunted, and he let it die on the lips of his tea-sipping mouth.

"So what else is there about..."

"How's the studies?"

"Ah, shut down once again." Instead of being embarrassed at the narration of the obvious, Zachariah simply nodded his agreement behind the lip of the mug.

I inaudibly grunt at him for shutting down the story sharing but know better than to press my luck. Our conversation had been hard won; the first year and a half of my training had me shut down for asking too many questions, and being scolded about the subpar work I'd done and how thoroughly wrong it actually was.

"It's good. I've got sixteen of the twenty down pat in the last workbook. Of the three workbooks it's the one I have to finish, but I'm finally getting there." Three workbooks. Three workbooks over the last three years, and I was within striking distance of finishing. Felt good, even if it had been an unbearable slog. "These things are taxing as hell, especially redoing everything from the beginning over and over and over again."

"Hm." Smug wasn't quite right, but it was grating how self-amused the man was. "That's a good start."

Always a good start.

"So what, if I finally get through these things and you teach me the rest of the kung fu, can I apply to this Iandor Institute?" Something cheeky inspired the pursed mouth that tilted to one side of his gentlemanly countenance.

"Janzen, those workbooks? They are for year-ones, and most of them finish in a semester."

Ah well, I couldn't say that that didn't hurt but as I reached out to the workbook in question and drug it from his end of the table to my own, I felt that old wellspring of defiance stir to life and I smirked at the pseudo-insult. "Yeah? Well, can they doodle like this?"

"We usually beat it out of them by the first year's end." The elder man deadpanned.

"Hitting a kid is proof positive you lost a battle to an adolescent mind," I didn't mean for the comment to come out as sharply as it did, and I inwardly flinched because of the way it literally stopped Zachariah in the middle of standing up. "Sorry, I ju-" The man had been nothing but kind to me, taken me in when I first fumble-fucked my way into this life, and despite my painstaking ineptitude at the finer points of Artificery he was constantly tutoring, mentoring, and shaping me. My apology was short-lived, a brisk hand waved to cut me off and I dutifully fell silent instead of pleading my case.

Zachariah, master of the silent spell, took the time to straighten up while staring down at me with a newfound air of practiced stoicism that told me nothing and hinted at even less. It felt like a lifetime, but the gruff expression broke into something tight and wry, a scathing chuckle disappearing into the tea with a last deep sip.

"Don't apologize Janzen. I don't teach you because you're a good student," The amendment didn't hurt as much, but my ego did bristle a little bit at the sobering realization that in terms of aptitude I was so far behind the curve it was probably a little foolhardy to have some of the aims I secretly did about where this talent could one day take me. "I teach you because you're a good kid. That, and damn if you aren't resilient."

That last comment was anchored by an affectionate look aimed at the well-worn, thoroughly sketched on workbook I toted around with me like some kind of sacred keepsake. Despite my perpetual pile-on of self-deprecating one-liners even I knew I was a stubborn, hard-headed, determined type. Life wasn't easy, and nobody was getting out alive, so somewhere along the way I realized I was going to live and die by my own hand.

"Our greatest glory is not in never failing, but in rising up every time we fail." The quote startled me out of my pensive state. Zachariah was making an exit, gathering the cane he used when favoring an old leg injury.

"Alright *Balboa*."

"It's Emerson, not Rocky." The chiding was a soft ribbing.

"Yeah, but you're more Rocky than Emerson."

It was the older Artificers turn to laugh.

"How so?"

"Because Emerson visited Thoreau in jail, while you're the type who would be sitting in the cell next to him. Emerson expounded convictions, Thoreau and Balboa lived them." At the time, it hadn't dawned on me that it might surprise people that I knew any kind of historical anecdote, let alone one pertaining to a famous quote. I was already gathering my effects for continued study, missing the small touch of something in his eyes I couldn't quite identify at the time.

Pride.

"That's why I let you teach me, Zac'." I turned the workbook over, dropping my eyes to the last four templates I was working on to ignite some semblance of energy into the blueprinted conduit splayed out on the rough-textured pages. With my worn-and-torn trusted pencil I started scribbling some of the power dialect I knew, feeling if any of it resonated in a way that would allow me to intuitively understand some of the sigils' power.

"You're a good dude."

***

With some hindsight, I could better recall how much that surprised Zachariah; even more surprising was how quick he processed it with a smile. My old teacher thought I was a good kid, and hoped I could be a better man. He was the first to believe in the fact that I was intelligent instead of just snarky. Zachariah never pushed me too hard or brought down the cruelty of his own experience and education when trying to bestow the gifts won from those hardships on me. It's like he trusted that I had the tough part down, and because of that trust, I could extend my own, so that whenever training got to the bloody and brutal parts I never doubted the necessity of it, and therefore doubled-down on my efforts.

Bleed in training, sweat in battle.

***

I remembered the tall fit model type guy being introduced but it didn't quite register. I caught Grove and saw some growing concern walking across his face, but it's muted somewhat by the intervention of Verrak; both of them were lingering near the entrance. The change of cadence in the talk going on around me brought my focus back to the silent interchange between the bartender and the woman in white. With a longer form inventory of the newcomer, I took notice of a particular ruby ring, a series of silver emblems suspended like trinkets on overlapping bracelets, and the unique nature of a pocket-watch chain tucked neatly into her vest.

She's pretty. Not just for her age, but in general. There's something penetrating about her eyes. They are a kind of whitish blue, not quite glacial but something near it. It's as if she knew not to even bother speaking to me yet. Knew that I was hearing everything, and that the noise incessantly ricocheting off the walls around me wasn't being actively listened to. There's a nobility to her features, an earned kind of stature, not inherited. The look I offered Gale let her in on the fact that I took issue with what was essentially an ambush, but I let it slide as I turned on the stool I was sitting on, and both Gale and I regarded the woman at the entrance.

As the two women locked eyes, I wasn't sure what to expect. Gale usually profiled as indifferent, though if you caught her on a good day, you might get intense. She wasn't haughty, nobody as approachable as she could be though there was an air of command to her presence. We saw her as royalty, but there wasn't anyone amongst us who didn't know that they could come to her in a pinch. Still, she was hard to hold eyes with, and known for being very aware of her elevated station ... So when she dipped a respectful nod to the human woman across the way it was not a small gesture. The nod not only acknowledged Helena, and invited her into the conversation, it pretty handily ignored my nonverbal complaints. Helena floated over to pause just within arm's reach of me. Neither of us moved.

"Mr. Robinson," it had a grade-school teacher resonance; less mean and more magical, "while I am sorry to have such a rushed, informal introduction, I'm glad to finally make your acquaintance." It was the way she sank into her words, her steady hands on the cane adjusting a little as she slid smoothly onto the stool beside me. Gale knew the order she'd make for this one, and in her usual unrushed manner set off to concoct the drinks. Helena tapped the cane twice, her smile broadening a touch. "And I disagree with Gale quite vehemently, you look nothing like a sun rotted burlap sack of spuds."

That sharp, refined chin rested exquisitely on her curled fingers as her head tilted a bit to the side. Even sitting it was hard to miss the condition the woman was in, and I don't mean that in a crude way; she was solid, and even though she used the cane as an aid, there was something so steady about her gait that I was confident she could still call upon a significant amount of strength at any moment. That quip about Gale landed just before the drink, which was a Guinness, with a shot of whiskey beside it.

I couldn't help it, I smiled.

"It's only because you're on my good side. This half?" Pivoting in my seat, I rotated to show her the other half of my profile, "straight car-wreck." There was no real change to speak of, but humor didn't have to make sense. I took a moment to take inventory of the guy who'd come in with her. Athletic frame, probably a couple inches over six feet, and every bit of his attire was perfect. I got a military-like vibe, though I suspected it wasn't the kind of service we usually thanked thick bearded men for. The Iandor institute did have a division of soldiers—Enforcers as I recalled them being referred to—but he didn't read that way. Slight difference, but it was an important one. The Iandor institute was the organization that Zachariah had retired from, or was forcibly excommunicated from, depending on how many drinks he'd had before you asked him.

I think of a dozen ways to signify some kind of exaggerated (see: obnoxious) expression to clue her into the fact I was waiting for her to say more, but I realized that she'd already taken up a rather comfortable pose as if expecting me to speak first. Silence is a hell of a weapon as any good salesman or negotiator will tell you, but silence is especially potent if you're a notorious talker. It can interrupt expectations, which is always a good thing to do in cold meetings.

I instinctively did a natural version of this, but Zachariah helped me understand what I was doing and why, which helped me shape it. Art of War meets Alan Watts type of stuff. Something about the way I smile at the realization wins a modicum of approval from the woman across the way, and just as I gulp down my shot and get ready to break the hold of quiet over us, she starts talking.

"It's a pleasure to finally meet you Janzen, my name is Helena Muranti. Sorceress, Master Artificer, Commander of this and that, and so on and so forth. And since Gale has been nice enough to drop me on you like a bomb, I was once married to your teacher Zachariah." She had swooshed her hand around at every moniker and title she named—a mannerism I not only liked but often employed—and managed to scoop the shot glass up and shoot it down in her last swooping iteration of the motion. It was as a salute to my old mentor, and I raised my own glass in response.

"Divorcee is probably the more accurate terminology, though if the old bat was any good with his money and had any kind of respectable estate, I'm sure I would jockey a little more for the widow title." It was fun listening to someone take a well-meaning shot at him; I never had anyone to talk about the old crew and this brought life to a lot of the memories living in the further recesses of my mind. Zachariah had done well enough with the antique shop, but any money he made was spent immediately on research, tools of the trade, experiments, or the local community. Now, judging from the steel-edition Rolex she wore and the designer brand everything she was in (not to mention how perfectly tailored it was), my guess would be that she wasn't hurting for money… but the quip was made in good spirit and relatable. I couldn't tell you how many times I had to cover for the old Englishman with debt collectors; some of them still called.

It was another wandering walk down memory lane, one that distracted me though the astute woman was wise enough not to try and talk or interrupt. I had the distinct and continual impression of her having a degree of approval of the usually grating daydreaming I was guilty of falling into. I suspect she knew this was motivated by our mutual connection, and that despite the divorce, she'd had a great deal of love for Zachariah…not the affinity you'd expect on a human level between two people who once had a special relationship that ended, but rather one born of a shared love that was still alive and well, even after he wasn't.

"What's up Helena?"

"Right. Good communicators know when to get to the point."

"That, and I am very curious how I can help a Commander of the so and so at the Iandor Institute, so yes, let's get to the point."

She asked with a steady look why I would assume she's here for help, a disposition I can't help but smile at. It took a certain kind of talent to be able to ask with pure expression, and I hadn't seen it done so flawlessly since the Englishman had done it to me.

"I'll just share some of my observations and conclusions with you: Your approach has a lot of ceremony to it. You seem genuinely happy to meet me, but I doubt you'd have been compelled by any inclination of your own to make my acquaintance given the estranged nature of your marriage with Zachariah. Plus, if you two had the type of relationship that allowed for more acceptable civility, my suspicion is that I'd have met you before all this. That old coot was dangerously likable and had more than his fair share of faces from his past that made the sojourn to our city. I could keep doing the deducing thing, but I suspect you're a lot smarter than me and it's not as impressive as I'd like."

"Common sense is so rare these days it now needs an explanation," the lament was satirical in spirit, and honest, "nonetheless, spot on. It's official all the way down to the shoes, I'm afraid."

I couldn't help myself, leaning forward a little to peak down at her feet.

"You don't have enough brains to forfeit them for your newfound good looks, Janzen." Gale managed to cut in while passing, punctuating the verbal dagger with a look and a fresh beer on the snide-by. My shoe-peek in response to Helena's own phrasing stopped, but not before I mouthed *thank you* to the Barkeep with the poise of a teasing grade schooler. Sneer and all.

"She thinks I look good." I couldn't help but echo as Helena straightened up, humoring my retort with a smile.

"How can I help the Iandor Institute?"

"We're opening an investigation into Zachariah's death, but perhaps more importantly, we're opening an inquiry into his work. Specifically," the hesitance was palpable—but she wasn't the type to mince words and it had a professional feel to it—"what brought him to Cleveland in the first place."

That was a lot to digest.

"We're here to investigate you too, Janzen."

Belay my last.

That…was a lot more.

Iandor wasn't much more than a myth to me. Something on the periphery of my periphery. During my tutelage I had gotten the quick and the ugly of it, and even some of the more thorough lessons about it were painfully abbreviated. I'd known about the House of Unet, a kind of governance in the Veil as well as the Masarou Tribe, the entity that served a similar purpose in the Abyss. Iandor was our answer to that. It had legacy wealth, bedrock level influence, and was the outfit that Zachariah himself served for the better part of two decades. I always got the drift he came in somewhere around middle-management, and that the break-up wasn't an amicable one. No point in bringing that up now, but I did put that old fact on the shelf to take a look at later.

"This is starting to feel like you're serving me papers, and I'm getting a big *we're gonna ask you to talk but it's not really an ask* vibe."

"It's not an ask, Janzen." Her surprisingly genteel tone was contradicted by an unblinking stare.

"Yeah, hard no for me."

The plus one she'd come in with had longer hair, but it was still fashioned in a very clean, well-kept manner. After you got over the actor's good looks, the fact that the shirt was straining to keep him in was a show of top-flight fitness. He took care of himself, borderline obsessively I think, or at least that would be my guess. My outburst finally warranted most of his attention, and Helena had to lift a hand and almost stop-swat his chest to keep him from closing the gap between us; though to Helena's credit she didn't flinch. I could see their own uncertainty was in response to my seemingly visceral response, but even in the face of our own magical answer to Big Brother I wasn't going to balk, back down, or take any more shit.

Cleveland was my city, and I had people now.

"Sorry, kind of a knee-jerk to authority." Halfhearted apology, halfhearted shrug was about all I could give her. "And the whole answering to people who haven't been around to help isn't a big priority for me. Not to mention your timing is…well…it leaves a lot to be desired."

"Told you." This time, the pass by from Gale was to refill the emptied whiskey. The comment was a subtle piece of advocacy for me, though I couldn't say exactly how I knew that; just something in the way the two women's eyes met. Gale was one of those people—debt or no debt—that I knew would be there if I needed help.

Helena held her breath, deliberating; I can see a hint of tiredness in her eyes. I knew because I'd been there. Hell, I pay rent there.

"Let's break bread," I interject, interrupting before she can resume. The pivot softened her, and after a momentary pause I was able to conjure up a whiskey with some creative pantomiming to Gale. "Put these on my tab."

"You already owe the bar money, Janzen."

"That's why I said put it on my tab, Gale, yeesh."

Gale's low, serpentine smile would usually scare a proper amount of life out of me, but I'd recently earned quite a bit of equity with her, and we both knew it. Strangely, I think my lack of backing down warranted a second more thoughtful once over from her.

"You still need a haircut."

I take what I can get, scoop the shot glass and hoist it up between myself and Helena.

"To the old man. Somebody who knew how to make a proper rule, ones worth living by—and equally important—knew how and when to break them. Zachariah was a good teacher for sure, but as I get older, I realize just how great a friend he was to me."

It took some cajoling, but she raised her own re-filled shot glass about halfway into my makeshift toast. Glasses clink, we drink, and she doesn't even flinch, as I squirm, gag and complain the whole thing down with a deep, eye-twisting wince.

"What was that, drain cleaner?" The protesting tongue stuck out at the glass, scrapping the biting taste off my buds with my teeth before depositing the lowball glass back on the rail.

"Anyway. Zach, friends, right. I'm happy to help. And fur-"

"I need your help finding out who killed Zachariah, and then I plan on ripping the life out of them."

Oh.

That stopped me. It wasn't just what she said, but how she said it…the conviction of it. There was a chill that spread across the room, and I wasn't the only one who noticed.

"Then we have to move on to why he was here. Given your recent exploits it's becoming harder and harder to ignore that there is something going on in this… City."

"Watch it." I love Cleveland, and even though it was a playful ribbing I did have to admit it was unexpected.

"The fact that these incidents seem to not only happen here but have a mind to repeat themselves is definitely cause for concern. There's also the emergence of creature sightings and attacks, though your own…company has done a surprisingly admirable job with that. Still, this place is becoming a magnet for these incidents."

"I would go with "Mecca for Monsters", but I don't think it'll get by HR."

My commentary was priceless, her irritable scowl be damned.

"And considering your own infractions…the fallout cannot be ignored—surrounding circumstances notwithstanding," she added. I could tell that she was trying to be somewhat diplomatic about this but having recently been the center of attention for law enforcement, and just getting out of jail, I was more than a little tired of this. Especially since it was the subject that Iandor ignored that opened the door to everything that happened.

"If you want to bring your happy ass down to Cleveland to help clean up shop, I am all for it sister. I know Zachariah was chirping about that for a year straight, trying to get one of your Inquisitors or Conquistadors or whatever the fuck name you got for them down here…." And then it hit me, and she saw it too, the epiphany that Zachariah had spent the last year furiously trying to get help from every power that be, but none would listen. That is what kept him distracted and detached during my last year around the shop; I always knew it was something important but had never imagined this. This thought killed the momentum of my tangent and clumsily led me into another thoughtful, beer sipping quiet.

I half turned to the exit, but stopped as I watched a few familiar faces start to roll in.

Nicholas Greene was the kid we'd caught with some Witch-Doctor juice juju, a substance that had been at the heart of a few of our headaches. He looked better than I remember, which didn't surprise me. In order for the substance to work it derived power from funneling your own life force, basically sapping you like all the best vices did. Obviously, he'd been off of it for a spell because there was a kind of quiet confidence about him now. Maybe it was just general rejuvenation, or maybe it had been the help he'd been giving us of late. I had it on good authority that he'd been crucial on quite a few of the accountability projects they'd designed for everyone. Nicholas was an accomplished coder and hacker, somebody who'd pulled in big money out in the real world; and he'd used the combination of those two things to help systemize a lot of what the group had been doing to help our locals. To say I was proud didn't quite express it…those of us who walk out of our own darkness are more gratified than people might imagine when we see someone else make it out of the same crucible. It was quietly reassuring on the best days, and openly motivating on the worst ones. Formerly dirty and disheveled hair was slicked back into a tight ponytail, and a pair of horn-rimmed glasses accented his square face. He's barely old enough to be allowed in the bar, and I was looking forward to buying him a beer.

Or, well…maybe he was buying me a beer. I was broke. Still, I was excited to drink beer while he was in relative proximity, which was a big thing for a guy like me.

As he spilled inside to greet Grove, Johnny B. was on his heels – looking as flamboyant as ever. The elven power-ballad-bard was a recent ally, and a damn good buddy. I was glad he stuck around. Taller than almost everyone, though just a hair above Verrak, Johnny was bean-pole thin—strong-skinny I called it; his frame looked like it belonged to a swimmer, though the outfit was some kind of homage to every generational outcast known to modern man, tied together in an explosion of acid-washed denim and rainbow bright color. Ever in the know, the *stink* face he'd given me was a comment on the company I was keeping, and with his notice of this impromptu congregation the usually imperious song-bandit tactfully took up refuge at the far end of the bar to make sure I stayed within eyesight. Far from the grown-up table I'd been tricked into sitting at, but present. The Soldier and the Hacker flanked him at the bartop after a quick round of civility with staff.

"So, what, we're going to get our own version of Lestrade finally?"

The Englishwoman finally broke, and the light smile was disarmingly resplendent, there was a kind of poise to her that was impossible to teach and effortless to watch; Helena was really a striking woman.

"That would make you Sherlock then?"

"Yes, thank you, Grove will be happy to learn about the doctorate." Watson was a fitting placeholder for Grove. Watson was the Samwise Gamgee of these stories anyway.

The woman laughed and shook her head.

"And let me guess, their first order of business is to try me on some kind of Kangaroo Court for the blown-up building downtown."

"Two blown up buildings." Gale dropped as she breezed by on her way to her son, our favorite Karaoke King. Out of the corner of my eye I saw the embrace and the easy repartee, and it made me smile.

"Helping or hurting, Gale… Helping or Hurting."

"Janzen," the soft tone was back, and I turned to regard a woman who I had every suspicion was about to tell me about some kind of very severe punishment that had to be served upon me. "We're not going to send anyone."

I felt Kaycee come in, and her route to me was a lot less circuitous than everyone else's. She was striding over purposely, with every intention of joining this conversation. In fact, I could see there was a part of her that actually wanted to interrupt. The half-elf was a welcome nugget of calm and serenity in the midst of all this, and while some of my pseudo-meditation prepared me for the prospect that I would step out of the jail and into a madhouse, the fact that it had literally been what had happened was a little jarring.

"It seems pretty obvious that there's a fight coming Janzen, a war of some kind." Helena Muranti; The Sorceress, Master Artificer, bona fide badass Mary Poppins decked out in the kind of ensemble you'd expect out of someone that came from money, had buttoned her set up nicely and now hit me with the big reveal.

"You've been conscripted. That was part of the agreement."

CHAPTER 8

Draft Day

Conscripted.
    Part of the agreement.
    I lifted my head in time to see and feel Kaycee lay a hand on my one arm and put her other arm around me settling in at my side. Kaycee was half-elf, though by the standard caricature of what we'd come to see as an elf, she came across as quite unusual. Pretty and charming as the day is long, there was a gravitas to the woman that had only become more pronounced over the years. She was thick, and the first one to tell you about it, and there were a few wisps of gray in her hair to offset the raven thicket that was usually tangled up into a messy bun. Cliche be damned, she would sometimes walk around in an easy sundress and apron while running the magic shop across the street and taking care of her kids. The shop was another Kansas City Shuffle so to speak; it was home to an actual magic shop beneath the made for the masses one. Lately, she'd taken to schooling locals directly, which was good because in terms of raw prowess Kaycee was actually quite an accomplished sorceress herself. Kaycee was over a hundred, but as was the case with any mixed breed, once the human blood started to win out and you began to age, devitalization began to catch up. She'd another hundred in her, but she was starting to gracefully glide into the proverbial back nine.
    She was my oldest friend, my rock in a lot of ways, and the only person who never had the luxury of falling apart because of

the cacophony of the demands of her world. On top of her own family responsibilities, she'd taken to being a steward of the lost and downtrodden, like some kind of foul-mouthed patron saint of the street.

She had a charming habit of being very country in demeanor and speech, and then shifting abruptly when aiming to hand out an ass chewing. I could tell she was blisteringly mad because the glamour for her ears wasn't up, but this was the kind of mixed company where that was easily overlooked. Fun fact, almost all those double takes you do? Probably from a slipped glamour of some kind. Maybe not all, but it's about half my caseload after you do some bubble-gum detective work.

"Hi Gale, really appreciate you keeping to the plan—you know, the one we all agreed on when we were talking this through together."

"He's almost forty Kaycee, got to let him off the tit sometime." These two had history, and it was the best kind of history because not a single soul knew a thing about it and neither of them had an iota of an inclination to bring it up.

"I'm not even thirty Gale." I said, balking at the bartender's retort.

"Ouch."

"Real mother of the year, this one." Johnny B. had not only managed to slide over to center stage in our makeshift circle, but he'd done it so surreptitiously that it was the shot at his own mother that announced him.

Gale opened her mouth to respond, revisited whatever horrific abandonment drama had driven such a wedge between herself and Johnny, and instead just shrugged while muttering "that's fair". Helena studied the way we all flowed so seamlessly; it was easy for an outsider to see that this group had spent more than a few nights and a handful of cocktails together, sharing new woes and old stories with equal ease. It wasn't lost on me that some of my people had started to tow-the-line in as much a show of unity as of force, and it dawned on me with some very real weight that even after my absence I was not only every bit a card-carrying member of this community, I was truly one of the Founders. With Kaycee holding court with Helena now, Johnny was happy to just lean that long back on the bar and keep his eyes on the proceedings.

"It's like Jem exploded all over your face Johnny B." I fired over my shoulder, commenting on his exotic eyeliner as he single-arm hugged me from behind and dropped an affectionate kiss on the back of my head, while never taking those made-for-mischief eyes off the other pair.

"*If only.*" the rocker managed to suggestively whine. I love/hated him, as I diligently edited out any image of a middle-aged Jem and Johnny B. tangled in love throes. I swatted at the studded lapel to shut him up but paused long enough after the impact to share a mutual smile of understanding, gratitude anchoring my side of it while duty anchored his.

"It's good timing Kay, 'cause Helena seemed to be suggesting we cap off my *welcome home from jail* party by making me a *copper* for the Umbrella Corporation over here." Before the orator of Iandor could defend their ranks, the leveling look I gave to my oldest friend still pressed to my side had a question mark. She knew why too. There's a host of bad byproducts to having a brain like mine and being a social-contract slayer (between the short attention span and the unintentional rudeness, and sometimes both at once) was one of my most cherished.

And I put pieces together really fast. "Apparently that was part of the agreement."

Suddenly, I realized that Johnny wasn't there to back me up with Helena, but instead to back Kaycee, who was looking across the bar at Gale, who was standing post for the same reason. "And what exactly is this agreement?" I could feel the first grasp of dread, shifting my look from my compatriots to the newly crowned Woman in White who'd started this. Anxiety can be debilitating, and I had to work to keep mine from rising up at the sudden degree of seriousness blanketing everyone.

Kaycee began to speak. "A lot changed after the trial, Janzen. A lot. There are questions still unanswered about why Zachariah took early retirement and relocated to Cleveland—that came up again obviously. Cleveland was basically witness protection for those of us in a bit of a jam at his behest after he'd gotten here and set up shop. Zachariah was trying to shine a light on all of these coincidences and happenings. Still, most of us are here under a kind of allowance, and that's directly from the very powers that oversee some of our oldest rules; the ones threatened by recent dealings. Everything with the Masarou Tribe, and the House of Unet, plus with—"

Helena actually reached out and touched Kaycee on the forearm, and it was another small moment with larger implications; an ask of forgiveness was there in the first moment, as well as a reassurance in the nod that let the elf fall quiet so the Master Artificer could try and put the pieces together.

"We're not sure as to the how of it, but Donovan was amongst those helping Zachariah. We suspect that when Zachariah tried to liaise with the other governing bodies after failing with Iandor, he went through Donovan and Ja'Sune. They worked against him and used the knowledge of what he was trying to do and what was going on to suppress anything from getting out. Both Masarou and Unet were grossly unaware of anything when they set up the trial, and the contingent sent only came because of old loyalties and some complacency. If we can figure out what Zachariah discovered, maybe we can get ahead of this, and start acting on it rather than reacting to it. I know your experience thus far with these agencies have been-"

"-Thick with corruption and layered in incompetency?"

Despite himself, the guy who was her hang around chuckled. Helena took a moment to make formal introductions. "Julian, this is Janzen. Janzen, you might as well have the name of the man who is constantly glowering at you. Julian is my former apprentice." Despite being embarrassed by his impulsivity, it was obvious that she was very proud of her hand in his development.

"Low hanging fruit, but fair." Helena managed to muscle through without laughing, but I was glad she smiled. Sometimes you think you're going for blood with an outburst, and other times you realize maybe you were just looking for a little acknowledgement.

"The IRS being assholes is low-hanging fruit, y'all are two day rotted apples on the floor."

"Regardless," the tick of irritation placated me, and while most would assume it's my incessant and unexplainable need to rub-someone-raw thing, there was a method to my madness." – there were some innocents involved in all that transpired, people caught in the crossfire of Donovan and the woman from the Abyss."

I resisted the urge to offer a more concise name for the fiend, like bitch or scum.

"Nobody wants blood, or anything archaic like that, but accountability and an effort to make sure this kind of thing doesn't become a mainstay in Cleveland is of paramount importance. If we can ensure at least that much, there are certain things we can acknowledge as just a tragedy and move on."

I flicked my eyes up searchingly, the urge to be scathing corralled by my genuine curiosity of what it was exactly—outside the things that happened to our people—that could be considered tragic.

"The dark elf for example, apparently he was just a guard doing his duty," Kaycee offered me as a lifeline for my aimless thoughts. I recall the combatant, the one who'd chased me out of the old courthouse and had been one of the most troubling enemies I'd ever come across—Blind Judge included.

My mouth opened to protest.

"The two goblins from the Masarou Tribe," Johnny ticked off. How I could have saved them I hadn't the faintest clue, making my already arresting shock send me into a stupor. In my turn from half-elf to the full bred rock-a-billy one behind me, I caught something of a grimace on the black-haired, black rimmed tag-a-longs disposition. I couldn't say why, but it convinced me to hold my tongue. People hurt by people shouldn't have to explain themselves, and while passing this conversation with us, I could tell this piece of the puzzle stung to the yet-to-be-investigated interloper a bit.

"There's also the matter of the property damage. You destroyed an older, valuable Blind Judge that has a higher responsibility to the cause than any of us." Julian added, reeking of company man bullshit; a corporate ladder climbing, merciless asshole if I ever saw one.

"Property damage…are you fuc-" Kaycee actually *clapped* a hand over my mouth, which was good because my eyes screamed when they turned to the next commentator. I was about to say that maybe advertising something as unbreakable was just asking for it anyway, but I didn't.

"The three Unet council-people weren't in on it either, so that's what…five?" Johnny, unperturbed, kept counting. "Alpha and Delta were pretty badly beaten and bruised; they were down for almost as long as you were. I imagine they want that in the record."

"Johnny." Luckily, with a controlled squeeze I conveyed to my oldest friend that she could trust me with my own faculties again and Kaycee had thankfully removed the manacle she'd turned her iron-grasp into from my mouth. The helping or hurting comment came to mind, and it momentarily made me smirk at how alike he and his mother were. My hands instinctively spread out and I stood up at some point.

"Okay, cliff notes version, we're all here because you're mad that I broke your monster and let your council die, the same council that was trying to sentence me to death for something neither I nor Gale did." Based on context, and being able to sniff out bullshit, this was hard for me to even pretend to stomach.

"You're here because Zachariah was right, and not crazy, and now you're covering your ass."

Helena had grown conspicuously quiet and maintained an air of watchfulness. "And you give me this bullshit rush job treatment because Iandor is one of those agencies, governments, guilds or whatever the fuck, that has their fingers in everything and hands on everyone so that you can throw your weight around, and the kicker is that even my own people are hoping I'll be diplomatic."

Julian couldn't help but smile at the way everything was going down, and I noticed there was a touch of response to my tangent that told me that if this had been a neutral audience, I'd have won them all over. "I've been trying to get here since there was a rumor of a Stalker passing over in a rift, so in a roundabout way I should thank you?" A shrug complimented the rhetorical statement.

Much like Helena, the guy had a few pieces; noticeably this wicked cool double-ring with the shape of a mace laden over the top of it. The craftsmanship was amazing, the replica feel of the weapon being depicted was so detailed and there was the neatest, tightest scribe-work of sigils across the heart of the main band. Pragmatic work, but just unbelievable; like the best kind of basic handwriting in the world. The simplistic nature didn't take away from the potency either, and the fact that the hand was so impeccable I imagine it charged and channeled the powers associated with it brilliantly.

"Plus, I got a promotion after the whole Judge debacle." Black eyes hiked up gleefully, seeming to be unfazed by the fact that this incident was something of an ongoing nightmare for the rest of us.

Ms. Muranti wasn't distracted by my outburst and was steadily tracking me with an assessing stare.

"All things considered, this is about as cool as I can be about all of this. Setting aside what was done to me and mine, you do offer food for thought." I finally said after chewing on the implications of the bigger picture. The vague gesture does a poor job of encompassing all of their points, and truthfully, I'd never put any meaningful thought into that side of it, even with nine months in jail and little else to do.

Helena, having adopted quiet during this part of the discussion, slowly shifted a look to Gale.

Gale, who looked perfectly mysterious and absolutely majestic with her arms crossed, and her cat-eyes alive with a power that I had personally seen answer the challenge of would-be Godlings, was posturing. She was posturing for me. That was why nobody intervened with my sentencing, or time inside. All of this felt like it was being laid out in an agreed upon, scripted fashion, and I was sure that that was her influence. She wasn't just tipping the scale; she was staking a claim on one side of it.

She wasn't kidding when she said we were even...that sucked.

"There's more to it than just their desire to police the situation, Janzen." Kaycee said, uncharacteristically cautious. I considered her the wisest amongst us and trusted her to prioritize the right tone over the one that she may have wanted to take. "Half the reason the community is becoming so tight knit is necessity. Not only are there random attacks that we can't explain half the time, but even some of our own people are starting to struggle. This stuff is dark and addicting, and as the gifted become the able there's a lot of stuff that's going unchecked. Iandor is suffering from a similar problem, but on a larger scale. Those problems began to escalate not long after your first run-in with this...*Woman*. It's likely that that wasn't the beginning of it either. We now believe that all of this has been brewing for a lot longer than we ever imagined."

Since our encounter at the lake, I had suspected that this woman, this unofficial Queen of the Abyss, was most likely responsible for the death of Zachariah and the team. Hearing someone else say it turned it into more than just a passing thought or suspicion; it was a fact. I bit my tongue to keep myself from saying something stupid.

"We can talk about it more tomorrow, maybe late in the afternoon after you've had a chance to settle in." That maternal instinct was running hand in hand with her very justifiable apprehension that I was on the cusp of saying something idiotic. Kaycee knew me the best of the lot and knew the only thing I loathed more than authority was being told what to do.

I'd already blown any chance of being some kind of rehabilitated zen-master, and while a parting shot would be on brand, I found myself exhaling through the smart-assery and instead tried to land on something a little more civil.

"Yeah," I offered after a pensive moment, nodding myself back to the present. "I'll see if I can clear my schedule." I emphasized the wrong part of the enunciation but didn't have the heart to really drag it out. With some effort I was able to not only keep the irritation from my face, but actually push it aside while standing with Helena.

We shared a sense of duty to one another, though I couldn't say why I knew that, or where my confidence in that suspicion came from. Zachariah mattered to each of us, albeit in vastly different ways, and I knew that if there was an opportunity to make sense of what had happened to him it might help with whatever closure looked like for both of us respectively. It was easy to get a feel for how unhappy I was at the way a lot of this went down, but I think I did an admirable enough job keeping the fuck you off my face.

"We'll be in touch, Mr. Robinson."

It stung a little, hearing my name in the English lilt.

"Use the paper cup phone, I didn't have a chance to get a new cell yet."

Helena did an impressive blink-balk hybrid, before opening her mouth to inquire, but instead shifted a look to Kaycee. The half elf shrugged and gave a confirming nod.

"He's not kidding."

I turned to the bar, breaking the dialogue and trying to drag my mind out of the cauldron of headaches that would inevitably be born of whatever this would become. Like all the most important figures in my life, I had spent a significant amount of time thinking of Zachariah during my time in jail. That was especially true when I was studying in my cell. Reminiscing in an almost daily meditative state, I was fortunate enough to walk through a myriad of our lessons and interactions together and was grateful.

Kaycee was literally dragging at my arm to shake me back to the now, and as her sigh melted into a more commonplace smile, we ordered another round of drinks and started to welcome the night in, while toasting my homecoming. It was a nice gathering. Kaycee never directly addressed the impromptu meeting I was blitzed with, but I knew we would talk it out in due course. Grove was a lot freer from his shell than I ever remembered him being, though it made sense since he'd served as a kind of glue for all of this in my absence. Johnny sang about a dozen songs despite never once stepping on the stage or being asked to. Eventually, even Patrick rolled in.

Despite my new concerns it was nice to be home, and for the first time since the era of my old mentor that was exactly what all of this felt like.

Home.

CHAPTER 9

From Hunch ...

The night found a good rhythm after the interruption. Strained small talk eventually got traction, and after I made it abundantly clear that I wasn't up for discussing the heavy implications of everything that had transpired earlier—even after a fourth and fifth round—it was pretty universally addressed anyway. Truth be told, the festivities with my ragtag crew got a little livelier than expected, and it became pretty obvious to me that they needed a blow-off evening much more than I needed any kind of Welcome Home party. Throughout the night I got small insights into what they had been dealing with lately. They had definitely been busy... though nothing anywhere near as traumatic as our inaugural battle with the Abyss intruder

Nor had anything been as violent as the brawl that had landed me in jail, and taken the life of Xander, the original doorman of the Last Love Bar. Still, it was a little jarring to hear just how much activity had been thrumming throughout my city. Apparently, the unification of the abnormally large number of people in the know about our world was fueled more by random attacks, troubling disappearances and other insidious coincidences that had been piling up recently. The city was lucky it had been left in such capable hands, but I could feel the battle-fatigue in almost everyone. Kaycee, an already perpetually exhausted mother, friend-group chaperone, and surrogate for every lost soul I knew, was now doubling-down on her already overwhelming responsibilities with this school she had started. Her students were gifted, but it wasn't as if she could churn out effective foot-soldiers. The schism between someone able to cast a spell because of innate ability and a battle-ready wielder was so large it was almost impossible to quantify.

Grove, with the surprising help of Nicholas, had been developing custom security systems that would alert the growing community with communication, contingency and escape methodology while also alerting him and a few other key players as to the whereabouts of the disturbance. Of course, that kind of exertion came with an often-unacknowledged commitment; meaning that whenever he wasn't fielding a job, working a job, or training, there was the city-proper to be patrolled, people to check-in on and failsafes to be regulated and maintained. Even Gale seemed more reserved and resolved, and when I had made it a point to let everyone know I didn't want to get too deep into the details of what had just happened with Iandor, I did let her know that I was curious about why there wasn't any debt to be named between the two of us.

Johnny B. and Verrak appeared to have fit right into the Last Love Bar and were able to interject enough personality to cover down when Gale felt a little muted, presumably at the loss of Xander, who was her life partner. The place was doing well, and when the hour turned to night proper, I was pleasantly surprised at how many of the occupying denizens came over to offer some form of appreciation for our collective efforts and take some time to welcome me back. Admittedly that didn't suck but given that self-deprecation was my go-to for humor, protection, and deflection, it was hard to really accept in any meaningful way: I was still incredibly reticent about things, and getting acclimated was not that easy. The inevitable challenge and moments such as these, felt like the real first canary in the coal mine of my self-esteem, and were leading me to the irrefutable inevitability of my own value.

Patrick seemed the only one who was unchanged, which wasn't that surprising. The Concrete Monk was a self-possessed, world-weary vagabond; somebody who swam in the deepest parts of these treacherous waters. Not as outright knowledgeable as a Gale or a Kaycee, the cut of his jib was a lot closer to my own, and given our similar origins, it was hard not to have a kinship with the Street-Saint. A couple inches taller than me, Patrick was a thick bodied, husky sort; fit enough that you had to wonder how much of the girth came from the ragtag layers he wore, and how much was well insulated strength. Truthfully, I'd never seen the strong frame in anything other than an almost cliched, homeless-esque uniform; a hand-me-down burgundy beanie, paired with a faded long-sleeve sweater, and navy cargo pants, punctuated with a black bandana neatly tucked in his back pocket and taped up outdated new balance running shoes. What a look.

The red head was a protector of those that had nothing and no one. Even though some people thought the homeless community didn't deserve a champion, the truth was that they did in fact have the best protector in the city. The talk about people that went missing led me to think of Patrick, both because of his affinity for being the type to defend that very group of people, and because the homeless served as a second-to-none information network. I knew Grove, Kaycee and everyone else would have trouble getting that kind of information out of him; primarily because nobody thought to ask…and there was also the fact that the man had a strange method of measuring people and was only inclined to help very specific types.

I think I inherited the loyalty Patrick had for Bhalore. They were thick as thieves when they weren't trying to take each other apart in training. There was history there, the kind that deserved an epic tome no doubt, but as men such as they were ought to, neither ever spoke of it. I respected that, and Patrick and I honored that legacy during our last foray into the impossible together. I wanted to understand more of what had happened and was going on, so I set up a time for us to talk the following evening. It wasn't that I wanted to be secretive, but easing into this newfound network was going to take time, and I had a few things I wanted to check out first.

Everyone understood my wish to head home early; the stunning sincerity of all the guests was both uncomfortable and nice at the same time. So I headed out with Kaycee who walked me across the street to her store so that I could retrieve Max—my very favorite family member. I was quick to cut-off any attempt she made to discuss what had happened by plying her with a constant smattering of questions about my dog. We both knew it was avoidance, but I was a master at it, and kept the facade of exhaustion front and center to explain my sudden aversion to sharing.

After assuring her I wasn't upset or even caught off guard, I cut her off for the last time by opening the door to Max. Time was funny…nine months wasn't as long for people as it was for our furry friends. For Max? A pitbull flirting with a decade, it was a much more consequential stretch of time. It hit me a little hard to see the gray spotting on that once steel-blue pelt, and while excitable, I could see a measurable stiffness in the couch-dismount that preceded him jogging over to me. Still, that old land-shark hit my flank with gusto. It was the first uncomplicated surge of goodness that I felt since I got out. I leaned down to take hold of him.

I promised my oldest friend, quasi-mentor, and surrogate sister Kaycee that we'd get into the nitty-gritty of everything after I slipped into a small coma. I felt a little guilty about how good it felt to get away from everyone, and that was reinforced by the fact that I knew every one of them could tell that there was a change about me, one I embarrassingly hadn't even really grasped until this very moment; something to think about as Max and I headed home.

Max didn't exactly heckle up, but the break in that aloof, airy prance-walk that was his signature cued me into an unseen shift in the energy. The short-legged canine curled a look toward a nearby alley, one about five feet ahead and just outside the entrance to my efficiency. I'd actually only gotten to move into the place right before sentencing. Cheaper than my apartment, and attached to the shop, it was ideal; especially since the office doubled as our home when we were on a case anyway.

"Gale sent me," the familiar voice of Verrak was surprising but not startling, and the way she just blossomed out of the blackness was a stark reminder of her lineage and abilities. Verrak was not only one of the *Cura'Sha*, the woman happened to be one of the biggest and baddest of her tribe. She moved in a soundless predators' saunter stopping just to my left in the center of the sidewalk. Leveling me with a look, and standing in companionable silence, I held court with her stare well enough to let her know—without words—that that wasn't a good enough explanation. We stood the last few feet from my place but given that she wasn't telling me what it was she was actually doing here, I begrudgingly pulled a reluctant Max into the street in an attempt to get past her. I was about to stride by, calling her bluff, before I heard her rather theatrical sigh that carried a toothy muttered *fine*.

"She noticed you spit almost every shot into your beer, and barely finished any of those." The question mark in her stare was met with a blink, and another bout of silence, though I had slacked the leash enough to let Maximus bulldoze into her denim calf and demand some acknowledgement of his own. I thought of deflecting the insinuation with some witty quip about twelve steps, which would make some sense given my well-known struggles with booze, moderation, and generally any sound decision making, but I reminded myself that cultural and topical references tended to elude even the most engaged human-pretenders, and Verrak was far from involved or studious in her efforts at blending. She watched my mouth open for comment, the processing thought getting worked over, and instead my answer was served up in a spiritless half-shrug. Unbothered by the stoicism, the warrior knelt to give some deserving adulation to the mutt mulling around her feet.

She answered my apathy with an approving grin, even if she was for once the more expressive of us while scratching under my dog's chin and whispering sweet, guttural-tongued encouragement to him in her native dialect.

"Change is hard. Even more so when we're the changed one." I surveyed the scene of Verrak and Max thoughtfully, before giving a slow-burned nod as if to both agree with the point punctuated by her follow-up quiet and even encourage her to continue. Unrushed, it wasn't until the Stalker stood that she continued speaking. "You have changed Janzen Robinson, in ways your people can only scent but are far from understanding." There was an implication behind the vagueness of her statement, and I could smell it and sense it with this newfound wisdom that was hard, and ugly won.

"Gale asked me to make sure you got home tonight." There was a kind of seriousness to the prowl that pushed her past me to my apartment door, and she reached above the door frame to grab the hidden key tucked behind the woodwork, "-which is good for us."

"Us?" I bit, a little subconsciously, but it was honestly fascinating to watch her deduce not only my intentions but sniff out the irregularities in my pattern of behavior.

"Well, given her wording, all I have to do is make sure you're home, which means I won't have to tell her about wherever it is we're going, so long as I can get you back here in relatively good health."

Shocked rather than surprised at this go around, the glamorized, death-dealing super predator had been able to deconstruct the actual motive of my evenings' behavior with disarming ease, and an accuracy that transcended some of my oldest friends and confidantes. How she knew I'd planned to go elsewhere was beyond me, and the fact that she'd been remarkably accurate in her assessment was so obvious that I didn't dare try to conceal any of it, as I followed her into my home.

Home felt like a generous description of course, given the fact that I'd only spent a handful of nights here before sentencing. It was a studio attached to the Circle Protection offices on one side, and Grove's efficiency on the other. We thought it was efficient— pun intended. My tribe had made sure that it was ready for me. Max dutifully trotted over to the food and water bowl, which I quickly filled, and after making a slurping crunching mess, eventually slunk off onto the criminally fucking comfortable hand-me-down couch. I mean, it was a petri dish of disgusting I was sure, but damn if it wasn't able to steal you away into a soul-stirring slumber at will.

"Where are we going?" I pry tentatively, even searchingly, as if I was actually worried, she knew where I had intended to go in the witching hours of this evening.

"I don't know…I think it's above my paygrade." There was something a little too self-amused in the answer for my liking.

Still, relief flooded over me as I realized she was being honest. So the sage Stalker hadn't sussed out where I was planning to go, she was just sniffing out the fact that I obviously hadn't intended to end my evening just yet. Honestly, I should have guessed that, but I think I was so thrown by the initial observation that I hadn't recovered all the way. Whatever lie I was going to freestyle died on my tongue because of the withering look she gave me for even entertaining such a thought. My sigh is a bit more defeated than her own irritated one from earlier, and with a literal *bah*, I wave off the futility of trying to evade her and instead trudge by the couch-and-television room to the wall where some of my old artifacts were mounted in an ornate, display.

"It's nothing really."

The second withering look aimed at my back is placated by my own expressive glance. Verrak had been routine with her jail visits, and even though they were a little stilted and awkward at first, it wasn't long before I came to look forward to and enjoy the consistent reprieve from the daily slog that prison-life was. We passed the time with her telling me about the Abyss, about how wide a variety there was in her species and how plentiful the tribes, clans and differences were. In return, I became her unofficial tutor on human interaction, shaping a kind of informal curriculum as well as helping her work through the contradictions of our behaviors with her own customs and more primal nature. Somewhere along the way we became friends.

"Nothing yet. A hunch maybe. A thing I kept to myself about something that happened while I was in." I couldn't help but laugh at the first artifact I plucked off the wall, my trusted but violently unfashionable leather wristband; a throwback to a short-lived alternative-rock trend from the early 2000's, a fashion trend already a decade behind when I crafted the thing. It soothed me to feel the familiar thrum of shaping power in the item as I slipped it over my wrist, the fit was a lot better than it had been. Since jail I'd lost the weight I put on during the boozy-pity-party sabbatical I'd gone on after the deaths of Zachariah and company.

When I turn, there's something darkly intriguing and dangerous about the look in the inhuman eyes of my once almost-enemy. I could tell she's debating internally, and while I would guess she didn't subscribe to traditional social contracts, it wasn't hard to see that she had a kind of loyalty to Gale now that had been forged during my absence.

"*Dak-durn.*" I'd had to dig into my mind to find the word and seeing the momentary confusion that walked over her face, told me I hadn't pronounced it as accurately as I'd hoped.

"*Mak-hurn?*" She asked as much as corrected, her piercing eyes fixing on my own.

"*Mak-hurn.* Yes." I confirmed the word and recalled a little more vividly the lesson that had come with it. *Mak-hurn* was the phrase she'd used to describe the oath her tribe made to one another. It obligated them to one another in a way that was outside human understanding; a debted oath more serious than a simple bond. We would try to quantify it inadequately with words like revenge, loyalty, or a blending of the two. It was a promise she'd struggled with not keeping when she opted to join me in my crusade against the rising threat presented by this psychotic demigod, rather than put me down for killing one of her own. It helped that this same fiend had for all intents and purposes enslaved not only her tribe, but a few of the other nearby enclaves of monsters. The first time I came across one of her kind I stumbled upon it mid-hunt. After hitting it with an SUV, a dozen elemental spells, and dropping a building on it I finally was able to dislodge it from my friend's tail, sadly to no ultimate avail.

That had been my first introduction to the woman from the Abyss. She was obsessed with both my city and my dead friend Maria. Unaware of her own power, Maria was a Wanderer who'd had the misfortune of catching the attention of the Black Queen. I met her while making a delivery to her house in my previous career. The Black Queen tried to use Maria as a conduit to open a portal from the abyss to our world, which would have been catastrophic. At first, I thought this was a tragic case of the damsel in distress needing help in a city fresh out of heroes and that this was slated to be a manufactured tragedy ... But I was wrong. This city wasn't out of heroes, they just needed a reason to step into the light. Maria was one of those heroes.

Thanks to her sacrifice, we were able to save the city, though sadly, she paid the ultimate price.

Verrak's clan had been subjugated by this enigmatic Black Queen, and apparently the Cura'Sha sent after her was one of their more decorated and celebrated members. The shared threat of this mysterious, deific woman who'd announced her presence in the Abyss by trying to breach the In-between and escape was initially our unifying call to action and had now turned into a kind of crusade.

Mak-hurn was a blood oath between people deserving of it, a word that forged a bond to avenge any of your ilk unfairly taken from this life, to support and safeguard their left behind responsibilities, or something equally honorific and archaic.

"*Mak-hurn.*" This time, when I repeated it, even I was a little surprised by just how much malice had bled into my fixed enunciation. "Before the attack on me in the jailhouse, when Kaycee had first come to visit, I had a hallucination, or maybe a vision..." I waved off trying to define the episode. "It was Her. Maybe not her... directly... but I saw her." I flash to the memory of the glimpse, the way it wrapped around my entire consciousness and seemed to trap me in an impossible moment while simultaneously suspending my body from any ability to try and physically, let alone mentally, escape it.

"Vision isn't the right word for it, it didn't feel prophetic, but there was something unnervingly real about it. At the time, I took it as some kind of weird astral trip or maybe a trauma response of some nature. The incident with the ghouls happened so long after it that I hadn't even really thought about them being connected. Hell, even when I got around to entertaining the idea that they could be related, all I could really think of is why would someone like Her use ghouls? The whole thing felt off." This Disney villain gone mental proved that she had the ability to capture, twist, and torment anyone anywhere, which meant (I suspected) that there was a far more menacing catalog of monsters she could command. Granted, there was something to be said about the caste of the type of monster she would use for her higher priority endeavors, it certainly confirmed a kind of intelligence and understanding of what wouldn't interrupt the normality that's ascribed to a prison as violently as saw a Troll, or an Ogre. On second thought... an Ogre might work too, given how big and ugly a lot of the inmates were.

I could tell that Verrak was mildly interested in what happened to me that day but was trying to connect how this brought us here, to the moment where she happened upon me walking my dog before heading off into the city well past the time that any reasonable man should be out there.

"The attack on me in that place was brutal. I tried to stay as steady as possible when telling everyone about it, and I made sure the lawyer kept as few of the details as possible from spilling over, but I would be lying if I didn't say it got ugly. That attack didn't just kill a nameless few prisoners and a random guard... it took a good man. A friend. Somebody who'd helped me stay sane, and saw me for who I was, despite the nature of our imposed dynamic. He's the *Mak-hurn*. I owe him. He saved me during that attack." Verrak had witnessed firsthand my suicide-king streak of willing to step in front of it for a friend, and though it happened in short order, I really liked Beau and was already a little heartbroken that we'd never get a chance to connect on the civilian side of the world. The guard was my friend, and in my eleventh hour had stepped right into the metaphoric fire without a moment's hesitation; a good friend, and an even better man.

The soul-baring was ripe with sentiment, and while it would have chilled most to see their confession seemingly go unacknowledged, I couldn't help but appreciate the matter-of-factness of the Stalker while she kept a bead on me with her own unblinking stare. Despite my openness, the bonding and how this connected to my after-hours excursion was still the question, and there was no doubt she was waiting to hear how it all came together.

I heaved another breath before continuing.

"I saw someone before the hallucination, a vision, whatever you want to call it." A flash of the chubby, short, black-haired visitor in the lounge I locked eyes on before being transported, came to my mind at that moment. "I realized who it was about a week ago. It was Frank, a cult member of the group at the lake." This cult had established a connection with the dark mistress who then co-opted them to use Maria up as a vessel to open a rift so that she could cross over into our world. "Frank was a journal writer, he wrote about everyone and everything, and I've read it cover to cover over and over again."

I turned my back to her, looking at the wall of my old stuff before pulling the equipment from the wall piece-by-piece. Verrak was suddenly beside me, not a whisper of sound betraying her approach to stand shoulder-to-shoulder with me as I started to tactically situate some of the gear on my person.

"I recognized him, and even though he was with the cult that was weaponized to use Maria, he seemed like one of the good guys. Maybe not good exactly, but absolutely in over his head, if I remember correctly. I need to talk to Frank, but he's dead. The next best thing I think is that there's something about another guy in that journal we grabbed from the burned down evidence building we broke into during the Blind Judge fiasco." I don't know why it helped, but I knew squinting helped jog my memory. "- And when we were at the bar, I remembered who it was…it was a guy named Thomas, and his address is in the journal."

Verrak was up to speed on most of the details and people involved in our growing epic. She had heard a lot about it from my own team by now and given the trials they had faced in my absence; I was confident she had learned a lot about the parties involved on her own. Plus, it wasn't lost on me that she probably had a perspective from the other side of this to some degree. Verrak didn't strike me as just a foot-soldier, even if enslaved to a cause that wasn't her own.

When I turned to face her, we were a little closer than I expected, and she's even leaning into my personal space a bit, though there wasn't anything suggestive about the motion. It was lethal, and pointed, as well as engaged and attentive. It screamed hunter to me, and coming from an apex predator if you weren't well forged that could have you forfeiting a lot of confidence and wetting your pants, being face-to-face with it.

"After me and Frank locked eyes, I had the vision. Hell of a coincidence don't ya think? Almost as big as him randomly being there. I'm certain he was trying to tell me something. Should have seen that sooner, in hindsight. What happened at the lake and what happened to me in jail are connected. I can feel it. I didn't want to bother anyone about it until I had something more substantial. Plus, with all the bombs I got dropped on me tonight I figured it would hold until tomorrow." It wasn't like Verrak to be the one to plot out much of anything, so I was relatively certain she probably had no idea about the little ambush earlier in the evening, but I was willing to bet she'd heard about it by now.

"And yet you're getting dressed to handle it now." It's hard to miss the eye-narrowing indictment attached to that rhetorical statement. I probably liked it less because of how dead-to-rights it had me.

"Beau was a good dude. That was the guard. He's actually the cousin of one of our local lost-girls." The Peter Pan reference was wasted on her, but to my surprise something of recognition flashed over those eerie, steely eyes. "He didn't deserve that ... So *Mak-hurn*." This time, I tried to match the nature of her own tone when speaking in her native tongue as if to drive-home how serious I was about my suspicion and my urge to immediately investigate. *Mak-hurn*, the oath to a blooded tribe-member, was my attempt to relay just how serious it was to me.

"The theory is thin," I warned, as if already knowing what she would insist on.

"Right now it's an inch-thick branch kind of thin." My perpetual use of 80's buddy-cop era movie-metaphors were really not hitting home with her, and to be fair she was making it very clear that she wasn't the audience for such schtick. Naturally, I started to subconsciously double-down.

"Brittle," I clarified, before continuing. "So before I stir up any shit, I need to investigate some stuff, maybe talk with Thomas and ask him if he knows exactly why I saw Frank right before all that shit happened. Coincidence isn't really a luxury we can afford to ignore, but just because people are in our orbit when something off happens doesn't mean we can immediately dismiss or condemn them. We're a magnet for madness at this point. Plus, checking in on the last few hang-arounds from that group might not be the worst use of our time, what with all that's been happening since I've been locked up."

"Whose car are we taking?" The finality of her question was reinforced with an attitude that told me in no uncertain terms that she wasn't taking no for an answer, and that offering to tag along was her compromise for allowing this to go on without reporting back to the worried group back at the bar beforehand. "Yours," I tried to put a touch of gratitude in my smile, nudging her as I pivoted toward the door we'd both just poured in from in an attempt to steer her that way.

"I don't have one." I tried to spin it like a brag, knowing it was anything but.

I, Janzen Robinson, Champion of Cleveland, head of the first people-powered magical alliance to emerge in centuries, slayer of a Stalker and victor over a Blind Judge, can't even afford the uber I need to get to where I want to go…at the moment.

The jokes just write themselves.

"It's just a talk though Verrak, and I say that as the one with the dead friend that I'm angrier than hell about. We don't want to make this an incident with all those adult-types in the city suddenly, plus it still could very well be nothing." Just as she'd put her foot down in that nonchalant, unequivocal way, I returned the favor with a bit more heavy-handed directness.

"You stay in the car just to be on standby, but I'll share whatever I learn if there's anything worthwhile that comes of this." Half-barter, half-demand, I watched her deliberate over the terms and conditions I'd put out as we continued to stand almost nose-to-nose in the tight-quarters of the dark efficiency. After a period of consideration, a blink brought her back to the present and a slight nod signaled her agreement.

I finished adding the last tidbits to my outfit, throwing my weighted, leather jacket on and strapping the broken bat to the low part of my back while pocketing a few other knick-knacks. They'd constructed a workshop in the Full Circle office for me, and it was populated with a few of my more recent tinkerings and experiments, but the classic equipment was all housed here. Max got another healthy helping of food, as well as a stepping stool to make the couch more accessible to my aging compatriot.

CHAPTER 10

... To Headache

The nondescript house that I found in the notebook was just outside the downtown area, and smack-dab in the heart of a blue-collar neighborhood that was a stone's throw from some of the most challenging parts of Cleveland. I actually remembered Thomas; I had knocked him out on the boat at the lake. Frank and this way over-detailed notebook had a dossier written up about him that helped fill in a couple of the other gaps. Thomas was able to commune with spirits, and according to a note he had made, that ability had first manifested in pretty terrible ways. He was a newcomer to the group whenever the last entry was made, and the generally kind way Frank wrote Thomas led me to believe he liked the guy.

"Alright, give me a few minutes," I said. As maternal as the sharp look from Verrak may have been, that hard countenance beneath this shape-shifted glamor made the expression a touch more daunting than she may have intended.

"*Five* minutes," I said, decisively opening the door, and quietly stepping out onto the sidewalk. My lingering back hand sprawled open to display a flat palm shielding her own approach to speak, each finger prominently blocking a piece of her admittedly intimidating scowl. "Let me work. This guy is a lightweight even by my standards, and if my reading on Thomas is right this is going to be a guy already scared out of his mind and in way over his head."

"Just let me do my thing, and whatever you hear, give me five minutes to get him to talk. Your version of bad-cop would probably shock him into a catatonic state." There was an easing tension as we fell into a strained accord, signaling compliance with a nod.

The waning cool was the first clue of the seasons change; we were coming out of a mild winter and into spring. It still warranted a jacket, even if my heavy-duty leather was a little on the extreme side for what it was. Shrugging deeper into the studded, Billy-Idol era piece I side-eye the framework of the house, scanning for surveillance devices or anything that showed whether or not someone was monitoring the outside, and did see an expensive security system in place. Paranoia would no doubt be the expected response to the kind of trauma Thomas had been through, but this felt a little militant, almost operational. Although the idea that he might have wanted to stay home for the rest of his life after the shit show at the lake sounded pretty reasonable to me.

The porch was dimly lit; absent decor and very uninviting—except for the unlocked door which allowed me to just let myself in.

What can I say? Old habits die hard.

The single-family home had a ceramic-tile floor, and public high-school type fluorescent lighting, which was a strange touch. A small kitchen was the first room I stepped into. On the left was a hallway to what I assumed was the more private side of the home, and to the right was a blacked out living room.

The perfect spot for an ambush in a grade B horror flick.

While my dozen or so concussions had left me with an alarming sensitivity to light, and a fuzzy recall of my most formative years, they had also forged in me a deep appreciation for everything that could go wrong. The leather buckler on my wrist came to life, and I palmed a few of the marbles I had tucked away in my breast pocket before grabbing the handle of my severed bat. After taking a pair of breaths, one to center myself and the other to give a moment for my sight to adjust, I forged ahead.

I had fallen into a ready stance, and started to come out of it as soon as I saw the silhouette of Thomas ambling in. His surprise at me being the first thing he saw as he came out of the guest bath was met by my own surprise at how he looked. The Thomas I'd first encountered was the kind of skinny-fat you saw in guys who made their living sitting down for the majority of the day, and his head was topped by shoulder length blonde hair that was almost disarmingly luxurious and cut into a shag. Today he was gaunt, sunken, and so pale that even in the low light I could see an ashen quality to his skin. His signature hair was stringy and flimsy and had totally lost its luster.

The fact that his shirtless, gangly body was riddled with scarring was alarming enough, but it was the gnarled, thorn-riddled branch encircling his throat that really grabbed my attention. It looked like a collar of sorts, and I could see that the thorns had pricked his flesh creating circles of irritation and sickness. I opened my mouth for what I am fairly confident was going to be a great one-liner when I felt the air explode out of my lungs as somebody smashed into me, sending me careening into the wall just next to where Thomas was standing.

As I started to reorient myself, I was surprised to see Thomas standing perfectly still, and taking inventory of his expression I saw raw terror smeared across his face.

"Janzen Robinson ..."

Fuck.

When they say your full name like that, you know you're in for it. Nobody who knows your name announces it without either celebrating seeing you for the first time after a long while, or to castigate you as they secured your skull to the guillotine.

***

I heard the door close as I pulled myself upright into a sitting position to look back at the thing sealing the exit. For a moment I was reminded of Verrak when she had broken her stalker husk to fit into a humanoid shell in order to parlay with me at the lake. This thing was tall, disjointed, and stiff, with a patchwork of missing hair, which made the fact that it appeared to be female all the more disturbing.

After I'd hustled to my feet, I found myself looking up at her, and noticed that the robe she wore had a ceremonial flavor to it. As my eyes adjusted to the wall behind the creature, I saw a series of glyphs and sigils that were quite unlike anything I'd ever seen. I could identify some of the work, but nothing beyond the fact that it was a type of ancient magic you shouldn't tamper with—though I could see the roots of my own teachings in the structure of the design. Interestingly enough, this new enemy wasn't moving, which was fine by me. I was still trying to get my bearings while shuffling a half-step in front of Thomas. The risk was a calculated one. We all know that hurt people hurt people, but I could see that this guy was a victim, and during my time in jail I'd really squared away the prospect that if I die while in service to others it would have been a life well lived.

"*You...*" It gurgled, and I watched as the outline of other hieroglyphs illuminated and hissed to life around the same door I'd just used to come into the place. The narrowing menace of those eyes was unnerving. I balanced trying to measure my opponent, keep some attention on any movement Thomas might make behind me, and get an inventory of what was going on with the magic writing scattered across the walls. Multitasking was a strength of mine having lived with full-throttle ADD for the majority of my life, and while I wouldn't recommend living with a frequent threat of death looming overhead, it did cultivate a useful ability to funnel adrenaline and utilize it in a meaningful way.

"... are supposed to be dead." The hideous female spit out as she craned her head to look past me and lock onto Thomas, who at this point had rolled from a mewling statue into a mouselike position, literally scurrying behind the living room sofa as if that meager impediment could keep this foul thing from killing him.

A circumspect glance kept my visage locked on her but allowed me to glance at the face of my watch, a watch I wore on the inside of my wrist, taking the practice from Grove and Beau.

Three minutes, forty-five seconds.

"You're not the first woman to be underwhelmed by my ability to deliver."

For once, I immediately regretted my pithy rejoinder as an unseen gust of force came to life out of nowhere, triggered by a soft nod from the thing across from me. That nod was coupled with a snarl revealing fangs that snuck out of arid lips. My left shoulder clipped the wall, and while my buckler ate the majority of the hit the way the force spun me around in the hall made it so that I had to bounce off either side of the hallway fighting quickly to my feet; lucky I had the wherewithal to do that much because this thing was on me.

It was a vampire, so it was faster than me and stronger than a ghoul. That, with the fact that she seemed to be a competent conjurer, and that we were sealed in here together, gave me an immediate flood of regret. The reaching hand was boney, and the way my broken bat took a sizable chunk out of two fingers and her palm was darkly satisfying. I didn't get to enjoy the shock on the face of the thing for long, because my off hand followed my striking one and sent my shield smashing into her face, half-hissing at me for the second time in as many moments.

These things preyed on fear; they petrified their victims, often using their understanding of fear to subjugate them and get them to do heinous, awful shit. Unfortunately for Thomas, an undead vampire sorceress was a big ask for anyone to deal with. Fortunately for Thomas, I was over being on the scared side of things. As she reviewed the boney hand with missing digits, I sent a shield-bash across her face. After which I rammed the bat into her exposed midsection all the way to the hilt, sadly missing my intended target which was the heart. The splintered, broken-bat slipped past her magically enhanced armor, metal, and durable dead-flesh with equal ease, and with all those protections in place, it was a shock to her system that she felt the bite of the blade.

The original intent of the weapon was to assimilate kinetic, and concussive energies, and then unleash them once it was brimming with power for a more whack-a-licious home run style hit. Luckily, when the Stalker had rendered the bat in half with its magically enhanced talons, the weapon actually absorbed the trait, and even in its current cut-in-half state, was as an incredibly sharp dagger that didn't care for any kind of defense offered by an opponent.

Physically more capable, magically more daunting, and in any other metric of power this thing was by far the more domineering of us; but after losing two fingers, eating a face-full of shield and then being gutted I could see a flicker of something mortal-esque in those abyss-black eyes, and before it could process retaliation I sent a brass-knuckle bolstered haymaker straight down the pipeline. The next hissing sound didn't come from a fork-tongued primal cry, but rather an audible searing sound eating at the dead-skin of the vampire as I hit her again with the pronged brass-knuckles I'd surreptitiously slipped onto my assaulting fist before landing the blow. The religious symbols carved into the brass represented the four most prominent religions occupying our world, and while each worked on its own, printing all of them across the bitch's forehead seemed like the most sure-fire way to guarantee it wasn't a miss.

The beatdown barrage had pushed us into the hallway and out of the room it had attempted to sequester me in, and with that last blow I sent the living dead back toward the inscribed wall at the entrance doorway. I re-asserted the grip I had on the holy-scribed brass knuckles and rotated my wrist to re-align the buckler on my other hand. I would be lying if I didn't say it felt good to be back in the fight, and while this was far from equal footing, I liked my odds against some of these predators even with antiquated weapons.

Another nod sent a gust of energy at me, but this time the creature was right behind it, and the bone-breaking grip that grabbed me on each shoulder would have broken through normal leather and even with the protection I knew the mangling grip was going to leave vicious bruising. As the pain flashed white-hot in my head, I focused on it so that I could push through the sensation, acknowledging the agony and choosing to operate outside it. Thankfully, the grip hoisted me up, and as the incoming bite came for me, I was able to intercept it with a crisp knee to the bottom of her widening maw, following the head-lifting hit up with my own crown crashing down, sending the hardest part of my head into the softest spot on her own.

I broke a breath I didn't realize I was holding as that death-grasp relented, and tried to suppress my smile as I watched her crooked nose leak black-ichor all over the floor after it had masked half of her ugly face. A sorcerer or wizard would cook most novice practitioners, and to be honest even most seasoned warrior-caste with magically imbued abilities would be hard pressed against a proper conjurer…unless locked in a small space, where their more powerful spells would be a detriment to their own personage, especially if caught wholly unaware. Confidence flooded my body as I surged forward.

Of course, as quick as confidence came, it went, and while my charge felt like it was secured by sure-footing I felt something crash into my lower back and slam me brutally into the ground. That recently gulped down air flooded out of me, and as my arms sprawled out beneath me, I heard the tell-tale clattering of brass-knuckles skitter just out of reach. Even worse, whatever hit me from behind was still pile-driving weight into my upper-half even as I felt an inhumanly strong grip wrap around my ankles. The relief that was felt from the pinning assailant who'd tackled me from behind was short-lived as a second one joined the party and used the hold on my lower half to fucking swing me like a ragdoll up and off the ground and hurl me back down the hallway from which they'd just emerged.

I managed to stay conscious even as I pinballed off the ceiling, ricocheted off the wall and collapsed in some kind of linen closet, breaking the bi-fold door as the blankets thankfully broke my fall...after the ceiling, wall, and broken closet door combination.

The familiar taste of copper in my mouth told me that I'd either be down another tooth, or there was some internal bleeding looking for a come-uppance. Misery garnished the shit-sandwich when one of the two newcomers dragged me out of the closet with a bone-breaking grip, with enough strength to hoist me upright without any assistance on my part. Ghouls were human desperation level strong, but vampires were preternaturally so. I vaguely wondered where these two new ones came from but...I had no time for superfluous contemplation at the moment...

It was another vampire, and unlike the other one I had tangled with first, these two were not very old, and appeared to be following orders.

"The Mistress will be most pleased to kill you herself." The quality of the voice was decidedly not human and a part of me wondered if it was imbued by some kind of magic. It's the byproduct of being an Artificer, you can't help but wonder how everything works. Zachariah long postulated that anybody with a love for craftsmanship and a healthy dose of worldly curiosity could become one, it's why he so loved the profession. Even if someone like Iandor wouldn't allow it, there was theoretically almost no barrier to becoming one, even if that meant decades as opposed to years.

I held onto the thoughts and memories of my old mentor as the two male vampires took hold of my weakened arms and held me up crucifixion style. The robed female had a growing green-hue in the depths of her ink-black eyes, though its presence was considerably more muted than I would have expected.

There was a jostling noise behind me, and I was able to turn my head enough to see the branch-collared, broken body of Thomas shakily brandishing the discarded bat-dagger he'd found on the ground. My gaze dropped to the exposed stomach of the dark sorceress, noticing that she was covering the wound with her hand as a dark, putrid smelling blood-like substance oozed out.

She was sicklier looking than the two males that were holding me up but was still the strongest of the three.

"Let him go!" Thomas stuttered, his bravery a pure and noble thing—because to be courageous you had to overcome fear. Shaken and tear-streaked, the broken bat looked surprisingly steady in his blanched hands, holding on for dear life. "You've taken enough! Just go God damn…" He was cut off as a stronger pulse of black blood with a sizzle came to life on the holy brands punched into the leaders forehead as another gust of energy tossed the broken Thomas into the wall. He yelped and dropped the weapon while crumbling to the floor in the corner of the darkly lit living room.

"She wants you alive," annoyance was written all over her, and unfortunately for the vampiress she was the two things I annoyed most; an enemy, and a woman. "... but that doesn't mean I don't get to extract my own pound of flesh first." That irritating hissing noise returned, and despite my own brazenness, I admit that a part of my heart sank watching as the smatterings of wounds already began to heal slowly and systematically all over her.

I caught a glimpse of the branch-collar, the one with thorns piercing Thomas' throat, just in time to see a few symbols flash red, and realized that she was siphoning energy from the moaning unconscious man. This was some kind of sustained feeding no doubt, and while I suspected it had other purposes as well, I knew now wasn't the time to play aspiring Tinkerer. Focusing beyond the vampire I started to scan the wall, trying to make sense of something inscribed across the face of it. My effort was rewarded with a jarring, brutal smack, one that sent a denture-fashioned tooth out of my mouth. It tickled my captor; that ugly look of satisfaction was one I'd worn myself a few times.

"It's hard to believe something like *you* has been such a nuisance," she said, timing the insult with her palm striking me a second time, this one on the opposite cheek and then again with the back of her hand before pulling it close to her own face and gruesomely breaking her dislodged nose back into place. "Aggressive rodents often die because they forget themselves, and foolishly aggress against larger animals." The explanation was rhetorical, and I could see an old, humanlike arrogance in the mage as she half-shrugged at the assessment.

"You know, you basically just called me a honey-badger."

As a man who was usually a decade behind, I could tell this woman was even more painfully unaware of any cultural relevance to the reference, so much so that the slight expression on her face born from her confusion at the reference was almost human. Quietly, I mourned that my witticism would die in front of an unengaged audience.

"Janzen Robinson, in five minutes you have been taken, beaten, and are about to be made an example of. Had you any kind of sense, you'd have left the first time luck broke your way, and like the rodent you are, you would have dug a deep, dark hole to hide in while the inevitability of all this comes to pass... and instead?"

The last rhetorical inquiry was outright grand-standing, and the soft glowing green dwelling in the furthest depths of her eyes was churning a bit brighter, as if fighting to come to the surface. The diatribe felt a little off brand for her ilk, and admittedly my knowledge of vampire, ghoul, and all the creepy-crawlies was just a depth better than surface, so it wouldn't surprise me to learn there was more to it than I'd originally thought. My suspicion was her hauteur heralded from the Mistress, as ego and insane rage were a kind of calling card for the Abyss-trapped demigod...and I didn't miss the rodent dig either.

"You're right about everything," I managed, spitting out some bloody phlegm so that I could continue. "...except one thing."

The amusement glimmering in her smug face was grating, and the preening bitch even folded her arms before tilting her head to one side as if entertaining whether or not she'd want to hear my caveat. She would of course, because egomaniacs are as predictable as stupidity, and one should never underestimate the predictability of stupidity.

"Enlighten me, honey-badger."

"It's been three-minutes and forty-five seconds."

Sadly, I couldn't enjoy her insult because quite frankly, every piece of my being celebrated being called a honey-badger. I had to ignore the small victory and focus on the bigger picture. The questioning in her eyes in response to my statement was answered as abruptly as it was asked. To her credit, my original rejoinder hadn't landed, but the fact that I wasn't ripe with fear, or any kind of deterrence clued her into the fact that something was amiss. To her further credit she managed to duck and roll away just as the double-window at the front of the house blew out with a wild gust of air. This push wasn't the attack, simply an announcement, and before the vampire on my far arm could process what had happened, Verrak hit him with the gusto of a professional linebacker, his hold on my arm evaporating as the impact tossed him across the room.

It was the kind of power that was hard for a human to quantify, let alone process, especially when the vehicle was seemingly another person. The reinforced leather jacket shielded me from any injury the extricated death-grip would have given, as my arm was freed. The surprise put the other vampire in a momentary stand-still, which is a fatal mistake in a fight. They were dangerous for sure, but surviving, adapting, and learning lessons from failure had made me the more deadly one. Before it had even processed the interloper dislodging the other one, I had spun and tucked into him, negating its reach and strength, and managed to stuff his shocked-wide mouth with a handful of marbles. My leading hand lifted the ensnared jaw, pointing the things head toward the ceiling, before collapsing my straight arm and sending an elbow into the little button on the mandible that could easily break in a human opponent.

Not so with a vampire, but it was still hard enough to crack the pair of fire-charged marbles I'd force-fed him. The mildly concussed expression shifted to confusion, which gave way to panic as a soft red-glow started to give the sunken cheeks an illuminated profile. I was able to free myself as the dead-skinned vampire started to claw at its own fire-catching flesh. I caught Verrak in my periphery just in time to watch her Stalker claw hand blow out the back of the other vampire she'd first attacked. The claw hand emerged holding a black, decaying heart in its grip. I thought it interesting that the rest of her had remained human during this maneuver, watching as she almost disinterestedly cast the dead one's heart to the ground.

We shared a nod, and I appreciated the once-over she gave me to take inventory of my status. In a short period of time we'd become surprisingly close, and I was one of the few people in her orbit that deeply understood that her very nature was outside our human operating systems and understanding. I had to remember this. Things aren't always as we think they are or wish them to be, and they don't always align with our beliefs about them. Bears aren't cuddly, and very often they eat their young without provocation; but that doesn't stop us from imagining them as a Jungle Boy's protector and best friend.

Truth is, Winnie the Pooh should eat Christopher Robin and not think twice about it—but he didn't—that's the story we make up to be OK with things we're not OK with...

Shattered windows let the reigning moonlight pour in, the ethereal glow giving the undead vampire/sorceress a much more distinct outline and revealing just how macabre the portrait actually was. Slight, and the only word which kept circling to mind was sunken, as if there was a vacancy of life stitched into the very fabric of her being. The smell wasn't putrid but for some reason her proximity invoked a familiar, almost retching aversion to her presence. The soft glow of green in those dark, cold eyes had abated, but the litany of injuries had also been more swiftly healed.

I could hear another low moan echo weakly out of the corner that Thomas' crumbled body was folded into but forced myself to key in on the opponent in front of us. The clearest indicator that I had to not charge was the fact that Verrak remained still. The Stalker was about as big as her ilk could get, and they were themselves versed in rudimentary, but impactful spellwork. Verrak was not only an icon of the Cura'sha, she also had quite the working knowledge of magic, and in terms of formidability, I would put her right up there with Kaycee when it came to prowess and power.

"Traitor,"

"*Bru-maga.*"

Luckily, I didn't need to look for an opening, because the vampiress crouched low and erupted forward only to unexpectedly dissipate into a wisp of toxic-tasting smoke and pivot away from us and out the blown-out windows that now decorated the living room floor. Neither Verrak nor I moved initially, I think that our experience taught us to wait through the stillness and bolstered our once grudging mutual respect. It hinted at a venerability that very few had lived long enough to earn. Only when we were sure the threat had removed itself did we spool out of our tense crouches and shake off the intense readiness, in her case, literally shaking some of the strain out of each limb.

"*Bru-maga?*" I asked with both the question and the lift of an eyebrow, all while picking my way over to the corner that she'd folded Thomas into. "Would you like to share with the class?" Small but noticeable differences existed in the dead vampires at our feet, though my cursory inspection was hurried as I moved over to the fallen cult-member. My fear was confirmed when I plucked a chair from on top of him, quickly deducing that whatever the last pull of power from the collar was, it had cost the former zealot his life. Kneeling to inspect the corpse and collar, I stopped myself from beckoning my make-shift partner over for this newly minted crime scene when I caught her rather studiously scrutinizing the two dead vampires I'd stepped over.

"Life-force vampire." Whenever not in mixed company, Verrak spoke in a deeper octave that had a gravellier quality to it yet still decidedly feminine. It was also a tell, hinting that some of her more primal qualities were closer to the surface than her more unassuming glamor might lead one to believe. "Rare," her own bewitching eyes glazed over while she dug into one of the deeper recesses of her memory, as if trying to lay this out in a comprehensible fashion while keeping it succinct, "very rare. They're Magi, who slowly turn to darker and darker magic to keep themselves alive. There's a master, and usually an underling, a subservient second who is usually strong as well.

These were strong and they were gaunt, like Thomas, but I'd been able to make headway against them. I rolled to a knee and reached deeper into my jacket retrieving a pair of second-skin gloves. Fingerprints wouldn't be an issue with the cleanup that would probably have to come, but there was no point to complicating the issue of evidence.

Prison was a university for criminals. I'd probably learned more about crime there than in my two decades as a hustle-savvy street kid. "Okay, so our resident enigma-enemy is leveling up the help?" I carefully gathered the branch-collar between two inspecting fingertips, pulling the prongs out of the flesh when I was sure it wasn't booby-trapped or alive with some kind of enchantment.

"That's not what's bothering me," I heard her say distantly. Luckily, she wasn't repeating herself, and I had the wherewithal to keep some of my perpetually split attention focused on what she said as she searched their bodies. The sigil work wasn't terribly complex, but it was very precise, which was kind of odd in my opinion. Zachariah had discussed how some of those who know our craft are incredibly capable in one space, and just refine that strength in another; meaning that their sigil carving and calligraphy could be immaculate, even if their understanding of the magical collaborating symbols was stunted. As I disengage the collar with a small pulse of my own focus into the binding clasp and break it, I store that little curiosity away.

"*Bru-maga* draw from their apprentice while their apprentice tries to figure out how to learn everything from them before dying so that they can kill them instead of being killed," I hear as I rope the thorn-torture entrapment to my hip.

The startling interjection came from Johnny B. who appeared out of nowhere.

"What are you doing here?" I asked.

"A little birdie called me about 10 minutes ago. Said you might need another pair of hands," he replied with a shrug.

He didn't ask about any of the happenings that led up to this moment, and instead helped us figure out what some of the irregularities meant. The half-elf was tip-toeing over the broken debris, even exaggerating the step he took to enter the room. Whatever coy quip or clunky observation he could have ribbed us with was taken care of with a faux-sigh of mock exasperation. Before diving any deeper the quirky elf pulled out a crank-wind box and did as the name implied, placing it dutifully on the broken windowsill, and before any of the melody could even finish its first circuit, a wash of illusionary magic helped put together the shattered remnants of the houses facade to make it seem completely unmolested.

It bought us time, and I was grateful that he had the mindfulness and skill to protect us from prying eyes. Between my gloves, and his common-sense contribution to us staying as camouflaged as possible, I was proud to see our pedigree as criminals so universally elevated.

"Break it down for me, music-mage."

Johnny flat-out frowned at the moniker.

"Song-Sorcerer?" My tone and ask were a touch hopeful as I went back to regarding the hallway that the two bodies had emerged from.

Johnny B. was drawing a loop of circles with a finger, as if telling me to keep cycling until something more fetching caught his famously fickle fancy. Thankfully, he didn't need any more prompting to begin his explanation as Verrak and I turned our attention to the ingression I'd been fixated on since I got here.

"The apprentice is a slave to the Vampire that initiates them. The Vampire draws life force from the apprentice, and at the same time the apprentice learns magic from the Vampire. It's a kind of cycle, and as the apprentice is tasked with getting them more victims to feed off of, the more plentiful their magic is, the more the apprentice is sustained and the deeper the Master Vampire will feed off of them. I'm not an expert and admittedly slept through the *weird* subcultures of magic and vampirism class."

I chewed on that a little, edging closer to the hallway that led deeper into the house. Verrak shifted her attention more directly toward it as well. "Worked for the Sith." My newly crafted aviator glasses fit obnoxiously well, if I do say so myself, and with a murmur the night-vision enhanced bespellment on each lens activated and I scanned the corridor.

Johnny chortled and Verrak, who missed the reference, actually keyed in on the Karaoke-King who softly waved her off as if to clue her into the reference being pop-culture and not social-contract. "It's not...wrong exactly, but it's off, and the apprentice is usually a response to weakening, not strengthening..." Johnny's teetering hand swiveled left and right as if to sign that the analogy was apt but not ideal.

Johnny, Astute as he is aloof continued, "Having two apprentices and still being strong enough to fight you two off? That's a lot. Plus that", pointing to the collar at my hip with a questioning glance. "Whatever the hell that is."

"I don't know what it is yet. It's crude, but it's expertly done. I could give you my shotgun assessment, but I've really got to dive a little deeper into it when we have it back at my workshop." Suddenly, we heard a low, guttural rumbling sound from the hallway that stopped almost as soon as it started. The Stalker moved past me down the hall we'd both just come out of and listened.

"Johnny takes rear." I say, immediately regretting the phrasing and smothering the boyish snicker with a tempering scowl. "I'll lead. If we run into anything I'll skunk it, you punk it." The Stalker balked a little at the reference, and Johnny groaned at the rhythm. Thankfully, I only dignified one of the responses with an answer.

"I'll hit it with a distraction, and you'll hit it as hard as you can," I clarify, moving to the front of our little trio. I gave Thomas one last look, wrestling with the fact that my feelings on the matter weren't terribly complicated, or even conflicted. Maybe this last sabbatical had irrevocably hardened me, or maybe it had simply forged a tougher interior. A part of me wondered when it was that I stopped mourning someone who still qualified as a victim by most standards, while another part was quietly glad to feel my first impulse was to move on. The hallway had a guest bathroom on the left, a closed door on the right, and an open door that brought us into a cozy office/den hybrid.

It didn't take but a quick inspection to find a crudely dug hole with a makeshift stairway. It lacked some of the foreboding with my enhanced glasses on, but that didn't deter the sense of dread I had as we followed the pathway. Verrak stopped me from immediate descent, sniffing a little at the stale air before turning a look to Johnny B.

The Stalker signaled to Johnny in a complex series of gestures, and after digesting the message with an unexpected somberness, the steady elf's mouth pursed to the side before his spellbinding eyes lit up with a eureka moment. He took his phone out, pantomimed to make sure my own was silent, and sent me a rapid-fire text.

Two more downstairs.

I look at the message, scrunching my features, before quickly writing back.

When did you two learn sign language?
IS THAT REALLY IMPORTANT RIGHT NOW?

Cap locks from Johnny are the pinnacle of irritation, and with my job safely done I walk down into the nest of vampires beneath the dead-guys house. I didn't bother telling him that I was already well aware that everyone had started to learn some signing as a courtesy to Grove.

***

Below was a strange mix of things both surreal and jarring. We found a carved-out catacomb about twenty feet in diameter, shaped in a half circle, with five upright concave columns dug into the wall. The one directly in front of us at the center of the five was obviously assigned to the master. Though I wouldn't call anything in this place luxurious or comfortable, there were some items in the area that led me to believe that this was the spot dedicated to the spell-caster. Two of the niches flanking it were conspicuously empty, and I did not miss the reaching prongs of thorny branches germinating at neck height in those standing, coffin-like spaces. During my inspection, I noticed five sigils, at the top of each niche. These corresponded with the symbol I saw flash to life on the center of the vampire-mage's chest.

The last two were occupied by more full-bodied, fresh-faced looking types locked in what appeared to be a spell-bound slumber. While I was relatively confident that the two apprentices we'd faced had been men, these were also identifiable as male because of their still human resemblance.

They were fresh converts, and they still had these branch-like, thorn burrowing collars around their necks. Their stirring was light and sporadic, and when all three of us filled the space of this underground dungeon we measured one another with the kind of look that spoke varying levels of concern. We didn't say anything, and after we realized these two combatants weren't about to become animated, we set about investigating the chamber. Sadly, nothing of importance was there, and I couldn't find anything that spoke to their identity or purpose, outside the usual suspicion you had with a vampire.

After assuring the fourth and fifth symbol on the collar I'd taken off of Thomas coincided with the markings carved in the last two suspended vampires own wooden-chokers, I put the eternally damned down for good with a pair of broken-bat thrust into their undead hearts, eliciting a death-rattle from each. Once we were out, we combed through the den, the living room, and the bedroom; unfortunately we found close to nothing. By the time we got back to the original scene of the fight it was near-dawn, and the once obstinate night was about to give way to daylight.

Before we left, I gave some instructions to each of them, filling Johnny in on as much as we had figured out to that point, as well as my own weird hallucination in jail. Why I had seen Frank troubled me, but the vision had reminded me of his journal, the journal had led me to Thomas, and Thomas had of course turned into this debacle. The fact that I had just glimpsed Frank before being whisked into a hellscape where I had to stare down our enigmatic enemy from the Abyss was at best a loose connection that felt vital yet unimportant at the moment, even if I knew it wouldn't stay that way for long.

The shared silence in the Stalkers truck was as amiable as it was somber as we waited, only pulling out when we saw the fire we'd set start to spread to the rooftop. The illusionary music box kept the worst of it from being evident until then, but as we pulled onto the road, the voracious flames began to light up the yawning skyline devouring any evidence of our activities. Of course, none of that really mattered, the shock-value of committing felony arson was offset by the gnawing suspicion that this was once again a harbinger of something so much worse than what any of us could imagine.

It felt like the first heralding of War.

CHAPTER 11

The OGs

The fact that I slept didn't surprise me, but it did trouble me how easily I found it after the night I'd had. We'd gotten home just shy of four in the morning, each of us breaking rank and agreeing to let everyone get a little rest before we started disseminating the troubling update with the rest of the crew. Grove was of course awake within an hour or so of me getting back, and I hated myself for being grateful that he couldn't hear, because without his disability, I knew the man would wake up every time I came clamoring in like a drunken sailor on a mid-tour leave. Max rustled awake and thumped out of bed the way a heavy old dog does, with my own heavy ass following suit. After feeding him, I push into a shirt, yawn into a coffee, and shoulder open the door at the back of my barren apartment.

The door that led into the sprawling back room of our office at Full Circle Protection, the one that housed my workshop tinkering station and our own supernatural safe room. It was also where we trained and sparred. It had been almost a year since I'd been here, and while I wasn't taken aback exactly, I did immediately recognize how foreign this once familiar place felt. I'd picked up on a dozen differences almost immediately. Upgraded computers had a brand-new sheen, the wooden weaponry displayed now had a series of staffs added to it – telling me Grove had either coaxed Kaycee to come down here for some training, or the half-elf did so at her own behest to help cheer my partner up. Some monitor screens tucked into each respective corner that watched not only the front and back of our shop but several key vantage points throughout the neighborhood were a nice addition. Luckily, by the time I dragged my feet across the high school wrestling mat that once gave us ringworm because we'd foolishly not washed it before our first use, I began to settle. If I was ever going to acknowledge a strength of mine without a self-deprecating zinger immediately following up a self-compliment it would be my adaptability.

I paused short of dropping into one of the chairs when I heard Grove coming back from the gym. I hoisted my coffee mug up to him in a wordless salutation. The hyper-observant warrior had nearly dismissed it with a nod before catching my mug-holding hand. From there he glanced at a few other spots I was sure sported fresh bruising and light blemishing from last night's skirmish. Without much prompting, I brought him up to speed on everything that happened last night verbally, getting used to the practice of facing him directly, and mindful of every enunciation.

How'd you track down this Thomas guy?

Retelling the story had me susceptible to losing myself in thought about it, but when the stone-still soldier suddenly moved, it rattled me enough to keep that from happening. "Oh yeah. *That.* Well, I had a vision of Frank – remember the cult dude who didn't all the way suck?"

Grove deliberated, not because he couldn't recall, but because he wasn't sure he considered Frank to be one of those all-the-way-don't-suck people. I found it easier to qualify something as redeeming, I suppose, usually the benchmark of a guy in need of that very thing. After the categorizing Frank and his character bit passed, the part about me hallucinating was addressed by an openly skeptical look.

Go on, the deft fingers invited me to continue while the man foraged a mini-fridge for water before closing the distance on me as if seeking a better understanding by way of proximity.

"So, I didn't put any of it together. Seeing Frank in that vision, triggered this kind of living nightmare where I saw the woman from the Abyss, and then snapped back to the visitor's room. I didn't think of it until the ghoul attack, and because they were basically marionette dolls, I knew the symbols I found on them had a different meeting. That, and the fact that they were possessed…a very unimpressive possession if I must say. The Stalker we first fought did a version of that, using a kind of hive mind to get the vampires to act in lockstep with its intentions. This was a messy, weaker, clunky version of that."

"Anyway…all of this?" Gesturing vaguely up and down my body where some of the fight was still worn on my skin. "Kind of shit luck more than solid detective work, I'm afraid. Between the hints Kaycee had been dropping about the problems you guys are having, the big-league magic PoPo finally coming to town after ignoring Zachariah's countless requests, and the attack, I just went on a hunch. I mean, Frank was dead, but I knew about half a dozen cultists escaped from the lake that night when Maria died, so I went looking."

We could finally pass the subject without it being anything more than a dull ache. Grove sat, prompting me to do the same in the chair across from him. I inhaled to continue but Grove lifted a hand to pause.

"You okay?"

It was a fairly simple question. As is often the case in our world, the surface of a thing was very rarely the totality of it. The breath I'd brought in for another tangent was released in quiet, as I gave the question the gravity it deserved. I appreciated him asking, and I know he appreciated that I was taking a minute to do a little self-assessment and honestly check myself out before answering.

"Yeah," I say with a slow nod, finding a little more security in hearing myself say it, just as I felt the familiarity of solid footing when I walked on our wrestling mat. "I'm thrown a bit by how okay I actually am…It's kinda weird," My hand gestures around the room, and even though there were changes and it was dressed with more stuff, the truth was that the bones of the place—the foundation, the soul of it was the same—it's signature decidedly mine and my partners. There was great comfort in that. "Yeah, I'm very okay, and glad to be back."

Without invitation we both leaned forward in our chairs and dropped our heads on each other's shoulders and half hugged. I chuckled at my urge to say something, only Grove wouldn't have the faintest clue at what it was I had said. He laughed too, though why on his end I couldn't say, and we both just sat and celebrated being together again. It took a lot of emotional intelligence, and maturation, to identify this as a kind of intimacy. I think being separated after finding someone who covered your deficits could be great for forced growth, but there is no substitute for having an old friend back in your orbit. He offered a light shoulder squeeze, I signed off with a pair of sturdy pats, and with a sip of my coffee and we settled back into our office chairs and did our damndest to suppress the excitement we were feeling over having an opportunity to get back in the fight.

"I figured I would check on one of the two still living cultists I didn't think were completely scumbags. My brain flashed to Frank because he kept that obnoxiously detailed journal, and I knew it was the best resource we had for checking up on that bunch. That, and a part of me suspected that the ghoul attacks were piloted by one of them. They would have been the easiest help that bitch could reach out to after the Blind Judge fiasco, so it kind of fit… and the attack just felt amateurish."

Grove embodied patience, and it never ceased to amaze me how perpetually unrushed he was. I'd never met anybody who seemed as completely in control as he did. I'd ripped a few dozen drinks back with him and we'd talked about old wounds, toxic behaviors, and bad habits at length, so I was aware that my partner and best friend was in fact the gold standard of being a soldier, and still very much a man. Despite that, his steadiness was impossible to duplicate, and was the personification of an even deeper, more resolute character. Before moving on to what happened last night, he meticulously questioned me about the fights in the prison. If I didn't know him so well it would have been uncomfortable, but I knew the interrogation was just trying to ferret out how much of the information was usable intelligence: the brain was after all a wonky beast, littered with crazy, biased, inaccurate processing at every turn.

After fielding a second more broad stroke inquiry, I returned to the comparison I was trying to make. "The prison stuff was brutal, but it was amateurish."

"Personal."

Me and Grove may well have been singing in stereo when we landed on that conclusion. I nodded and added that "Thomas was surprised to see me, and the attack wasn't a planned one, it was in response to my showing up." I felt the theory coming to life, swiveling left and right in my chair as if stirring my brain with the freshly consumed tar we called coffee, though it didn't pass as such to any respectable human being.

"The person who attacked me in the prison wasn't Thomas. Whoever it was is still out there."

Oh good, he signed.

"So Thomas was part of a hive of – what was it?" The beard gave him a very dark, antihero aesthetic that I didn't hate but also was still getting used to.

"*Bru-maga*," I offered, sipping the coffee and hating myself for doing so.

"Right, *Bru-maga*. Rare, life force vampires that are not acting as they should normally, correct?"

"That's the gist I got. Could be it's time to stop asking for the cliff notes. Verrak will be here early this afternoon, and I suspect our friends from Iandor will be swinging by before that. We'll see what we can get in the way of answers from the collective."

Do you trust them? He signed. Grove knew my history with Zachariah, and my history with authority in general. In fact, on one of those bottle-bleeding nights we'd gotten deep into that history so the picture of what I am, and the why of it, was a lot clearer to him than it was to a lot of other people; people who'd known me a lot longer.

"Fuck no. Double fuck no. Stack every fuck you can find in Cleveland and use that as a point of emphasis for how little I trust them." The joke never landed, so Grove wasn't a fan as I beat the already dead thing to death in front of him for my own amusement.

"No," I reiterated, softer and with a more somber tone. "I don't. Zachariah did, and I know he wanted me to contact Helena if something ever happened to him and had intended to do something himself if he ever got any hard evidence about whatever his suspicion about Cleveland was." As usual, very little got by my battle-buddy and when the admission that Zachariah had wanted me to reach out to Helena was read off my mouth, I could tell that it took him a little to digest that. I couldn't really talk through it, nor did I want to, but the half-shrug was my way of showing I would give it a shot.

"I never did for a thousand different reasons, one being that it was too difficult to be the one to tell her that he died. Iandor had a lot of shit about it that wasn't cool, ask anyone on the outside of their circle what they think. My original instinct was to not trust them, and while I do like Helena, I'm sticking to that. And we're 0-2 when it comes to the governing bodies of all this shit, so why would the human one be any different?"

A messenger of some kind appeared on the monitor, forcing my partner to make sure it wasn't anything too serious before pushing me to take another run at explaining all of this. "We'll see what they'll say, try and figure out what they're actually after, and who knows, maybe the shit is finally bad enough for them to step in and help. I sent Johnny B. to fill Kaycee and Gale in and give them an invitation to do the same with Helena. They're here to help, so I want them as close to me as possible." I turn back toward my room, ruminating on whether or not I should grab the thorn-collar and get to work on it.

Luckily, Grove had a much better idea.

We spent the next hour talking about fitness, the upgrades to the office, and how this newly-formed, tight-knit community was working. I'd pretty firmly relied on his guidance to finally get in shape, and while I still wasn't quite on par with the Golden Boy, I was finally able to take my shirt off without feeling the need to puke immediately in my own mouth. Truthfully, I'd managed to really get on top of my physical health, which was never quite as lackluster as I'd often insinuated.

Nicholas had built a cheap, fun web game; a white wolf fantasy kind of thing. It was a multi-player that was by invitation only on the same server that hosted all of our stuff. It took place in a fictional city that just happened to be identical to Cleveland right down to the missing Jim Brown statue. There was a social media forum to swap stories, ideas, information, and reach members. The best part? It was disguised by being in plain sight. The game was a modernized version of dungeons and dragons, and the forums were designed to profile as if the users were writing as made-up characters and not themselves; online role-playing as it were. With the ability of this game to heat-map the location of each user, everyone was geo-tagged to assure fast responses. They'd even built in a partnering system and replacement matrix if there was a scheduling conflict or any complication so that everyone in our circle could always opt to be with another member. And to cap it off, behind some kind of super technologically-sound innovation, were complete dossiers on all of our people. Here we kept track of abilities, innate talents, core day-to-day competencies and locations.

Kaycee and some others also monitored their growth and noted any irregularities in that. Beginning five years ago, the number of magic-inclined people in Cleveland had doubled.

And then it doubled again.

Not only that, those who were adequate practitioners had started to become adept, and the adept had started to become quite formidable. Nothing powerful enough to turn the tide, but they were now capable enough to be relied upon to supplement efforts, and no longer profiled as a soft target for almost any predator. As much as this was reason to celebrate, the fact that so many of these seemingly dormant powers began to emerge in much older wielders was not just historically rare, it had never been known to have happened before. I button mashed on the game, very aptly called The Land, skimmed the social-media boards inside the thing and thumbed over a couple of the files. Grove also upgraded the vehicle, downloaded logistics and schematics about everything from escape routes to rally points, and even showed me how to activate a program that would locate algorithm protected eight-digit grids, grids that had smaller weapon caches.

After that, we trained, ate, and went over everything we'd discussed earlier to fortify our mutual understanding, and stress-test some of our working theories. It felt good to be back at work, and while there were moments that I couldn't help but feel a bit left out of this new growth, I had to admit the evolution was great and the way everyone was coming together filled me with a surprising degree of pride. I decided to end the half-day on a good note and go shower before taking a nap.

Good thing I did, because I was ripped out of a deep sleep by rancorous shouting from the other side of my apartment door. It was so boisterous I was hoping it was coming from anywhere other than the Full Circle Protection offices, but before I could recalibrate and crawl out of my repose, a peace shattering roar confirmed my worst fears, and I exploded out of my bed to not-so-gracefully land face-first on the hardwood floor, my feet failing me spectacularly.

Whatever wise-crack I was about to make died on my lips as a second, booming roar echoed a moment before I hit my door like a fucking battering ram, head down, ready to kill whatever had been dumb enough to step inside my house and try to bring danger to our doorstep.

CHAPTER 12

Growing Pains

The destroyed door did nothing to impress our newest visitors, though it did manage to startle the hell out of Kaycee, Johnny B., Nicholas (who almost fell out of his chair), and even Helena to a degree, though she'd the constitution to not jump.

Her bodyguard, or whomever the towering, muscled up piece of hunky-man-meat was, had respectably imposed himself between her and the two-hundred dollar expense I'd just racked up for myself because I couldn't tell the difference between an other-worldly monster roar, and a digital tiger in our community-based video game, which was being shown off by its proud developer while everyone waited for me to wake up. I'd heard a third damning roar and knew emphatically that it was coming out of the pricy speakers and not the mouth of some horrendous beast or monster.

Half-crouched over, my shoulder hurting a whole hell of a lot as the adrenaline wore off, I awkwardly cleared my throat before daintily picking up a shard of wood and the busted doorknob. Nicholas looked horrified, Kaycee was entertained after a puff of air cleared the hair from her face and she got over the initial shock I'd given her, and Johnny B. gave a very girly half-yelp before collapsing into the side of Helena's most distractingly attractive counterpart, Julian.

"This is Julian everyone," Helena's voice was soft but never timid, and even as she offered, without me yet inquiring, it was interesting how easily it carried all the way across the room. The introduction didn't fill in any gaps but did ease some of the anxiety that comes from meeting new people, especially for us middle-of-the-road Millennials. Julian was a good sport about the suffocating side-embrace from Johnny B., even letting the musician walk exploring palms over his arm to pry himself off rather than just stand up straight. Judging from the reaction of our resident song-sorcerer, whatever lay beneath the sleeve was as impressive as what we could all currently see. "And Julian, this is Janzen Robinson."

After dawdling in that dusky, door-shattered clearing for a bit, I just kind of listlessly tossed the doorknob over my shoulder before walking over to everyone. This was not quite the assembly I expected, though I had confidence that Grove would make an appearance before we sorted any of this out. Julian and I exchanged a handshake, and I'm bummed to report that despite the fact that he's about a head taller than me, considerably more handsome, a few years younger, and a decorated member of some elite Iandor strike team; he's also a better artificer than me. I carried a lot of enchanted gear from all over the spectrum, but this guy had very few obvious pieces; pieces for breaking bones or beating ass. Begrudgingly, I had to admit it was really sound work, like the kind of immaculate work you'd expect in anybody but this kind of guy. Seeing just how capable he actually was can inspire a deep, loathing hatred —most commonly referred to as jealousy.

Luckily, my ego's ass had long since been kicked, so I took it in stride.

"What's going on?" The open-endedness of the question was baiting by design, an attempt to interrupt the tension in the room. When my phone went off, the flinch of relief I saw wash over both Kaycee and Helena confirmed my suspicions—suspicions that something had been going wrong even before last night. For the last few months I'd been frozen out of the actual issues happening in my city and was instead fed strained small talk. I made a show out of taking the device out and silencing the ringer, calmly placing it face down and dropping my undivided, expectant attention back to them, and waited for a response.

"He wants to know what's going on?" Grove shouted over my shoulder, slipping in from the Full Circle side entrance with Verrak in tow. Leave it to Grove to read the room simply by body language and understand enough about everyone in it to say exactly the right thing. Verrak paused at the door, exchanging a look with Kaycee before making her way over to my side of the office and then retreated to the furthest wall as if doing her best to stay on the periphery of the issue. It would be unfair to call Gale being there a surprise, given our relationship; our trials with the woman from the Abyss had unintentionally created an even stronger alliance than anything we had ever had in the past.

As Kaycee began, Nicholas swiveled completely away from the computer to join the discussion. Julian looked at me like a vague disinterested predator not quite ready for a meal. He had an air of competence with violence, similar to Grove, even if his was a lot more polished. Interestingly enough, Helena had taken to drifting around the room, taking a keen interest not in my workshop itself, but in my notes, concepts, and sketches.

"We've been having pretty regular attacks for just over two months now."

That hit me hard. Even if there was some part of my mind that knew something was out of whack it was a shock to have it confirmed. I could tell that she was hesitant to tell me this, and that they were expecting a much more animated angry response from me. Sure, I could be salty as fuck, and livid with outrage, but right now wasn't the time, because I was absolutely clear that we had once again slipped into the thick of a crisis, and that it had somehow managed to sneak all the way up on us.

"We all agreed." Grove took some of my guard down by not only being in on the decision but damn sure sounding like one of the signing members of the committee. Given the depth of our knowledge of one another it was probably impossible for him to miss the *fuck you* stamped across my forehead but I stiff-upper lipped it for now and nodded, waiting for a little more detail. "You weren't going to be able to help us out here, and we couldn't help you with the problems you'd run into in prison, so it made sense not to tell you."

His response caught me a little off guard and I was genuinely impressed. I pivoted my attention to Kaycee and saw that her eyes were wet from holding back tears; this decision had been hell on her, probably as hard as hearing about me under attack in the one place she couldn't get to without making some kind of scene. Seeing people who loved you upset was rough; seeing them distraught with worry for me deflated a lot of the ire I'd found welling up. The explanation was like a bucket of cold water, and posturing aside, I grumphed my ornery ass over to my oldest friend and wrapped her in my arms.

"Water under the bridge."

Checking the assembly of faces and giving my sister-mom the opportunity to gather herself, I saw a glint of approval from Johnny B. and Grove. Nicholas and I hadn't yet forged any kind of bond, but I could tell this alleviated a lot of his worries. I imagine keeping me in the dark about this was the source of a lot of conversation and debate, knowing how most of us would feel about being left out of the loop on something like this. I knew the decision was the right one, and I appreciated the soundness of the reasoning and the courage it took to do it.

Meanwhile, Gale looked like she was miles away, Julian looked like he couldn't care less, and Helena's demeanor seemed clinical and pragmatic.

"Attacks have been going on for about nine weeks," Grove added, as he picked up the thread again. I gave Kaycee's hand a squeeze and dragged my pajama-covered self to the center of the room. At first the impulse to move to the center felt like it was a product of my attention-deficit stuff, but I also have to confess that there was still a part of me that wanted to be the focus of everything, but it was more than that. I needed to receive all the incoming information before developing a plan and executing our response. It was a physical metaphor: I was stepping into the middle of the problem, because I'd stopped running.

"And while we haven't had any fatalities, there've been a couple of bad injuries, and we've been missing a pair of people for the last two nights. We have reports of things behaving differently. Everything from more aggressive to way outside historic behavior patterns."

"The per capita number of people capable of using magic is far, far greater than at any time in the past or anywhere else in the world." Helena added that tidbit with practiced ease, and even though I had just imparted forgiveness for the duplicity I could tell she saw a flash of irritation turn the corner of my mouth.

And I could swear my flash of annoyance amused her.

"She's right," Kaycee said, her internal strife put to bed. The powerhouse I knew and loved was moving purposefully into the discussion, "and I know Grove and you talked a little bit about it, but some of our students are getting better, faster and with more power than I would expect. Normally, that would be the point, but magic works a little differently than weight lifting for example. We usually have a pretty good idea of how much power you can throttle out from the beginning. From there we aim, shape and even enhance it but it's all within a pretty expected range. But people are just becoming even stronger than I would expect them to. They seem to be...."

"Brimming with power?"

Almost everyone sat up or narrowed their gaze at my statement. The intent behind it was to focus their attention on what I'd just said, knowing that the word fit, even if nobody had thought to describe it that way. Verrak and I exchanged a look, and from that look I can tell that she's going over everything that happened to us at Thomas' house but hadn't yet keyed in on the connection that allowed me to make such a leap.

"The *Bru-maga*,"

"The what?" Helena and Kaycee interrupted in tandem.

"An undead sorcerer."

"A lich?" Kaycee asked.

"No, a vampire."

"A vampire mag; a *Bru-maga*."

"Janzen, that sounds like a mix of witch in Spanish and Latin." Helena said evenly, and despite the feeling of condescension that comes with such an implied correction I could sense a touch of bemusement behind it. I mouth over the words, tasting them instead of saying them before turning to Verrak who scowled at the insult.

"I don't know your word for them Helena, but it fits." An unapologetic shrug was the best I got from the Stalker.

"It was a vampire, using a specific kind of life draining energy device." Helena and Kaycee exchanged a worried look.

"Yes, there's—wait, do you not know how many different types of vampires there are?" I asked. Helena suddenly looked a little puzzled, tossing a look over toward the half-elf before getting confirmation by way of a half-shrug, one not unlike Verrak's.

"There's the Dergund, and the Bri-"

"We usually use *monsters* and abominations, but since you all seem so keen on keeping mixed company we thought it best -"

"To shut the fuck up?" I fired that straight between the eyes, and when her enforcer bristled, I made sure he saw just how thoroughly unimpressed I was at his attempt to defend or explain. "Yeah, why don't you return to your usual mode of behavior before your attempt to unfuck a situation goes any worse."

For all my insult had cost him in face, both Helena and the warrior saw just how antagonistic that comment was to my people, and while their tribe might have been bigger, my gang was bloodied and ready to do it again if need be.

"I get it. Two types of vampires. One that gets warped because they use dark magic to steal life force, and one that becomes warped because they do it with fangs. Fangs are fighters and tougher, but the life-force ones are bigger power houses; there's just fewer of them. According to Verrak, *Bru-Maga* -" I make sure to eyeball the prince-charming type as I drag the working name for the vampire across the conversation with the tact of an M-80, "- usually only have one apprentice at a time. *One.* This one not only had two, it had two more in the oven so to speak; we found the other two in hibernation mid-transformation. Let's add that to the list of creatures crawling around Cleveland acting differently, along with the fact that more people are popping up with abilities here like never before." This was stuff we'd gone over, and over again, and by re-hashing it aloud myself I could tell that everyone in the room at one point or another had been aware of this conglomeration of troubling facts and happenings without drawing one thru-line conclusion.

I moved to the sturdy hand-me-down desk from my mentor and banged on the left side panel to open a hidden compartment and fish out the thorn-branch-collar. It was an insidious piece of twisted deadwood; the thorns hooked maliciously and seemed to elongate, hungering for flesh and caustically reaching out for it. After rolling it over in my grip once more, I returned to the center of the room and managed to pull a good number of the onlookers in with me.

Knowing men are creatures of egos, and good soldiers were hard finds, I extended the collar-contraption to Julian for his examination and thoughts. He was probably an even more capable artificer than me, and Helena suppressed a covert approving smile at the gesture knowing it was not unlike offering a literal olive branch. "Look at the sigils and tell me what you see."

I was a little thrown by the confusion it prompted, though after rolling it over in his fingers I could see flashes of recognition and even the beginnings of an actual understanding. Helena was also examining it, and she had a much better grasp as to what the device was doing than her protector/apprentice, but even she had a gap of understanding that she looked to me to fill.

"A few things: strength, spirit, and there's a vampiric element to the magic—a draining effect. I think she was draining his life force, his very soul." Incredulousness was wrought all over her, and with a searching look asked Kaycee and Gale if they had any opinion about it.

"That's far too high level for even a capable Bru-maga," the mother-hen said, tossing an applauding supportive glance at Verrak who actually bristle-beamed a little, which was adorable even if you knew she was actually an eight-foot man-eater. "Plus that kind of magic wouldn't give anything. It's more the kind of power that is driven by intent. The apprentices would have to not only offer their soul, they would have to really want to give it. Gale?"

"That's how I understand it too." The woman murmured, actually startling me when I realized the damnable bartender had somehow soundlessly ended up right beside me. There was a purr in the smirk she gave at seeing how I responded, but I swatted that down with a scowl, though secretly I was glad to see her more engaged.

"There's a summoning...clause I would almost call it. I've seen it before."

The foreboding quiet that often followed a moment like this was stretched out for effect, but when I lingered on finishing the sentiment it wasn't for theatrics – it was to take the time necessary to quell the hurt of the memory while speaking so openly on it.

"It was the sigil that Jackie carved into Maria, on the sacrificial table."

Everyone looked stupid with shock, the kind of quiet a pin-drop could crush, and the only thing more jarring than having to speak the realization out loud was the fact that not only did Gale already know that—she expected me to make the connection.

CHAPTER 13

Confessions

Wildly enough, out of all the questions I expected from that declaration, the first and loudest was the one I hadn't entertained.

"You can read all that sigil-work?" Helene asked as she carefully plucked the thorny collar out of my grip and re-examined it. She was quick and clear-cut, and as if remembering her role as teacher, passed it to her apprentice after finishing her inspection.

"Yeah...I couldn't duplicate it maybe, but I do understand the foundation of each of the sigils. The base is encircled with a summoning element, one used to break into or siphon from the In-Between. If I had to guess, she was using Thomas to super-charge herself and make more apprentices than her own energy would allow, even though Thomas wasn't strong enough to battery-power such an undertaking; but he had changed."

I kept my eyes on Helena, to see if she had any other questions about my ability. Truthfully, I was a little unsure if her own skepticism was a form of condescension or general surprise, but for now that wasn't important.

"Changed?" Kaycee shouldered a little closer. "How so?"

"I don't really know that yet, but if I was gonna take an Evil Knievel type of leap, I would say that somehow the In-Between has been leaking into some of us. Maybe it's the lake itself? Maybe it's being exposed to the opening? My understanding is that's a really, really rare type of power that only a Wanderer can tap into." Team Iandor stiffened a little at that. As I scanned the rest of the faces in our little group, I could see Kaycee reflecting on some of those fights. Gale appeared to be struggling with what I suspected was more information about this than she was letting on, and I knew pushing her would gain no favor nor bear any fruit. "This symbol is used to either harness or call on that energy." I said, pointing at the base of the collar. "This collar was around Thomas' neck, and she had the same symbol etched directly into her chest. We found four other collars, each with the same symbol, and they seemed to speed up the transition of her apprentices. This is how she kept them in line and remained connected to them so that she could draw upon their life energy." I felt the frustration of losing another person to this evil business. True, Thomas had been on the wrong side of this, but we all make mistakes.

These people are my responsibility.

"She used that connection to pull the life out of them and keep herself alive."

"Alive-*ish*."

It's hard not to love Johnny B., and even I couldn't help but let out a laugh. Gallows humor was fair if there was greater than good chance you were about to square up with a metaphoric firing line, and if something was about to go down there wasn't a doubt in my mind that Johnny B., would be fighting steady as a hair-band-ballad solo right beside me.

I use the small gasp of levity as a window to take the collar back, wrapping a second exploring hand around the opposite end.

"This is the same energy that made Maria into a target; it's the same energy that Donovan was after. The same energy she was drinking from Thomas during our fight through whatever conduit this collar created. I saw a glimmer of it in her eyes. Maybe it was a mix of this energy and his life force energy, but if I am reading it correctly, a single human wouldn't have given her enough power to do everything she was doing. Am I right?"

Helena had something very unnerving in the quality of her stare, and I knew this because she'd locked eyes on me since the beginning of this conversation and was yet to relent: clinical, not cruel, and thoroughly objective. Verrak and the silver-haired

Artificer nodded their agreement. This working theory was coming to life in front of everyone's horrified eyes and had a troubling sequence of happenings and suspicions, finding a disturbing pattern that it was falling in line with. Kaycee and Nicholas looked mortified, and while Johnny was quick with a joke, the elf was equally swift to address the weight of this implication with a more withdrawn countenance. Verrak and Grove were served well by their stoicism, and try he might, I saw a crack in Julian's bad-ass armor which gave us a glimpse of earnest apprehension as his understanding caught up with the clues.

I turned to look around at everyone, hating my hypothesis even as it poured from my mouth.

"Somehow it's infected these people. I don't know if it's only those of us who've been to the lake, or if it's anyone in proximity to the city itself. It may be just the original cultist group, but I don't think so." That half-wince, half-eye-narrowing thing I did clued everyone into the fact that I was roaming my memory trying to reconcile this with the number of new people showing up out of the blue with talent. It wasn't much of a stretch to believe that this thing had a much longer reach than we had initially thought.

"That energy from the night at the lake is part of this. The rift that bitch has been beating on for the last few years is leaking stuff into our world, and just like radiation poisoning, it's having an impact on people with latent talent along with people that have never exhibited any kind of talent at all. It's like a living bridge, this In-between. It divides everything, right?" I turn to Gale this time, the only one of us who'd had regular experience traveling between realms.

"Yes. There's the energy of the In-Between, which most suspect is... not alive exactly, but still deeply sentient." Gale had begrudgingly given me an abbreviated breakdown of these other worlds, so I had a rudimentary understanding of them. The Abyss, she had told me, was not quite hell, not quite forever dark, but a world of monsters that hunt, and beasts that kill anything less than them within claws-reach. The Veil was the genesis of magic, home of elves, mythical and magical creatures; a little Alice in

Wonderland meets Middle Earth if you will. As cool as some of that sounded, there was a very strict separation between these worlds. Those who wanted to migrate from one world to another had to get permission, and then travel through the In-Between... and the In-Between eviscerated anyone who tried to circumvent the rules.

As much as I didn't completely understand all of this, I did recognize the fact that something had changed. There were hints that rifts and breaks in this magical boundary had happened before, and that something like it was happening now. In fact, gauging by Gail's reaction, this one measured as not only the first on our world in thousands of years, but was amongst one of the largest as well.

When I'd asked Gale why she couldn't make the workings of it clearer, she asked me if I could explain red to a blind person, or thermodynamics to a dog. It was the kind of gulf in context that couldn't overcome limited understanding without having a much broader experience. The bar-keep actually patted my hand, a motion that last year would have caused me to jump, but now offered comfort. This newfound stillness I possessed was keeping me in my skin as the living nightmares came to our doorstep once again.

Her fingers untangled the murderous collar from my grip, lifting it to align with her sight-line before twisting it left and then right.

"How can we be sure these actually worked the way you say they did?" Julian asked with his nose in the air. He was arrogant and disinterested, looking to discredit me and the seriousness of this discovery...to what end I couldn't say. The implications of what I discovered were a clear-cut indicator that something much worse was coming.

"Janzen retains everything he's ever been taught and knows the basics of almost every one of your little talent trees." Kaycee snapped, and while the talent-tree reference was a gamer jab I could also tell whatever she was using the term to explain was something that Helena understood completely. I was deeply intrigued.

"I also saw the magic." Verrak said managing not to add the words *you prick*, but conveying it, nevertheless. Even though Julian was an egocentric turd and a bully, I knew that even a bully could be brilliant at times, so I did not discount his question out of hand.

"Janzen is better at understanding the workings of Artificery than even Zachariah was," The finality with which Gale made the claim was a bit alarming. The compliment was just too heavy handed to be true, but I couldn't deny a swell of pride upon hearing it. "And ever since jail forced him to sit still and stop playing on his damn phone he's gotten even better."

The claim was believed by my people, and when Gale's eyes met Helena's steady dubious ones, the two momentarily squared off. "Donovan Unet said as much, I had him report to me weekly on their progress."

"Ah yes, the outcast of the House of Unet. He did seem a reliable type, especially when in service to you. Look, I respect that you are all proud of Mr. Robinson," I knew immediately she wasn't trying to be insulting, and was instead trying to appeal to the fact that in a world of much bigger and badder things, I was a relative nobody, and that relying on my unverified expertise might be a mistake. The searching look was measuring each of us, before locking on me with something of an apology alive in her eyes.

I liked her. A lot.

Her tone had been sharp when insulting the peace-keeper of Cleveland, as was the insult she had hurled. For a moment I hated being at the center of this little contest where these two much more powerful women had found themselves at odds with one another. Truthfully, I was about to clumsily interject anything—accusations of mansplaining be damned—just to turn us toward a more productive conversation. I even timed it to cut off the small break of an olive branch offered by the Artificer, but Gale wasn't finished, and as usual, had a surprise ending for us.

Handing the vine-deadwood collar over to me while murmuring a low-pitched agreement to my assessment, a stride carried her just out of Helena's reach. The fire-headed, green eyed mystic and resident heart-breaker of Cleveland cleared her throat before a triangle insignia flashed on and around her throat. At the pinnacle of the triangle was one initial, the base sat beneath her esophagus, and the sides flanked what would be her Adam's Apple. This symbol was unknown to everyone....

Everyone except me and—I suspected—Helena.

It was the self-made brand he'd used for his crafthood signature; a secret way for us to sign our work. Normally, an Artificer only does so on a prized piece, and for Zachariah, I'd only seen it on the fire-invoking glove he'd made and adored.

You know, the one I eviscerated...but hey, it was for a good cause, right?

When Gale spoke next it was with a pitch-perfect simulation of Zachariah's voice, and while at first I thought she was just mimicking him, as she continued on, I realized it was not only the man himself but that this was something of a last testament, highlighting the section about me.

"And of course there's my apprentice, Janzen Robinson." Not only was the tone pitch-perfect, I immediately recognized that Gale had fallen into a small trance and was even emoting the way he would when he wanted to emphasize a point. Judging from the soft lilt in the speech, I would guess that this was done—this magic-made recording—after a few well aged drinks that I couldn't pronounce and had been barreled up for a few decades longer than made any kind of sense to me.

"My friend."

Gale copied that pensive, far-off look I'd gotten from him so well, before clearing her throat with a disarming amount of masculinity and just leaping back into it. "Mr. Robinson will buck the leash so to speak, so if this does not go well, I want you to keep an eye out for him and just make sure to leave a light on for when he's finally ready to come back home." The flinch of emotionality underlying the instructions told me that his proper

English etiquette was failing him, and that half the reason he was forging ahead was to keep from appearing even slightly human. Of this I was certain because Zachariah thought sniffling in a sad movie was histrionics.

"I have kept from constructing traditional structure around my curriculum for Mr. Robinson, trying to instead harness some of the strengths that come from his unique upbringing and background. In doing so, he's taken an interest, to varying degrees, in a bit of everything. And I have done my best to foster it. He has an imaginative mind, is a quick study, as tough and brave as any young man I've ever met, and so much smarter than he thinks he is. Janzen has an incredible ability to understand the way a thing works, a talent that has to be nurtured; a talent that I have never seen matched except maybe in some of the most elite Tinkerers from some of the most celebrated Gnome families in the world. It's remarkable and tragic, because a school such as the one I came from would never entertain taking on such a pupil. Janzen has the capability to develop a base, or foundation set of sigil work in every pillar of spellcraft we taught in that school and meaningfully charge them. He doesn't understand how spectacular that is, but it's something I've only seen some of the most seasoned instructors at our institution be able to do."

There was a pause, a light hiccup which Gale mimed brilliantly. "I can't do it."

I saw his mustache on her lips while she thoughtfully pursed her mouth and chewed over what to say next in a perfect homage to his own mannerisms. "While he's yet to get into the deepest workings of each respective pillar, this broad-spanning adoption of understanding has led him to crafting tools that on the surface aren't yet fully optimized but are truly the seedlings of great innovations. This ability has to be fostered. He is the embodiment of a Renaissance Man. While I know it isn't a lot, Gale, I need -"

The *recording* abruptly shut off, a stabbing one-two shake of her head right to left and the spellwork was dropped and the invocation died.

"You might not trust his judgment," Gale said, as she took a step back. She looked over her shoulder at us, and finished saying, "But we do...and Zachariah did."

Helena was a whirlwind of feeling, and my respect for her grew considerably while witnessing the woman acknowledge, process, and compartmentalize her emotions without ever once losing composure over what was just shared. Me?

The only thing that kept me from spinning into a mental freefall was remembering the moment I was in...and then my phone shrieked. It was almost comical, and I silenced it with a slap and an embarrassed half-smile.

"So we have that." Kaycee was such a mom, the woman had managed to punctuate the conversation, and pivot the discussion to frame how we were going to handle what was happening. She literally turned and took a step toward the desk Grove and I used. Before long, we all surrounded the desk and faced one another, and as I went over to sit in my old, broken-in-leather chair I stopped half way to pulling it out and said, "...and it seems like we have as close to the why as will ever make sense."

Helena nodded, and Gale took a second uneasy breath. "Now we just need the who."

This time it was Johnny B. who wrestled some of the stage that our poor-man round table was fast becoming. Watching him and Gale perfectly illustrated how all of these creatures, magics, monsters and people could both co-mingle while so deeply, and vastly misunderstanding each other. They had mended the broken fence that was the result of whatever had severed the ties between them, but there was an almost peer nature to their interactions, and underneath that was an almost primal communication and affection that they shared. A prompting shoulder-nudge stirred her enough that she unwound from her tightly arm-crossed defensive posture with an audible breath.

Usually, I was able to get ahead of the script, and it was almost impossible for cohorts to get much of anything completely by me, but for once I was searching the respective faces to see who here had a firm grasp on where this was going. Johnny was posturing as if in support of Gale, who looked as human and uneasy as the day she showed up at my doorstep covered in blood and running for her life.

The soldier beside me was watching, and Helena looked as if she was eager to get on with things, which told me that she had some idea as to what was going on…but nothing had prepared me for what came next.

"I know who the woman from the Abyss is."

CHAPTER 14

Abigail

The revelation dropped like a hammer, and apparently my subconscious was able to navigate my ass into a seat that apparently my body felt I suddenly needed. Grove, Verrak, and I were completely slapped, though I had to say judging from the reaction on Kaycee and Helena's faces that it was evident these three had been discussing quite a bit about this in my absence. My mouth felt dry like the Sahara, and I could taste the word arid.

Grove was mad, and I knew that because the sentence he signed at Johnny was one I didn't even repeat. It was a rather poignant reminder that Grove spent a significant amount of time around the men whom the phrase *curse like a sailor* was coined for. The half-elf who'd been with me and the soldier from day one was able to calm any further soundless insults from being hurled as her hand captured his signing hand in mid-motion. Once it was secured, she kept it firmly in her grasp, and by her side.

There was a murmur between Verrak and the Bard, and Julian looked as arrogant as you would expect while shouting a demand for more clarity. Helena, who I could totally see as being able to hold court with Zachariah despite my dumbfoundedness, not only shut him up with a snapping look. but was able to actually compel him to sit down with her brutal glare.

Even in my catatonic shell-shocked state I heard that surgical, always talking voice note something curious in my head; these women had discussed this, and with some of the new information

I'd brought to light we'd be able to—maybe for the first time—see all of this from a bigger picture vantage point, but that wasn't the epiphany.

I realized that Helena must have been here for quite a while now.

I wondered why she didn't visit me in jail, which felt silly, but I also wondered why Kaycee hadn't informed me about any of this. Then I wondered if I was looking for anything to wonder about so long as it avoided the realization that Gale knew who this woman was. It re-aligned so many things in my head, even without hearing another word. As I sluggishly clawed my way back to the conversation, I heard my surrogate sister slap everyone into silence.

"*Stop!*"

I realized that several of the strained whispers had turned into chatter and actually bled over into a little bit of arguing. Blinking some of the haze away I found that Gale was not only waiting for my acknowledgement but looked sincerely apologetic and sympathetic. She disguised it well, but I caught a wince while shuffling to sit upright. Most people wouldn't have caught it, and those who did would discard it as some kind of misread given the posture and prestige of the Peace-Keeper, but I wasn't most people.

Hurt people hurt people, and those who'd been abused could recognize their own from a mile away.

Gale in that moment looked truly human to me, and so with another steady mental cadence of *one - two - three* I was able to bury my ire behind a mental firewall of compassion and patience. I sat it right next to my own sins, as if needing that reminder to keep myself from saying anything too shitty. It was harder than I cared to admit, and some people might assume it was a bit presumptuous of me, but before prompting her to continue I took a moment.

For us…Gale and Me.

"Talk to me Gale, it's alright. I trust you too."

The word trust was layered and carried a lot between us. I kicked a seat out for Grove, the motion was the best way to grab his attention, and as my battle-tested partner quietly sat down beside me, the hint for everyone else to join him was taken. There was a small reprieve in the tension; an almost cute look passed between Johnny and Verrak as he retrieved his own stool while dragging one along for her. Kaycee wasn't all the way out of the woods with me for hiding so much of this, but if I trusted Gale, whatever I had for the half-elf was twice as rooted and cherished. Given the hell I'd put her through, I had to acknowledge that turnabout is indeed fair play.

The last generation of rustling was folding into quiet, and Gale was now the center of our attention and our collective focus. Funny enough, for a moment I thought it was the grimace that made her feel more human, but in this light as she grabbed up that mane of red hair and stretched her arms out in front of us, I could suddenly see half-a-dozen scars that had been earned over the last few years.

I also noted a general sense of her. Where she used to radiate power, now it was more suggested. I thought of the inhuman but still valid bond between her and Johnny, a half-child of some kind from a complicated time in a long-ago life, and I had to say I wasn't at all surprised to find his unblinking stare locked on me as I thought this over. I met the penetrating look from the Karaoke King with equal measure, and as the Bartender and proprietor of the Last Love Bar—resident Peace-Keeper and friend—finally made herself ready to share this long overdue story, I turned my full attention to her.

"When Helena first came here it wasn't long after the trial and the attack on the city. She was joined by Julian, not only to get some kind of understanding about what happened and who was involved, but to help figure out what we should do about it." I look-check Helena but the woman could give the word unreadable a run for its money. "I've known Helena a long time, but first, we need to get to Abigail."

Abigail.

My skin crawled a little and a vague uneasiness passed over me.

Gale dropped her eyes to the center of the table and went a million miles away, even as the most basic part of her stayed here to narrate all that she was reliving.

"Every thousand or so years a rift of some kind does open, but it's not *exactly* a thousand years. Those from the other worlds care not for the way Humankind measures things, and it would be impossible to adhere to them. Anyway, the reason it's hard to identify what I am is because once, a thousand or so years ago, I was human." I was surprised at how unsurprised I was, her faint smile as sad as it was serene. "The last time there was such a rift, it was bridged to the Veil. Back then I was a part of a coven of witches, we practiced druid-type magic that was close to the natural forces of this world, forces that have a direct connection to the Veil. Our sisterhood was vast and far reaching. My chapter was from what is now southern Scotland. With every passing solstice in the decade leading up to the rift opening, more and more half-breed creatures and energy were able to escape the Veil and start influencing our world. The Veil doesn't seem as terrible as the Abyss on the surface, but I promise you, the Sidhe, the Fae, some of the ancient elves, and the sentient magics and monsters that live there are every bit as capable of cruelty as those who call the Abyss home." She was too steely spined to falter, but the terror she spoke of passed her eyes and I could see the depth of it. I could see how traumatic and scarring it had been, an awfulness that was still haunting her centuries later.

"Abigail was the leader of a sister covenant, the largest of our Order. When we realized not even our collective power could heal the rift we came up with a plan," Sardonic and regretful, the teeth-baring smile was thick with regret, and I could already tell this plan was where the story went south. "We all traveled to Northern Ireland just before the turn of the twelfth century. We were young and foolish. We were the strongest generation of witches ever born." She came out of the reverie enough to rejoin me in the now, as if putting the memory on pause to help connect a missing piece I'd unwittingly brought to light.

"It wasn't until what you just said Janzen, that I realized the reason for this strength was our constant ceremonies on the rift. It's also why we were able to survive the journey through the In-Between."

That bit perked everyone up, and I could tell that even though she'd filled Kaycee and Helena in on some of this, they too were hearing about these details for the first time. Having unknowingly contributed to solving this mystery I listened as she resumed the story.

"We were the strongest generation of witches ever born. Our duty was to this world, and this rift threatened all of it. Her name was Abigail, and no, I didn't know her well. She was far too important for me to regularly consort with, but as I was the head of my little chapter, she was civil and aware of me. Abigail was by far the strongest of us, taking on challenges like communicating with the creatures beyond the rift and negotiating the plan. You see, Abigail had been able to forge an alliance with a group of creatures who had the power and means to heal the rift and close it off, but they lacked the motivation to do it."

Gale finally retired to her seat, but still commanded our attention.

"The entire Sisterhood gathered, and while Abigail designed it to look like a willing pledge, each chapter head pledged a century of servitude to these things, in exchange for the closing of the rift." Suddenly, being able to read between the lines was a curse, and I was glad that Johnny was beside her to secretly take a hand and steady the proud, square-shouldered woman. "At the next ritual, each of us slipped through the rift, and as each of us passed, the broken barrier healed as was promised. Abigail was the last of us to pass through. These creatures, the Sidhe, did actually close the rift but the alliance was obviously a lie. Abigail had tricked all of us naive, foolish, little witches, and had actually sold and traded us to these cruel masters. In exchange, the rift was mostly closed, and Abigail had a bridge to go between our old home and this world at will, often bringing ignorant newcomers to the covenant to trade them as slaves."

"Every chapter leader has the ability to absorb magic from our surroundings. It's a subtle gift in this world, but a very pronounced and valuable talent in a world like the Veil. Often the Sidhe just siphoned and drained us over and over again when not implementing other sadistic practices for their perverse pleasure. Abigail, to her credit, was the strongest of our kind and so the more time she spent in the Veil, the more magic and knowledge she absorbed; her aptitude for housing power grew." At that point, I experienced a disconnect, as if running headfirst into a wall and now suffering from the brain-breaking aftermath. Suddenly, I understood that whatever complication severed her relationship with Johnny had been born of this tragedy and was probably a lot easier to forgive with this new understanding.

No one pushed, so I had to.

"Why now, Gale?" I didn't want to ask too much, but we had to know. I trusted that she would have a good reason for waiting to divulge all of this, and I watched as she realized that she hadn't even filled us in on the most important part, the *why* of this retelling. If I ever questioned what a struggle this was for her, I realized by the look of horror on her face what a thicket of soul-crushing trauma this experience had been for her.

"Yes…right…. After some time, I escaped from my captors. That's actually how I came to know the Iandor Institute. When I got out, they tracked me down. This was back when they used to more actively monitor and police breaches of the In-Between. Actually, I was able to get out of the Veil by way of House Unet, if you can believe it. They ran their own version of an Underground Railroad."

"The Iandor Institute has a kind of witness protection; a program we use to relocate people who get caught in this sort of slave trafficking. We'd relocated Gale to New Orleans in the 1920s, and I actually was her custodian for a few months in the late 70s." Helena added, the two women sharing a smile between the half-smirk they offered one another at the mutual recollection.

"Anyway, Abigail had herself overstepped with the Sidhe and finally grown a little too big for her britches, so to speak. I heard she was forced to undergo the same fate she'd sentenced us to, and after a long spell with a particularly sadistic Sidhe prince, she led some kind of rebellion or resistance that was smashed down and cost her her life. It was all rumor of course, passed down through unreliable channels, but I hadn't seen or heard of her in eight, maybe nine hundred years so I thought well, maybe...." I readily identified when somebody was using rhetoric for thought-stirring statements, so I let her chew over the question herself while trying to button up a finish.

"How she got into the Abyss is beyond me, and truthfully, it's hard to trust my faith that it's her because of just how changed she is. Honestly, it wasn't until the trial beneath the courthouse that I even realized that it could be her, and before I told anyone, I wanted to use every resource I could to try and confirm it: anything about her whereabouts, or what had actually happened to her." There was a small deflation, which told me without the need for her to say it, that they couldn't get any such confirmation. "It was her human image that day in the trial when I recognized her. The way she's been absorbing the powers around her to fuel her attempts to break through; the way she manipulated the cultist, and even the way she was trying to use Maria. I've seen her do it before..." Gale paused, and thru clenched teeth on a pained exhale said "I'd felt that magic before." Not one of us who had been present that night on the Lake could have foreseen this revelation.

"It's Abigail. I know it's hard to believe, but a thousand years ago she was human. She isn't any longer, and if she's anything like she once was, all she cares about is getting home, damn the cost or the consequences. It's her, I know it."

The quiet after was scene-stealing, and not a single person assembled at the round table had anything to say. Helena was the most inquisitive, but she'd the tact to use that curiosity to think over all the newly shared details; I could tell she was doing this, because I was doing the same thing. At our core, an Artificer is when an Artisan and Engineer mind-meld with magic. It took a very particular type of person to become one, and even though I was very susceptible to my emotions, I almost instinctively defaulted to pragmatism and logic when faced with just about any challenge. Helena was doing exactly the same thing now.

Julian wasn't, and I could tell that judging ran deep with that dude, because he was doing a shit job of concealing what was very obviously a deep contempt for Gale. Just as he'd done with Verrak, which given her lineage was slightly understandable—even if I hated to admit it myself. The fact that he didn't like me was equally understandable, and perhaps the sole indicator that he had any sound judgment. While this was jarring and a little destabilizing, as I knocked the cobwebs and dust off my brain to reassemble my understanding of everything considering this powerful revelation, I could finally construct a thru-line of logic.

Abigail sure as *hell* didn't like me because I kept getting in the way of her coming home; stopping her in her tracks. So far she'd tried to get the drop on a Wanderer and take Gale out after recognizing her involvement in all of this, and she'd failed at both attempts.

"You said you were relocated to New Orleans?" Compartmentalizing was great for being meticulous in the details and taking the emotional temperature down in the face of trauma, though I had to admit that I heard myself asking as I actively thought about the question. It was enough to drag me out of my own fog though, and hearing all of this was akin to overeating after already being stuffed, so I was glad to see my head was still able to work.

See what happens when you avoid a concussion for over eight hours—it's remarkable. Now if I could keep the streak alive for another eight, but it had the smell of that kind of day and didn't look all that promising.

"Sometime in the late 90s there were rumors of the In-Between leaking out here in Cleveland. It called to me so much I picked it." A look bounced between Kaycee and Helena, and I knew that at least one of them hadn't been informed of the next tidbit. "When Zachariah came here and started regularly visiting the

Lake and talking about what it was he was finding, and digging out, I suspected I was drawn here. That, and I could tell that the boundary was thinning again. I wasn't sure of it until he finally started sharing some of his findings with me.

"Did he tell you what he was looking for?" Helena beat me to the question, but we both leaned forward at the same time.

Gale stoutly shook her head. "He discussed irregularities, oddities, and asked a lot of questions about events around town and in the neighboring areas, and they were very selective. Zachariah was more interested in finding information than sharing, and it's not like I had a right to give anyone hell for doing that."

"As you know, when I left New Orleans, it was in the dead of night, and I tried to stay as out of the way as possible. Iandor was pretty clear that if I left the city I couldn't be assured of their protection, though by that time I'd finally gotten back on my feet, regained some..." She trailed off, but recovered quickly, "Back then I was even more secretive than I am now, and to be fair, Zachariah had been shot down about his concerns so regularly that the man was more obsessed with finding evidence of a breach than bouncing theories off of anyone. He didn't share much with me until the last six months, and by the time we started to open up to one another he was…struggling." It wasn't permission Gale looked for when meeting my eyes, but when I nodded my understanding, I could see her relax by a degree.

I remembered that time, and still mourned it. Zachariah had become a borderline recluse, and while the paranoia was becoming more noticeable it was also enervating a lot of other stabilizing qualities. The man was disheveled and unfocused, attributes usually attributed to me. Not to mention, as was often the case with a lot of people who stare into the ugly of the unknown, toward the end he'd begun the bad habit of retiring into a bottle most evenings.

"I never said anything back then either, because outside of having some experience with a rift opening, I hadn't a clue about anything else. At least not yet. It felt different as much as it felt the same. It's a world away, and this one leads to the Abyss, and

I didn't see anything hinting at someone pulling at strings behind the scene. Even now, sure as I am that it is Abigail, I can't fathom how it is she ended up where she is or what her role is in all of this."

I had a name now, and the sickening twist in the pit of my stomach was met by a slow rising of determined, well forged fury. It battled that unease back down into the bowels of nothingness, stomping it out along with every other shred of doubt I harbored about seeing this fight all the way through. Of course, a second rumbling in the pit of my stomach came from pangs of hunger and not the sixth-sense unease born of being around some supernatural mega-threat. Reeling at the information dump was enough, taking all this on while lacking sleep and sustenance was a task too tall for any mortal.

"Alright, first we eat, then we start to unfuck all of thi-"

My phone rang, and this time I glimpsed the number and name scrolling across the burner Grove had given me. Nicholas set up a system to mass-text all my pertinent contacts anytime I got a new number, a similar program they'd used for Grove at his insistence. Good friends, but man these over-prepared madmen were even better partners. Of all the numbers I could have guessed at, the one ringing me for a third time would have been at the bottom of that admittedly short list.

It was the church and father Handy

More troubling than the who, was the fact that I didn't even have to speak after pressing accept.

"Get to the church." Father Handy was on the other line, and while I was sure whatever was parading around as a man beneath the veneer of a priest had the power to rip me out of reality and drop me beside him on a whim. I was also keen to the fact that there was a kind of limitation to what power could and couldn't be practiced. The urgency is what really bothered me, and I responded in kind.

"On my way."

CHAPTER 15

Behind The Curtain

All it took was a look. Grove smoothly stood, and without any prompting half-jogged to his side of the office to gear up. Gale registered it, but the walk down such a hellacious memory-lane had completely exhausted her. Johnny was doing an admirable job of being a steady, soothing presence for Gale and he peeked at me, ready to spring into action. With a suppressed, reassuring wave of my hand, I had him stay and keep doing what he was doing.

Kaycee, meanwhile, had the audacity and clout to just outright ask.

"Where are you going?"

"Church," Half pithy, half to disguise the connection, though I was about to find that point moot.

"Father Handy?" She asked.

Helena and Julian both perked up at that, and Gale—despite the circumstances—did stir minutely. While I was aware of his powerful presence and had at various times unwittingly run my friends into him, help from the unpredictable enigmatic priest hadn't really been discussed. Nor had his connection to this, which we all knew wasn't a coincidence. The shrewd agent of Iandor had resources and did a lot of due diligence before she had blind-sided me at the bar.

Helena frowned at my tight-lipped non-response, even as she peppered me with a snide remark, hoping that it would be bait enough for me to talk about my unexpected ally. I maintained the silent routine until I stepped off myself to gather my stuff and get ready.

Or I had intended to, until Julian, calendar-esque frat-boy turned Iandor enforcer blockaded my pathway with his head-taller frame.

"You sure you wanna do this, runway?

"You may be able to speak to every Pillar of Artificery, but I am of the two that make up the real power of our gift."

I size him up, steady myself to blink once, and lock eyes with this impressive, clean-cut magic-cop.

"I don't understand the majority of that sentence, and even less the threat in it."

My ability to get under the skin of someone was legendary, but even I had to admit that an audible gnashing of his pearly white teeth from clenching his jaw so hard was a new one—even for me. Julian wasn't doing his brethren any favor by having such an uneven temper, and while I suspected the man could walk my ass up and down the block in a straight fight, I couldn't help but be unimpressed with the rest of him. Helena intervened with a scalding look, and even with an open desire to test my mettle against this fellow Artificer, I hadn't any desire to get any further onto her bad side. As he walked to the far wall to await further instruction, I caught a glimpse of a steel gauntlet that hung off his left hip, and more than just taking in the design, I was able to discern some of the craftsmanship that enhanced the spiked, steel glove. It was brilliant, formidable stuff, most of it a collection of strength enhancing, endurance elongating glyphs that considerably reinforced the thing.

It was better in quality than anything I'd done, though it lacked…diversity? Something about the lack of complexity bothered me. Limitations ensured that in a pinch you'd be relying on brute force over cleverness, and as much as I would like to be the heaviest hitter in any of my engagements, to date I'd never been on the winning side of that equation before squaring up with a problem. I suspected the theme was going to be a constant one.

"You like poking bears."

"I like antagonizing assholes," I clarified with a flat expression and droll tone.

Helena didn't bite, and perfectly disarmed me by responding contrary to my expectation. Her expression blossomed into something mildly amused and equally impressive, surrendering some of the posturing that usually went into these back-and-forths, making me feel like a perfect asshole if I didn't join her in a more civil interaction.

"We're here to help, Janzen, even if you don't like me knowing about this curious priest or the reckless ways you've avoided all of this from coming undone in the past."

"Alpha or Delta?"

Helena was a pro, and didn't give an inch, not even the slightest hint at which of the two had dimed me out about the up-to-now secret resource of the priest from parts unknown.

"I bet you're a nightmare at a Poker table."

"Bridge."

"God, Zachariah must have been putty in your hands."

"And me in his," She confessed, even looking a little whimsical in the process. "It was Alpha," she said; a truce offering. I could tell by the restrained hopefulness in her eyes that she desperately hoped I was going to take it.

"Ah, Alphie… Alphie, Alphie, Alphie." The tsk-tsk-tsk after was a little heavy handed.

"At least Delta is of the ride or die sort." I intoned thoughtfully, pausing in my retreat back to my apartment so that Kaycee could join Helena and me.

"They both concealed it as much as I think people like them are capable of, if it's any consolation."

"It is."

Meet people where they are and don't expect seismic shifts overnight. Sounded like Alpha barely wrote about it and Delta had left the entire bit out of whatever reporting system they had for the Unet Household.

"Who is he?" Helena dropped the question between both me and Kaycee. The half-elf shrugged a little helplessly, for once turning to me for any insight I may not have shared up until this point. Funny enough, I didn't realize until now that I had made a habit out of staying rather mum about my interactions with the priest. As someone who had the reputation of being able to carry on a conversation with a duck as long as it occasionally quaked back, questions about the clergyman tended to be amongst the select few that would shut me up. Distantly, I wondered if that was some kind of subtle compulsion but disregarded treading into those waters while so much was still on my plate.

"A friend."

Helena took my measure, and my first inclination was to put on a little show and see if I could get some kind of half-truth by her with a tried-and-true gimmick.

I resisted the urge, and instead asked for her trust.

"He's a friend, or as close to one as something like him can be. For now I suggest we focus on our own issues and let me just check in on why he's calling me."

"Has he ever done this before?" Kaycee asked. While I was away, she had morphed into a teacher, resource, and constant helping hand to our entire community. Even now, as she sought to fill in some of the blanks, she'd waved Grove over and started to inspect some of the gear she'd brought for him. Multi-tasking as only a mother could, it felt like she was actually trying to figure out what it was that I was going to be doing tonight while simultaneously dressing a sibling.

"Justin? No. He's never even called before."

Kaycee out-paced some of the gray smattering in her hair in terms of sagacity, and I was fast growing uncomfortable with over-sharing, so the subject was dropped. Helena picked up the context clue and wisely did the same.

I hesitated to speak because of my inclination to start ordering each of them around but Kaycee gave me the kind of support an overburdened leader prayed for.

"What do you need us to do?"

"Use these fancy-as-fuck systems Nicholas put together to do a roll call of all of our people, and once everyone answers bring them either here or to the shop."

I could see Helena deliberating on whether or not to join in on the offered assistance, and while I liked her a lot and had a deep, fast-growing admiration for the woman, I could see that her stature came with a touch of ego. Luckily, she was the kind of person smart enough to know when and when not to allow pride a place at the table. When we met eyes, I was reassured by her tight-lipped smile.

"There's a bar - restaurant by the public encampment beside Lake Erie," When I checked the time it was still mid-afternoon. "Post yourself up there and bring Lurch if you have to. Just keep an eye on the place. It was close to the big tear in this rift, so if something is going on out there, you'll probably be able to get a sense of it from where you are." I signaled to her phone, and took it out of her hand and quickly punched my number in.

"Text me on the hour every hour, no matter what." I glance over at Kaycee. "You too. When I get back from the Church, we'll for once get our whole tribe read in on this and finally try to figure out how to get ahead of it." Halfway into handing back her phone I stop myself, exaggerate an eye-roll, and make my inner moody-teenager proud by protestingly putting Julian's information in my phone as well. Helena caught it and smiled, the glint of approval obvious.

"You really were a pupil of Zachariah's."

I gave her a Boy Scout Salute with my fingers as I peeled off to go get my gear. *Be prepared always*. The old man, who in proper hindsight wasn't all that old, preached that above all else. Our job was to be prepared, to work out contingencies, and be almost infinitely adaptable. Julian was rigid, and Helena seemed a lot more of a traditionalist; in fact come to think of it so was my mentor, but my experience and tenure under his tutelage was surprisingly loose and dynamic when compared to what I had come to learn about where it was that my mentor had learned, and how his peers had been trained.

***

Helena walked the workshop with me as I got outfitted, interested in the variety and volume of knick-knacks and things I'd built or was in pre-production on. After making sure Johnny would not only stay in service to Gale, but that they both would be helpful with what Kaycee was doing, I showed Julian and Helena where on the map of Lake Erie the incident had taken place, giving them the location of the woods and the previous skirmishes we'd had there, as well as suggesting the cheese fries for consumption so that I could live vicariously through them.

I'd been out for almost a day and a half and all I'd consumed was half a light beer and the decaying waft of a vampire nest. Grove grabbed the lever-action, silver-bayoneted rifle that had served him so well. The bayonet was less a bayonet and more a half-ax, and the lever-action rifle fired low-caliber bullets; the bolt-assembly stamped a sigil on every round so that it had the nasty, searing, and weakening bite of silver on every bullet. I also noticed a less overstated but equally enchanted burnished jacket, a pistol half-concealed on his right hip and a healthy sprawl of neatly filed magazines on his left side.

I'd yet to have an opportunity to really build any new equipment, though I was elated to find that Kaycee had mended almost all my standing stuff. The full-size aluminum bat was staggered with elemental emblems that could contort kinetic energy into any of the corresponding sigils carved into it. My favorite part was the five or so minutes I spent swinging the thing like a madman against the asphalt and brick-wall, effectively charging it; not unlike loading a gun but with a lot more ridiculous-looking cardio. My wooden bat had been cut in half by a Stalker talon and had assimilated the magic that reinforced the biting edge of those malicious claws. Now? The severed bat was as sharp as those claws and served me like a dagger for close combat.

After shrugging into my own, much more overstated jacket, I locked on the leather bracer that I had come to have a lot less embarrassment over and attached a satchel of marbles to my hip. The last piece was an homage to the very mentor who'd been a mainstay in my thoughts over the last few days. The black glove was lined with menacing red stitching, and every digit sported an overlapping of the same three sigils; basic, streamlined and terribly effective. The glove could harness your power and produce a geyser of flames, it could also absorb certain kinds of magic, and with enough practice, you could contour the fire to do a lot more, though my mastery of such a thing was tentative at best.

For good measure I stopped by the kitchen on my way out and grabbed a bag of stale popcorn, dousing it in salt to make it edible, and pouring the remnants of the salt into one of my jacket pockets. Grove once again proved his uncanny ability to forecast needs and handed me a protein bar as I piled into our junker sedan to keep his still-new-smelling truck from what was historically our very destructive outings. My groveling stomach, impossible for him to hear, grumbled in gratitude. By the time we got to the church the first hints of night were starting to wear at the edges of daylight, which admittedly gave the stonework a handsome look. It was an old church, fashioned in tribute to some of the old cathedrals which celebrated the importance and character of the religion.

The location was a little curious; one side of the road was industrial, and the other had a lot of abandoned and discarded properties. It was curious because even though it was archaic, the building itself was a really gorgeous monument to the good old times, and I could imagine how proud the neighborhood must have once been to congregate at such a fine house of worship. I couldn't recall ever seeing anyone here before me, though quite a few people had come across the place after.

I felt my partner hesitate. Up until now he'd not really met the priest except incidentally, and with everything we'd just learned about what was happening here—the creatures we'd gotten tangled up with and how dire the situation was—it brought a different kind of weight to standing in front of the church as opposed to times past. As much as I didn't appreciate being watched or having my personal exploits chronicled by what passed as magic's version of government, I had to admit that for the first time they had me wondering a little bit about what the priest was, even while I couldn't help struggling with the compulsion to plead for his help.

I wasn't sure where Father Handy ranked in terms of power, but something told me it was a hell of a lot more formidable than the vehicle he'd been loitering around in would suggest. Whatever theory I was entertaining about the creature masquerading around as a man was usually abandoned whenever we laid eyes on one another.

Groves' glance at me would have seemed trivial to anyone else, but I could sense the worry in it, so I did my best to reassure him with a half-smile and directive nod, keeping a confident and steady gait up the flight of stairs. The landing at the top was pretty spacious and beside the heavy, carved-wood double-doors was one of those plastic boxes displaying a list of gatherings, sermons and freshly passed or upcoming events. Dawdling on the plateau wasn't based on unease, and even though I could tell that the priest had something time sensitive to speak about I couldn't keep myself from taking a quick scan of the block from that vantage.

It wasn't but three years ago that I had run/stumbled up these very stairs and threw myself through this doorway to try and find refuge from an unstoppable killing machine that not very long ago was the definition of a death-sentence to a lowlife like me. A year and a half ago—almost to the day—we'd escaped a burning building full of night-terrors brought to life as demon-possessed police officers and found our way into this safe haven. Sadly, a precocious girl had lost her second parent in the process, though the wealth spring of her talent was probably one of the first byproducts of the rift energy's many effects.

As much as I'd missed my people, and even some of the more punchy and zany cohorts of our camp while I was in prison, it was these shared silences with Grove that I had come to appreciate most. It was the utter lack of expectation that made him so easy to be around. In a world where everything seemed capable of winding you up or letting you down, the soldier was as rocksteady as the moniker suggests. Of all the people who'd stepped in to help me endure, survive and navigate this insane hellscape, he's the only anomaly because of his normalcy. A former public safety officer, and a down on his luck artificer doing the best they could with what they had.

"I can't believe you agreed to help me after seeing that Stalker back when." I kept my face aimed at him while leaning into the door. My laugh triggered his own, and he responded with the same nostalgia. "When I found out what a shit wizard you were, what else was I gonna do?"

The inside was warm and reassuring, with neatly lined pews bleeding into a beautifully spread backdrop of candles, carvings and decorative tapestries. Nothing was gaudy. All of it was immaculate and old, and as well made as it was well used. This was a church that was cared for and used by a still faithful community. The reverence for the place was matched by the appreciation of the place of the man beside me. Grove was seeing and feeling it for the first time, and I was learning to process it with a renewed respect for what was being brought to life here.

I caught the glint of a bald head down on the right side in the second to last pew before the Dais, and while I couldn't make out who he was with, I could tell that he was in prayer with the veiled woman sitting beside him. Tonight the pews held a smattering of people, and I was surprised to find that I was unbothered by the fact, and found it added to the warmth of the place. The quizzical look my friend kept aiming at me was asking who this mysterious theological benefactor was, and when the plainly seen cleric murmured departing assurances to the woman, I could tell that Grove was a little disappointed in the lack of a wow factor.

Justin Handy as I had known him was probably six feet down to the millimeter. If you told me the man was a well-seasoned twenty-eight, I would believe you; and if you told me that he was a fit, ageless wonder in his mid-forties I would believe that too. He was ageless in an incomprehensible way. Those in attendance very obviously knew him, and the clergyman's robes had an authentic aged quality to them (a fact that seemed to demystify him further to Grove), suggesting that maybe the man was not going to live up to what was becoming a rather far-reaching myth.

"Janzen, my friend." We clasp hands and almost immediately I relax into the familiar warmth that pervades the man's very being. Whatever form of magic or omnipotence he possessed, I was grateful for having him in my life. This peace I feel is a gift that I receive with a lot less reticence now, and when we closed in a hug it is impossible to describe how completely OK I felt. I'd missed him. He had been there as my only respite on the worst days of my well tested life.

He was my buddy; he was my friend.

"Father Handy, I would like you to meet Grove."

"Ah yes. The actual hero of the story, I hear you're the Samwise to our Frodo." By the time he'd turned to regard my partner we'd already let go, and so I pivoted to join him side-by-side. His appearance and approach didn't impress Grove too much, that had been obvious, but the fact that he could hear the priest when he spoke to him had struck him mute. Bewilderment flashed over his historically steady eyes, and while it was a testament to his own constitution how quickly he collected himself, you could feel the reverberations of awe coming off of him at the phenomenon.

"Hey…yeah… th-thanks." Not really known as the rabble-rouser type, it was nonetheless funny as hell to watch the Christian military veteran almost stutter into silence at feeling the miracle of being able to hear every utterance from this holy figure's mouth. I reassure him as to how eloquent he's being by winking and flashing an enthusiastic thumbs up.

"You ought to be thankful you ever lucked into such a friend Janzen Robinson." It was a lot frailer than when I'd last heard it, but I immediately recognized that voice. The fact I so quickly remembered it felt peculiar to me, given that I'd only heard it once. I knew her as Grandma. The black veiled woman now standing in the aisle was in fact the elderly woman who was the grandmother of the girl we'd rescued from the evidence depot that fateful night a year and a half ago. The girl was named Cat, and she had come to mind as had I walked up the stairway to the church. I was even more concerned now that I found myself in the presence of her grandmother.

"Penny, this is Grove, partner and friend to our own resident migraine, Janzen Robinson."

Penny, whose name I'd just learned, was now using a cane to help her stand and balance out a laboring stride. When I'd last come across her there was an undeniable spryness to the woman that belied her age and looks, but now it was if it had not only caught up to her, but had fast-tracked her to death's doorstep, robbing her of what I would have guessed would have been another two decades when I met her eighteen months ago. Grove was still a little stunned by the fact that every time Justin spoke it was as if he'd never lost his hearing at all; luckily after spending a few years with me he'd learned to adjust the limitations of what was possible by quite a bit. His reaction seemed emotional for some odd reason.

After quickly recovering, the soldier took her offered hand and escorted her to the seat she motioned to in the nearest pew, signaling him to sit as well. I stayed standing, realizing that the fact that she'd exhausted her energy to see us here indicated that this was an immediate kind of issue. Of course the fact that the priest had phoned me had encapsulated that in and of itself.

"How's Cat?" I asked.

"She's why I had the good father call you of course."

Fuck.

Today was not that kind of day. Even though nothing was set in stone, there was a foreboding to this that gave me a sinking feeling that there was about to be the kind of connection that didn't alleviate anything, but instead made this shit ten times harder. Justin wasn't big on misleading me (despite the episodes of cryptic talk he engaged me with whenever I tried to pry anything out of him), so the fact that there was pretty open concern written on his face worried me—a lot.

"Where is s-"

"I'm dying."

It's a deeply conflicting, and deeply human thing to be disturbed by the way you can juggle a pair of thoughts at the same time and have them be so at odds with one another. One part of me not only wanted to offer comfort, and wanted to sit with her and spend significant time with what I had every right to believe was an incredibly fascinating and well lived woman. The other part of me was engaged full throttle with everything that was going on, and I had to resist the urge to prompt her to tell me where her Granddaughter was for fear of how that would tie a little bow on all of this.

Chewing on each reality, I stiff-upper lipped away any response or rejoinder and nodded for her to go on. Grove was turning a little more in the pew, and after realizing her voice didn't register to him, I quickly signed what she'd said so far to catch him up.

"Cat hasn't been taking it well, and after what she experienced with you and her own natural proclivities, I fear she's not only been toying with powers she shouldn't be…but has somehow managed to make contact with one of them." I felt some of the blood drain from my face. My fast-moving brain was jumping between a wide myriad of possibilities, finding each one more daunting than the next. The fact that Penny was this sickly, and actually looked like death warmed over while talking about this felt like a bad omen.

Fuck.

"That's not all." Justin had a warning heavy in his eyes, so I knew not to push. I suspected his doing as much as he had was a lot more tampering than he felt comfortable with. Penny tapped the grip of her cane anxiously, a nervous tick to help her deal with some of her mounting unease at \ talking about this, and the very obvious concern the woman was feeling for her last living relative. Judging by the name of the hospital on her bracelet I guessed that it was cancer, and I'd be willing to wager that it was the worry over her granddaughter's well-being that was really affecting her.

"What else is it, Penny?" I asked softly, as a feeling of dread circled tightly around in the back of my mind. I was hoping for some kind of answer to the unease, and suspected that this was a connection I was not going to be happy about.

"It's not just the disease that's killing me, Janzen." The last time Penny and I had come across one another she had spoken to me with an unmistakable familiarity; it was something I noticed even now in the way I responded to her use of my name. I felt a subdued but ever-present familiarity about her that was gnawing at the back of my mind, like a piece of deja vu two days removed; or the memory of a memory.

"If somebody in my bloodline is gifted, or has any kind of talent, it's a little different." The act of speaking was laborious and I had another clash of contradicting thoughts and needs war themselves out inside of me, ultimately deciding on an inviting nod to encourage her to continue. "We're stronger than most practitioners. *Much* stronger. I wasn't, I actually only knew of my Power but never got to truly wield it until much later in life...but that's a story -" She drifted off, catching herself as she was about to complete the all too famous line: *for another time.*

Instead we come crashing headlong into the realization that there might not ever be such a time. I commended her ability to face that truth straight on, and with a deeper well of grit than most could claim she thinned her mouth into an almost daredevil smile. "Price of admission, I suppose." With a puff of air she finally shifted from a sickly, fading woman, to somebody with a last purpose that had every intent of carrying it out with high character.

"When Cat used magic it activated the power in her blood, Janzen, and that became hungry. It became demanding. It's been feeding on me for some time, and now she's drawn to the lake. She thinks she can save me I suspect, but ultimately, it's the will of the power in her blood trying to let it loose. This close to the surface it can't help itself." Grove wasn't lost but I could tell that the picture had crystalized to him the way it had me, and now I was taking the backrest of the pew in front of her while dropping my other hand on the armrest of the one she currently resided in, carefully kneeling down so we could be eye-to-eye.

"You need to go get her, Janzen. It's what you do, gather lost souls and lead them to the light. I need you to do that with her, and I need you to do it now. If you don't teach her how to harness this power, it'll consume her. She can't hide from it like I was able to. You have to promise me, Janzen, that you'll get her, and that you'll guide her." I wondered if Penny could hear how faint her voice was growing with every passing utterance. Part of the reason I'd crouched down was to assure her that I was taking this as seriously as she was, and the other part was so that she didn't have to strain herself by speaking too loudly. She relaxed by degrees when I nodded, and even though the woman was a warrior in her own right, I could tell a simple nod wasn't enough.

"Penny? I'm going to go get her, whether she's at the lake or in the mouth of hell itself. You have my word."

I didn't address the other part, and somehow, I could tell she knew why. I couldn't afford to be feeling my way around in the dark anymore. I respected the need to protect secrets, and we all knew a part of this life was having to live with everything from double-speak to riddled-answers but between people there had to be an equalizer.

Trust and community.

To date it was the only deterrent that I'd seen work, and the only advantage I could really count on from this building, a house of God, to what Kaycee and company had built that now served as a community and a farming ground for wayward practitioners. Relieved, the tear-soaked eyes of the grandma had a faint green hue to them.

"I was a Wanderer, Janzen. Not in this life, but...It lives in my blood and has taken root in my granddaughter. That day with you? The one where she first called upon the power in her bloodline? That was the genesis of it."

This wasn't a coincidence; the cosmos didn't deal in coincidence. A Wanderer. Not some kind of mutated, energy enhanced magic-wielder, but a real Wanderer. So soon after Maria, and the fact that it was the second one in this city in as many years, let alone lifetimes, made this unbelievably anomalous. I reiterate – the cosmos didn't deal in coincidence. I didn't know a lot about the Wanderer phenomenon but given how much of my life had been altered because of it I had done some digging. These holes in the In-Between had been having an impact on Cleveland, it only made sense that something like this might be in the cards. Maybe this power was simply calling to their ilk, and with the rift now so pronounced they could hear it more clearly than ever.

She could see the lingering questions in my eyes, but even a mind as voraciously curious as mine knew when to curb questioning; even the necessary kind. There was something knowing in the demure smile she offered in response, elaborating enough to give a little more of the picture. "I was lost in a world, one buried beyond the In-Between and at the center of all these pathways; these portals…"

There was a story there, one I was devastated wouldn't see the light of day. Something wistful flashed over her face, she seemed to be aging in real time now. "And I traded my power for passage home. I've recovered some of it, sure, but…dealing with the In-Between directly comes at a price, as is the nature of these things. So to sojourn home, that was mine."

Even in light of the tragedy playing out, that perked me up a touch, and I turned an inquisitive eye seeking a look at the priest who stood statue-still while watching the conversation. I couldn't help but feel that this was a final request before last rites, but I had to unwaveringly hold to the mission at hand.

God help Cat if she ever learned that it was her own growing power that was robbing the life-force from her grandmother. At least that's what I suspected was happening. Then again, it might be the inevitability of the moment that such a power awoke within her. Justin's blank face held nothing but sympathy for the fast-fading Penny. Whatever dictated his own power was probably incredibly strict on intervention of any kind, so I was sure that even phoning me was a version of fast-and-loose for the Priest.

My attempt to talk was cut off when Penny laid cold fingers over the expanse of my mouth and simply held my stare with righteous steadiness. The moment was objectively short but stretched into a long one for me. In vivid detail I felt my mind commit every detail of the woman to memory; noting that this was what I'd always considered courage to be. It wasn't until I felt a reassuring hand grip my own shoulder that I realized I had begun to cry. Grove didn't need to know the situation to show support, and while it was usually in the form of unwavering proximity, I was glad to feel the actual connection even as I kept my eyes on the black-veiled, dying woman.

"Life is pleasant, death is peaceful, it's just the transition that's so troublesome Janzen. I am off to my next great adventure, old friend." I was crying because I knew when she called me that there was an immutable truth to it, even if I couldn't identify it just yet. The talk invoked a light nodding from me, as she finished up. "Cat will want to turn to this power, to these monsters. You cannot let her Janzen. Not all monsters sleep under the bed, some of them live within us."

There was a listless weakening to the grip and for a moment I legitimately worried that the woman might actually leave this world right in front of our eyes, but just as I was about to count her out the steady grip provided by Grove on one shoulder was mirrored with a second one by her own hand on the other.

"Not all monsters can be fought, some have to be tamed." The grip was given a squeeze, before using the touch to actually aim me back to my feet. I didn't want to leave her, but I knew what I had to do.

"I've got her." Justin said, the reassurance carried by the telltale warmth of the church custodian. When I watched the affection living in those enchanting eyes as the priest looked down at the old woman, I knew it was true. I also felt, as much as witnessed, the sheen of an emerald light. It was of a richer quality, more resonating; like the frequency felt when being around a powerful signal source. Penny melted into our shared embrace, mindful of her weakened state but drinking in as much of the hug as we all could.

"You have to…" Penny weakly started to say, untangling herself a degree to look up at me as she sought to plead for my help anew.

"I got her." I echoed the same sentiment back that the clergyman had used with me a moment earlier, and the woman knew without a shadow of doubt that I'd lay dead, face down in that fucking lake, rather than come back without our girl. The only thing more surprising than the conviction of my statement was her unremitting belief in it. Faith of the utmost took a strength I couldn't yet find—but act as if you have faith and it'll be rewarded unto thee—or something like that.

Whatever the case, I was about to jump into the mouth of Abyss and test the theory. Our shared hands folded over one another, and I bowed my head as she nestled close to give my brow a departing kiss.

"Still a king of dirt, and better for it."

My ascent paused with our fingers still locked, and when I tilted my head as if to preemptively think of a question, she disengaged her grip and almost shooed me off, those star-touched eyes turning to look over the ornate display spread over the raised dais of the church. Grove took a moment to impart some of his own assurance, expectedly doing so with a lot less wordplay than I did. The priest was moving into the pathway that parted the two sides of pews as if parting the red sea itself, walking us out. This was priority enough to have him bending the rules, so I knew it couldn't wait, and with another piece of the fast-assembling puzzle coming together, this very dangerous and dire situation finally got the match-and-wick combination it needed. On the way out of the Church I followed Grove's lead and took a dollop of holy water and made the sign of a cross over my person. We shared a look on the way out, with me signing.

When in Rome.

Grove chortled, keeping that same leveled amusement as we climbed into the old beater and he stroked it to life.

"There ain't no atheists in a foxhole."

The adage was a well-known one and given what I'd just done on a knee-jerk whim before staring down another life-threatening fight seemed to prove the old mantra true. The weather had the first flirtation of a chill, and the clear skies and setting sun cut a pretty picture-esque skyline ablaze over the spread of downtown. The soldier shifted uneasily, trying to debate whether to engage the holy man directly or just leave the riddle-spouting entity to his mysteries and get the car,

"So, are you ... an angel?"

"He's the In-Between, Grove. Or some kind of emissary from it."

My partner looked as if slapped dumbstruck, and even Father Handy perked up a little; not at the statement, but at the fact that I stood on the theory with the type of faith that we'd just witnessed in the old woman about to take on the greatest adventure life had to offer. The intensity of his stare wasn't threatening, it simply was; a hurricane didn't aim to be destructive, they simply were. There was a touch of humor to the double-take my partner sent from me to Justin and back again, then finally settling on the priest.

The roll of clamoring green energy that washed respectively over each of his spellbinding eyes from left to the right would have usually been enough to back me off a little but not tonight. Maybe it was seeing a woman stand in her last moment of life to beg for the well being of a loved one rather than ask for a reprieve, sanctuary or assurances. Could have been growth, too.

Maybe it was that devil-may-care defiance that surged through me from time to time.

"What, so he's like...?" If I was the guppy of the group, Grove had to be the tadpole, and so I felt a little bad that this recent revelation was dropped on him aloud, but to be fair, not a person alive wasn't aware that I lacked a filter. I couldn't imagine trying to outline just what the hell this guy could be but after having personally witnessed the paragon power so casually displayed for what amounted to a whim, it was hard to see it as anything else. Plus, he'd been here since the rift first gave way—ever since Jackie of the cultist group had pulled one of the Cura'Sha, a Stalker, across the In-Between to help subjugate her people and prepare whatever divination spell they'd attempted when sacrificing Maria to get this bitch Abigail over. My guess was that the opening had to be adjusted accordingly for the power it was letting over and that was why we'd had some lesser interlopers and enemies, but this Black-Souled Mistress had yet to cross.

It wasn't for a lack of trying though.

"We got to go buddy." Knowing that while Justin could overcome the injury-earned handicap of my friend with his voice and that I couldn't, I actually turned to impose myself between the soldier and the priest. This time it was my hand on his shoulder, offering some stability and confidence while our mortal minds processed all the impossibility we had coming down the pipe. The detached nod was suspended when his eyes went wide in shock as I started to walk down the stairs. I already knew that the priest was gone, vanished before offering anything resembling a satisfactory explanation to all that was happening outside what we already knew.

"Yeah, he does that."

CHAPTER 16

Battle Lines

The fundamental element of all this was the connections, and it was much bigger than just me and my part of the story. On some level I always knew that, but with this new information I began to get a picture of its vast reach. The thousand year old connection between Gale and Abigail, the revelation that Cat and her Grandmother were Wanderers, Justin being a part of the In-between, Verrak, Johnny B. Zacharia, Helena…all the other elements…they were all connected, and once again, this thing was going to play out at the Lake, where it all began for me and this makeshift community forged by caring and duty.

My hourly text came in from Kaycee, but not Helena. Still I texted each of them respectively that I'd planned to make a trip up to the Lake and that there was nothing of consequence to report from the visit. I called Kaycee and told her to gear up and get ready to adopt a defensive posture for the community we'd become protectors of. I debated on whether or not I would fill Helena and Julian in, but decided not to when she texted back instead of answering the phone. The Iandor agency people looked to be going into terse mode, and I wouldn't be surprised if the politics in all of this was starting to become an influence. Plus, all of this was still developing, and I didn't want to tip any hand, so I trusted if anything was happening, they would reach out.

"How long?" Groves' gaze held mine until I answered, watching my mouth for the answer even as I hooked my phone up to the still working screen and punched in the GPS. I think it was some kind of Honda maybe? Funny how nowadays even a car that was a decade old had all this technology in it.

"An hour and change."

I pulled out the wooden-collar I'd been obsessing about, turning it over in my hand thoughtfully before sending out a second text, after all, what's the point of having friends if you weren't going to go to them when your back was against the wall. I deliberated on the craftsmanship of the sigils once more, settling on what I saw just as Grove merged into traffic. The scattering of cars was a lot less aggressive and thinned out now that we were on the back end of rush hour. The ringing phone broke the silence, as we worked our way toward Lake Erie, the epicenter of this since the beginning.

"Hey man," the person on the other end of the line grunted "what" in response, and I said "I need your help."

After we talked about the details of the favor I needed, I swatted Grove until he coughed up a debit card with a look that danced between annoyed and curious. We put a huge order of food in for the local homeless shelter, before hanging up and traveling in silence toward the great frontier that had been at the heart of everything that was happening.

Rolling a gold, military coin across my knuckles, I couldn't help but think of the first time I'd been here. Kaycee was worried sick, I was beaten half to death, and up until that point we'd fucked up every attempt we'd made to help: Maria had been abducted, every skirmish we fell into we ended up on the losing end of, and there was still nothing close to the resemblance of a plan.

And just like then, the rumble of the car steadily put me to sleep, only this time it was tormented and uninspired.

***

I woke up about a half hour out, and war-gamed the outline of a plan to Grove. Some people might think that was a little capricious, and funny enough, in times past my lack of planning was more a source of laziness than foresight, but over time I'd come to learn that a plan tended to be a list of shit that just didn't happen. What we had was an objective—find Cat. Whatever else may come would just have to be dealt with; it was hard to craft a contingency in response to the unknown. See, the disjointed nature of all that was happening gave even more credence to my planning theory.

Be ready for anything and everything.

We pulled over in a small tree-circled clearing at the bend in the road before pulling into the lakeside pub parking lot. With the precision and diligence of a professional pipe-hitter (a military term for someone who will go to any length to get something done), Grove checked the custom pistol on his hip as well as his lever-action gun-ax, before steadily resituating the dozen or so quick-load magazines for the rifle he'd secured in a well-worn bandolier. I was surprised to see a rather sleek, well-designed sawed-off shotgun join the party – strapped to the low of his back in an almost identical fashion to my wooden bat-dagger.

"We got a plan?" There was a deadly seriousness as we locked eyes, and to our credit, both of us kept a straight face for about ten seconds before bursting into rancorous laughter. After instructing him to put the hazard lights on and drive a little deeper into the woods, we set off, finding our way to the quaint spot on the lake that we'd sent the two Iandor agents earlier.

The valley of death was dark, make no mistake, and it would be a bold-face lie to say that I wasn't afraid of what lived in the most damning reaches of that recess, but I knew I could face it with clarity and character because of those who walked beside me. It was fully into evening now, the night taking liberty to obscure most of the lake, being heavily aided by thickets of clouds that kept the starlight from helping us navigate a water-cast fog that began to swim out over the surrounding area.

The restaurant was empty, the lights had been killed, and as I checked my phone, I saw that only Kaycee had kept up the agreed upon timeline of hourly texts.

I signed *see you* to Grove, though I used a **C** and **U** instead of longhand much to his chagrin. It was impressive how quiet the former recon expert could be despite the hearing loss, but I suspected traversing the wilderness in stealth was pretty much second nature to him at this point. Not twenty strides in and I couldn't make out any of his silhouette, a marriage of the snipers' skill and the obscuring fog germinating from the lake and billowing over us.

Even with the aid of fog and low lighting I doubt they hadn't got a sense of me when I first stepped onto the front porch and started a heavy-footed trek toward the entrance. How the place was like a ghost town was a question that I didn't have the stomach to entertain just now, and I was a little worried about the fact that there wasn't any civilian presence here, but I had hoped that for once that would work in our favor. Barren but cozy, the place sported a sizable lakeshore area for seating, and a far-reaching dock that usually had four or five fishing boats buoyed to it. It had a very country style eatery vibe, and the fact that it was on the water just added to the appeal and tranquility; or rather it had. Now it was contaminated with this bad, deadland energy, the same kind that had pestered my city for far too long.

Surprise flashed across Julian's face when I walked in the front door. He was big and pretty, with an innate elitism. The kind of person you cast to play a comic book hero, or some well-known Godling from long ago. Grove was big, but Julian towered over him. If what I'd heard about the enforcer division of the Iandor institute was accurate, he probably had much stronger gear than I did. The Inside had been cleared out, and the usual set-up broken down; tables, chairs and all the other assembled furniture had been pushed to the far corners so that there was a clearing in the center of the room for us to occupy. Julian immediately faced me, proudly holding some kind of chain in a bloodied hand; a hand that now sported a sigil carving not unlike the one we saw on the Bru-Maga. And at the end of the chain, was a branched collar encircling the throat of a kneeling Helena whose mouth was gagged, hands bound behind her back, being forced into this subjugated position at the foot of her own megalomaniac apprentice. A healthy dose of blood caked her face, other than that she seemed to be in relatively good condition. Speculation led me to believe she'd probably turned her back at some point and was rewarded with a nasty blow to the back of the brain-bucket as a reward for her trust. The sigil I'd mentioned was at the front of her collar, an identical mark to the one that Thomas' own had sported.

Julian scowled and sneered at me, and while I usually celebrated how quickly I could get under the skin of people, I was genuinely surprised to see the raw hatred this guy had for me. Helena paid the price for that misplaced wrath, almost falling face-first to the ground when the threatening Artificer strode forward. Helena's furious eyes locked on him and were filled with accusation. I waited at the entrance, which was a small square area where guests could mull while a hostess got them sorted. I could tell that the betrayer didn't mind my unexpected arrival and seemed kind of happy about the opportunity to finally deal with me. He did seem to be confused about how I knew to show up here, but before the aristocrat of assholes could have the satisfaction of asking, I jumped in and answered the unasked question.

"I told her to text every hour." It was off-handed, as if that was a perfectly suitable place to start the dialogue.

"We did." Eyes narrowing into a crazed glare, Julian straightened up and stopped on the way to bum-rushing me; which wouldn't have been the worst plan considering his physical prowess, ability and the numbers. Still, the stall wasn't surprising—at least not to me. People hated fighting, even when they were good at it, and though not directly aware of it, most would seek any kind of out. Not to mention the fact that me knowingly walking into a trap was as crazy as it was jarring.

"Once." The half-shrug didn't abandon my point but also laid out a crucial difference. *Once.* I'd said every hour. Helena was a precise person, and probably understood just how important clear communication was. "She would have done it every hour on the hour." I'd learned something in prison that I carried with me now: aggression invites aggression. Posture and disposition are important in a fight, and paradoxical as it might have seemed, I wrapped myself in calm remembering how often I'd been tested before in my life.

I noticed the ghouls when the one closest to my left side shifted. The movement was subtle, and my answer to it was as weird as it was bold; I pointed at them with a pen-heavy hand, pressing the button on top of the thing while doing so; the audible click didn't do anything after pressing it a second time and I was confident that my warning paused any inclination on their part to immediately attack. I set it down beside me.

"So you drove almost two hours without calling...on a hunch?" This guy just oozed ego, the kind of abrasive arrogance that made you want to bathe. It was so condescending that even the way it was fashioned felt like an insult; maybe it was something about his face. Objectively attractive, but you immediately knew this was one ugly son-of-a-bitch underneath the facade. Of course I didn't miss the skepticism, and the insinuation that I wasn't being completely forthright that was written all over the guy's face. Leave it to a traitor to want transparency and expect opacity.

"Yup."

I clicked the pen toward a second ghoul, if only to antagonize them: like a nervous tick, I was showing off my jail-earned talent for spinning things across my fingers to give my nervous energy an outlet.

"Well, you're kind of an asshole Julian, and I never really trusted you." I said this with a shrug, and even the dejected and bloodied Helena laughed out loud. I knew she liked me and thought she may have even held a modicum or two of respect for me: I was unorthodox, but you couldn't argue with my sheer effectiveness. When people asked me what I was doing, I always answered with *my best*. Julian was much more capable than me, and the only thing keeping him at heel was the fact that even in his rampant distaste for me, the former Iandor agent wasn't stupid. He knew my reputation, and despite his inclination, couldn't possibly believe that I was absolutely without skills.

When I saw that nostril flare paired with a jaw-flexing clench I knew that my routine was wearing thin. I could feel the swell of energy coming off of him and knew that sooner rather than later he would make a move. There would be an exertion before he extended intent and power into the assembly of undead ghouls that were incrementally creeping around me trying to cage me in, and I was waiting for it.

Seizing the pen, I twirl it back to have the spire end point at the kneeling hostage and flip another switch to engage the actual laser pointer. The red-dot indicated the soul-pillaging insignia carved on the front of Helena's collar. "The sigil on the collar… it's amazing calligraphy really, and it's complex and powerful, yet crude. Obviously, it was an expert taking a stab at something they didn't fully understand."

A half-growl from Julian was nearly a breaking point for him, but I had hooked his interest enough that curiosity won out over ego, and the fighter peered down at the point that I designated. "It's why Thomas died. You're basically using a portal conduit sigil to try and siphon; the main symbol is a pulling one, and the base is a conduit to the other side, the In-Between, *whatever*, but they aren't put together right." I could tell Julian understood in broad strokes what I was saying but couldn't quite make sense of it. Funny enough, Helena was perfectly capable of hearing, and I watched her own mind try to line up everything I was saying to arrive at the same conclusion I'd come to earlier than everyone else.

"So because I was so good at Artificery you knew I had done this?"

"That's what you'd hear of course…" I groan, muttering a little while shaking my head. "…and yes, kinda. You're good at the basic shit, but you can't think on your own. Probably why your bitch ass was easy to turn."

Now *that* got him.

"Plus, you bozo, your knight's armor gauntlet?" I use the pen, this time with no light, to point out the iron-plated glove hanging off his left hip. "They're almost the same symbol. Honestly, I'm embarrassed I only figured it out a little while ago. Well At least my asshole radar is still spot on."

"I'm going to enjoy killing you." Julian literally blooded himself when tightening the sigil-carved hand around the collar, drawing an inhale of energy from Helena and exhausting the woman in the process.

"I'm going to enjoy turning you over to Helena." The draw of power enabled a more cogent command of the four dead-eyed foot soldiers surrounding me, and just as the two on the left collapsed my flank to attack, I actually dropped into a low crouch and tossed the incessantly clicked pen to the same side that was collapsing on top of me.

The last *click* turned a conventional light on in the pen. The pen was a surefire pen, an overpriced tactical thing, but with some modifications it was an incredibly useful tool. The tip had a reinforced metal casing that gave it the ability to break a window, or if need be, punch through skin. The laser pointer was helpful for my unconventional sigil lesson that informed Julian how I'd put the pieces together while we mouthed off at one another as men want to do.

The last interesting capability of the multi-tool was the ability to engage an infrared laser. Invisible to the naked eye, it was as bright as sunlight to someone using any kind of night vision assistance; whether it be through a camera mechanism, goggles, or a customized scope.

By the time our little banter had ended, I was able to light up two of the ghouls with the infrared and mark Helena with the pointer. That was as close to a *go* as Grove would ever need. When the second ghoul dropped, we'd only just heard the second of three shots.

One to break the window.

One to drop the first ghoul I'd painted with the IR light.

And a last one to split the skull of the second ghoul.

I caught the other two stationary ghouls completely unaware, knowing that they would be in a half-comatose state because Julian had tasked the other two with killing me. Even the powerful Bru-Maga was limited in what she could do with her minions, and Julian probably had considerably less ability and bandwidth than the centuries old vampire. That meant that if he was piloting two of them to attack me, there was a good chance the other two would simply be emptied out vehicles stuck in a stranglehold while waiting for commands.

The enemy Artificer dropped low to easily scoop Helena up, shamelessly using her as a shield while hustling a room deeper into the building. I was able to dispatch the third ghoul, its lifeless eyes having an almost lackluster quality about them as it obediently waited for its execution. I didn't have time to wait for Grove, and after I dropped the fourth ghoul with a well-aimed aluminum bat swing, I whirled around in time to see Julian half-carry half-drag Helena into the small lounge beside the bar.

I didn't have time to wait for Grove and gave chase, finding myself on familiar footing as I burst through the lounge. Up until this point even I had to admit how good it was to at least find myself able to capably challenge everything we'd come across, but when I poured into the backroom, I was immediately reminded of what it was like to once again be in over my head.

Julian hit like a bull and moved with the speed of a serpent. I'd come barreling into the room, bat high, and whatever confidence our momentum had won me got violently ripped out of me with the force of that first hit. I barely got my shield up and activated in time to catch a mace from crushing my skull, and it was immediately clear to me that this Artificer, built like a brick house with the striking reach to match, was not only a practitioner but a legit combatant.

I was able to roll with the hit, purposely forfeiting my stance to tumble away and back up onto a knee and a foot; he just kept coming. I'd swung my bat to punish this over eagerness, even exaggerating the motion to create what I thought was the illusion of an opening I could capitalize on with a counter-strike.

Julian was so damn fast that it turned into a real window, already haunting my space and managing to easily intercept the bat-swing with his own metal gauntlet. The seized bat stuck and stayed, as if the steel palm had gorilla glue on it. I watched as the conduit base of the sigils on the bottom of it came to life and pillaged all the latent energy housed in the weapon and transferred it to himself. As a point of emphasis, the man literally crumpled the weapon before wrenching it out of my grip.

I'd have been dead truthfully, and for a second I hated myself for falling victim to ego and allowing my own confidence to make me this reckless. Luckily, before the pity-party could turn into a proper send-off, Grove let loose another shot from somewhere off in the nothingness that struck the raised mace on the helm, tearing it out of his Julian's naked palm.

Still on bended knee, I wrapped a hand around the cowl of the shield and shoved it down with all my might on the leading foot of the Artificer, still neatly planted in front of me. I didn't get to relish the agonized howl because to his credit, he'd managed to respond with not only a shout but a raised knee that brutally caught me just on the cheek and was driven up with the kind of forceful conviction that might have knocked me clean out had I not such extensive experience with being hit in the head.

I felt my body lift, and heard it come back down for the hit.

Blinking the daze out wasn't working, and as my tinnitus started to ring clear as a bell in the struck ear, I silently lamented being unable to avoid another concussion for at least my first week back to work. Julian was mindful of the doorway that looked into the second room with the dead ghoul, probably concerned about the perched soldier waiting to body-drop him just as he'd done with half the help.

Unfortunately, Julian was more than just a domineering fighter and the metal glove that had stolen the kinetic energy from my bat was suddenly coming to life. That series of symbols on the bottom of his glove spun on a separate swivel, pausing to align and create an illuminating sigil on the bracer as Julian lifted a spreading hand and aimed it directly at me. The fount of fire hit my buckler, and there was something particularly nasty about the all-consuming element as it just enfeebled the warded leather and devitalized my own wards in the process. In fact, for the first time ever I felt what had probably become my most trusted and relied upon tool failing me as that searing heat passed the magically imbued protection and began to eat at my flesh.

There was a physical impact to the geyser too, and when the onslaught finally relented, I furiously clawed at the band to extricate my burned forearm, leaving me exposed for all intents and purposes. There was a growing madness in the artificer across from me, and it was almost startling to see how rabid he'd become. There was also an awareness at just how menacing somebody this large could be when they simply put their mind to the task. There was a remnant of green glowing in his hungry, cruel eyes, and I wasn't sure if I could ever recall somebody able to meet me at every level with such ease. Helena had skittered off to a corner, and to her credit, the steely gazed woman was trying to get out of the arresting binds so that she could start to work on the gag and collar, and hopefully offer any kind of help against this juggernaut.

That effort was abated almost instantly, and I watched the silver-haired woman suddenly swoon a little before her rolling eyes signaled an unceremonious collapse.

Julian was drawing her life force through the bloody palm, using it to recharge the metal gauntlet, mindfully cutting off the only path open to Helena. This time there wasn't any rotation on the bottom band of the gauntlet, so when Julian leveled it at me, I did what everyone would expect a smaller, weaker combatant to do against a weapon that had already humbled them.

I charged.

I met the fire head on, leading with my hand instead of my head as was notoriously my propensity, and catching the flames in the palm of Zachariah's well-switched glove that I'd cleverly slipped on beneath the concealment of my losing efforts. Containing energy was a labor, and containing destructive energy was especially exhausting; containing a fire spell supercharged by leeched lifeforce almost buckled me. I'd barely managed to even find my footing before wave after wave of convulsing spasms started to wreck me, my twitching grip threatening to collapse and negate the defensive posture—and this was only the beginning.

I hadn't realized how close the Iandor trained warrior was until I caught a glimpse of him towering over my spread fingers and by then it was too late, the bloody-naked hand already had gotten a clean grasp on my shoulder and throat, and with a terrifying, inhuman strength the much taller warrior had picked me up and violently shook me.

The blood was like a foul-smelling lacquer, a touch of green tinted madman eyes, and the metal gauntlet was curled into a fist as the bottom swivel rotated to give another elemental, or equally destructive sigil a chance. Luckily, I was still conscious enough to see my death.

See.

Julian cried out in surprise and anguish as a face-full of salt was smashed directly into his eyes, even collapsing my gloved hand on the one fused to my own shoulder and neck so that there was no chance for him to immediately disengage.

The hand on my throat and shoulder was the one with the sigil that was literally sucking the life out of Helena. That same hand was trapped in a clumsy hold by my own gloved one, and suddenly I had an idea that I knew would both hurt like hell and was conveniently too small of a window for me to take any time to think about. My will surged into the Zachariah fashioned accessory. A concentrated blast of fire burned me so badly that I didn't even realize I was screaming. Then it palpitated a second and third time at my command, and fighting with gritted teeth and hound dog determination, I burned not only all the skin off his hand, but damn near welded it to my own neck and chest, permanently scarring me in the process no doubt.

And eviscerating the soul-stealing sigil in the process.

Blind, enraged, and now branded, the Artificer finally got enough wits about him to lift an arm and prepare to drop it down on my head in an undoubtedly pulverizing, and repeated fashion when I heard the kind of impact you'd expect out of a car crash.

Grove had speared the big one and finally broke us off one another, unfortunately entangling them in the process. The next thirty or so seconds were a bit blurry. By the time I came to, it was to hear Helena shouting my name over and over again; evidently, at some point, she'd been able to wrestle the gag from her mouth. I knew I was alive because of the ear-ringing, as well as the fact that this now blotchy patchwork of skin with a little bit of shirt was screaming at me with such a piercing, reverberating thrum that it was actually helping me come back to reality with a little more clarity.

Somehow Grove had ended up with the mace, and to his credit the man was doing better than I was against Julian, but even watching the two of them fight I couldn't help but notice the difference in pedigree, training, and know-how. We had the toughness, and because of our exploits I'd wager that the pair of us were more experienced with this kind of thing, but being out-classed was out-classed and as Grove furiously weaved, ducked and dodged it was obvious that there was no ground being won, and what remained was fast being lost.

Distantly, I heard my phone chime, and in what would be my most millennial moment ever I actually checked the thing – before chucking it at the head of the Artificer who was now in a thoroughly crazed state and completely intoxicated by this corrupting influence we'd seen start to spread over our city. Drawing from those places of love and desperation, I burst toward Helena and baseball slid down to her level after crossing the threshold. With a smooth unsheathing I got the bat-dagger out and her binds off, before whipping around to the fight, and before I could even get it out of my mouth, the Master Artificer was already commenting.

"He took everything."

"Could have sworn I heard sor- *Fuck*!" She'd almost palm-struck my burn wound which was a testament to how fast-acting, battle-tested and unwavering she was.

The fact that I felt a cooling balm, a small thrum of revitalization, followed by a warming, reverberating presence throughout my body clued me into why having Helena here was such a big boon to our efforts and maybe our immediate needs.

She was a healer.

There was a particularly nasty impact, and we both turned to see the soldier being hit with a nasty right cross after barely avoiding the caustic edge of his rifle-ax a moment prior. Julian was a towering, imposing mass of blood, burned flesh, disheveled clothing and ill intent. The only reason he didn't immediately close in on us was to not only gather himself, but I suspected there was a moment of savoring taking place.

At that moment, the island at the center of the lake turned into a beacon of green, the fog giving way to whatever was transpiring there and clueing us into the fact that we were fast losing time.

Grove was getting up with an elbow and knee under him when we locked eyes. He'd probably sprinted the whole way across the field, and as I scanned his person, I knew he'd abandoned most of his equipment in a trade-off for speed. The soldiers' grimace was telling, and as Helena tried to help pull us to our feet, we could see that the still-standing Julian was happy to bide what little precious time we had left, in the name of keeping us busy.

This was the kind of kid who liked to pull wings off flies for no reason. I just knew it. People named Julian were either great dancers, beautiful artists, or just outright assholes.

"There's more of them," Helena looked sick. We both looked at her before managing to stand up. We knew the only reason the traitorous apprentice was allowing all of this to happen was because it was such a condemnation of Iandor. "They're probably on their way here. This was their plan, to trap you here and then just overwhelm the place in a swarm." I could see the prideful woman almost wilt, managing to still a quivering lip while hating herself for having to admit the next part.

"I was bait. They knew you'd come if..."

I hoped my hand on her shoulder helped the steadiness I saw in her after taking a moment to digest our plight. This one-man wrecking crew was bad enough, but if a whole host of baddies planned on descending on this place to keep us out of the water… holy shit.

Grove straightened up, wearing a look I knew all too well, a look I tried to reason with when I reached out.

There was a shark-like void in the expression of our assaulter, and the murderous glee hinted beneath that nothingness was impossible to miss. Suddenly, we looked like those flies.

Truthfully, I'd all but spent my inventory of weapons and strength, and even with the soothing of her magic I was still a mangled mess. This wasn't some cure-all elixir, it blunted the worst of it, but the human body could only take so much, and there were some kinds of hits you just couldn't shake off in an instant. Helena was fuming but stripped of her most impactful equipment, which limited her to the healing magic that was innate. Grove was fit, and ready, but as I turned an assessing look back at our enemy I caught the hint of a strength sigil on a torn sleeve, leading me to believe that there were quite a few enhancements probably codified on his person as well as his gear; the guy had hacked himself into a super soldier. Alpha and Daphne had been subject to a similar practice, and while it was extremely effective at enabling you to do incredible physical feats, it also eroded your vessel in irredeemable ways that would have a major detrimental impact on you a few decades down the road.

Julian probably got the promise of being able to utilize such enhancements without repercussion, consequence, or some other such fable. Might not have cost him his body, but it certainly wasn't worth selling his soul.

Helena, with the binding sigil burnt off Julian's hand, was able to pick each of the pernicious thorn tips out of her neck while unclasping the branch-collar in the process. Grove and I formed a half-wall in front of her, but we knew this delay was more a taunting tactic than anything meaningful. Her suspicion was confirmed when I heard the first grueling cries of the approaching beast in the waiting woodline, no doubt placed for the ambush Helena was reading us in on. Whether she saw them readying or overheard I did not know, but she was confident in the intelligence.

"Tell you what," Julian crowed, shaking himself a little looser, tossing the gun he'd managed to get from Grove during their tussle and trading it off with the mace he'd started with. "How about I let you pick which one of you goes first?"

"Grove, *no*." I snatched at him a second time as the bravest man I'd ever met prepared to march right down into the valley of death and fight this nightmare to his last breath if need be. Not one of us didn't know that this was a losing battle, but if this rift somehow was ripped all the way open, the larger scale implications were so catastrophic that I doubt any of us would hesitate sacrificing our own life if we needed to. The rage bleeding out of my best friend was palpable at my interference, but I could tell something in my eyes gave the warrior who was ready to die for the cause the kind of pause a physical restraining couldn't.

"Yeah Grove," The lazily spoken interruption seemingly came from nowhere. Julian whirled in response to the unexpected answer that came from someone else just behind him, and what was waiting for him was a ham-hock sized fist that hit with the same intensity the Artificer had displayed against us over and again. "- *don't*."

I wouldn't be stretching the truth if I said that seeing Julian sprawled on the wooden floor spitting out a tooth as he tried to recover, was thrilling. I'd be an outright liar if the flash of worry that contaminated his normally pompous face didn't make my whole fucking week. In the space between him and the guy who'd just sucker punched him lay the bloody dislodged tooth, and a couple of empty sunflower seeds.

Not that I was throwing stones mind you, I always said that if you found yourself in a fair fight it meant you were a shit planner... me, or Sun Tzu...hmmm?

Julian's stunned expression shifted to something darker as he turned to see who it was that had just mollywhopped him. The blow had ripped the illusion of superiority from him, and the man who'd done it was slowly shrugging out of his faded gray zip-up jacket. Most people would think this would be the perfect window of opportunity to attack, but Julian with a cracked jaw had a suspicion that there was more to the seemingly unassuming man interjecting himself into our all-out war. He didn't trust himself after the right hook he'd just eaten.

"I'll be your huckleberry...." The Tombstone reference was perfectly articulated despite having to do so around a mouthful of seeds.

Undaunted, and peerless, the brawny red-head looked every bit the thrift-shopper you'd expect anyone of his ilk to be. Guy J. Smith was the alias of the man who served as a de facto unofficial champion of the homeless here in the Land of Cleve. Dutifully patrolling the hovels and lesser-known haunts of our shared city, going from alley to alley handing out hot meals and clean blankets to anyone in need of them. It wasn't a stretch to call the surly natured vagabond a saint of the streets.

But that was only half the story.

His real name was Patrick Marinazzo, master of the Last Gate (still hadn't the faintest clue what that meant but it sounded badass), and affectionately known as the Concrete Monk in more initiated circles. I'd seen him take down battle-mages, maul monsters of the Abyss and get the better of a Blind Judge for a healthy stretch of time all with my own eyes. I'd inherited his acquaintance with the passing of my mentor, and I won his respect and loyalty after our first sojourn into battle together.

Somewhere along the way we'd become friends, too.

"Get to the lake." Patrick managed to perfectly articulate the directive while simultaneously spitting out a few more seed shells. When a growling Julian erupted back to his feet and lunged after the three of us, with inhuman speed the Concrete Monk was there to meet him, closing the gap with his own incredible physicality, and shoulder-checking the larger Artificer so bad it sent him sailing off his feet to careen brutally into the far wall, denting the structure in the process.

"She's right too, the lake is full of creepy-crawlies. Nothing we haven't seen before." Despite dividing his attention to fill us in on conditions outside, the martial artist kept up a beat down on the enemy Artificer while orbiting the room to serve as a physical impediment between our group and him.

Julian was suddenly small again despite his size, and as the brute shook debris out of his hair from the fall, I saw a look I was all too familiar with. Bullies fought the way they did because of their aversion to fear. To them it was like swallowing serrated steel, and they often sought power by any means to ward off that fear.

Grove was a far sight better at swallowing pride, but it was good to see the shared respect between him and the Concrete Monk as the soldier swiftly darted behind the burly brawler, retrieved his gun-ax, and on the pass back managed a swift but sturdy clasp of Patricks' shoulder in nonverbal acknowledgement. Julian made another attempt at us, but found his limbs trapped in a flash of bone-bruising blocks and meat grinding counter-punches.

I had to half drag Helena out. I knew that the hurt of her apprentice's betrayal weighed heavy on her heart, and would certainly warrant some retribution, after processing the initial shock. Right now, I needed her to shove that shit down deep and help us see the rest of this through. Inside, the fight of the century continued, Patrick going toe-to-toe with Julian and making headway, didn't mean that Julian wasn't going to make him earn it. Hyenas, coyotes, and even carrion birds fight when their backs are to the wall, and they still have teeth and talons enough to kill. It was hard to ignore the way the two of them collided, but as I worked the rest of the binds off of Helena, I hastily scanned my surroundings. The den they had turned into their championship ring was just beside the general dining room, and once Helena got free, she darted behind the bar where her former apprentice had stowed some of her gear. Quickly retrieving a silver walking stick and that silver watch I'd seen her check on during our first meeting, I heard her spit a curse at seeing that was all she'd been able to track down before hurrying back to join us in the main area.

"Janzen..." The soldiers' ominous whisper carried annoying well.

"I know."

Grove's familiarity with the custom rifle-axe was on full display as the soldier swiftly flipped it right-side up and began to rapidly feed the death-machine some of the specialty silver rounds from the bandolier. Despite the confidence, and nerves of steel, I could hear a slight tremor in his voice.

".. Janzen."

"I know!"

Grove spun toward the side of the bar he'd shot out of earlier, sending a round before quickly pumping the lever-action with practiced fluidity. Helena yelped as I grabbed her head in my arms while dropping us to the deck, clearing the way for the soldier to swing the barrel toward where we stood and send a pair of rounds toward the double door entrance. Each round hit something, and whatever purchase it found outside the door caused the creature on the other side to painfully groan before a heavy thud followed.

"I think they're trying to keep you from an island." Helena was prying herself out of my grip while filling me in, unsure of the information, but confident in its importance. For a second, I was actually startled still as the swift and sure handed woman managed to snag the bag of marbles off my hip and simultaneously slide the fire-glove I'd workshopped from Zachariah's design off my hand.

"They wanted you here, Janzen." Distantly, the idea that somebody wanted to distract me from an event out of fear of my ability to sabotage it was quite satisfying.

Climbing to her feet, I saw there was suddenly something so fierce in her that I was mesmerized. She stretched the glove over her considerably smaller hand, and with a whisper of power the fabric tightened. The portrait of her bloodied face fixed beside the finger-spread hand in the black stitched glove cut quite the image, and when the next two ghouls clamored up the stairs and started banging on the entryway, they got to taste every bit of her fury. This time, despite knowing it was kind of my brand, I decided to keep my mouth shut.

I was about to see a professional at work.

With a summoning word the Master Artificer finally got to show why it was they called her that, and when the unleashed fount of fire came out there was such an amazing, almost divine control of it I wanted to weep. The still captured energy from my back and forth with Julian served as the fuel, but the way she shaped and compelled it, turned the raw power into something so much more lethal. The channeled fire blew the double doorway wide open before it washed over the one ghoul and then the second, suddenly turning itself into a wild inferno and reducing them to a pile of bones and goop.

Whatever instruction I was about to offer for how to use the glove was immediately stifled; the display of her own talent was enough to show me why the level of schooling and precision of an Iandor institute student had value. With an almost wave-like wrist flick it looked as if she simply *let* the fire go. My still open mouth probably had me looking like a perfect moron, luckily it shut when the Iandor Agent turned her attention to me.

With one last sector scan Grove bumped me, and together we followed Helena as she strode out to the front of the lakeside restaurant and surveyed the scene outside. On the left I could see about half a dozen ghouls; two or three were moving with the kind of fluidity and deftness that led me to believe they were vampires. On the left, my heart sank when I saw a dark clouded apparition emerge from just inside the tree line. Dread rose up within me.

A Stalker. I'd hit one with a Hummer, cut it to ribbons, and dropped a house on it and still only just managed to get away. The Cura'Sha were the most powerful of all the proverbial chess pieces wielded by Abigail, the Mistress. Of course, not to be outdone, in the middle of this nightmare come to life was the Bru-Maga we'd tangled with earlier. The emblem ablaze on her chest tying the myriad of foot soldiers to her in enslaved obedience was hard to miss even at this distance, and just as the three of us seemed to understand just how unbelievably bad this was getting, out of the corner of my eye, I caught a particularly nasty Mace combination eaten by the Concrete Mask in his still raging battle with Julian.

Helena, to her credit, looked ready to go down with the ship, and Grove only scanned to take inventory of just how badly outgunned we were. Both of them had the character, constitution, and conviction to stand firm even in the face of certain death, and fight for what was right. I was proud to know them.

The Bru-Maga looked downright gleeful as she cackled some kind of threat, painfully unaware that given she was about fifty or so feet away none of us could quite make out what she was saying. It rose a little above some kind of disjointed background noise the closer she got, but that wasn't what caught my allies' interest as they readied themselves for a Spartan-like last stand.

"I get smiling in the face of death Janzen," I appreciated that Helena was smirking, though maybe with a little melancholia and bittersweet acceptance, "...but this feels a little heavy handed, even for an American."

My smirk spilled into a grin, my expression was not a mask of panic but rather steadiness born of preparation and confidence. That set-up was perfect.

"Nah... *that's* not heavy handed...."

Sometimes, just sometimes, everything comes together perfectly. Not because of happenstance or some never-to-be-relied on luck, but because these failures, these hardships, these great challenges all build toward something greater than self. Sometimes, if you weather the storm long enough ...

You become it.

"*This* is heavy handed."

And just then, faintly in the background, a low-pitched but unmistakable guitar-riff filled this fast-forming battlefield with a soundtrack of defiance, courtesy of some face-melting eighties death metal as a brand-new pick-up came screaming around the bend in the road and hauling ass straight toward us.

***

"Hey man," The person on the other end of the line more grunted than responded. "I need your help."

Grove and I had just gotten out of the church and learning that Cat had fallen victim to some kind of other-worldly manipulation was the last component I needed to know why all of this had finally come to life. Our enemies were weak after the last go 'round. I knew it, and with waning influence it was better for them to simply lay low. Lay low and consolidate their resources, lay low so that they could formulate a new plan. The moment they found someone like Cat, they struck, trying to take us out. They had to know we'd respond to something happening at the Lake; that we'd have eyes on it. Plus with her grandma, and their relationship to the Church, they had to know they needed a coordinated effort to accomplish what was ultimately their goal.

Tearing open the rift and freeing Abigail.

As we started toward the Lake, I knew without a doubt that this was a thing we not only had to get ahead of, but that we had to take some quantum leaps to surmount because of just how far behind the curve we'd fallen.

"Water is wet, we'll always hate the Steelers, and I'm pretty sure the fact that nobody even reacted when we admitted aliens were real is proof enough that people are checked out."

"Huh?"

"Tell me something I don't know." The joke went over my head, but as a guy with the acumen of a drunk third grader throwing a dodgeball two sizes too large, I let it go.

The Concrete Monk was a confidante and even managed to be one of my more regular visitors during my stint in jail. The depth of our experience together was so fast-paced I almost felt like we'd gotten to the heavier part of bonding without taking care of the everyday stuff. Luckily, we had next to nothing in common, and when not being hounded by the threat of death at every corner we found our only best form of communication was constant sarcasm.

Patrick rose gingerly off the park bench he'd been napping on, clapping that strong-jowled mouth of his as if trying to get the taste of sleep out of it. After another grunt for me to continue (I spoke fluent grumpy Monk), I read him into what had happened since I'd gotten out and what exactly went down in the attack. That stretch of silence was an indicator of contemplation.

"Any theories?"

"Nope, and now I've got an emergency out at the lake, and there's no way they aren't connected. I feel like just because I didn't catch this thing in the beginning doesn't mean it isn't there."

This time it was my volley that passed over his head.

"Huh?"

"Sorry," The strangest thing in the world was to try to explain to people that at times my thoughts came to me in shapes. I still couldn't explain it, though I did recall it was precisely that fact which pushed Zachariah over the line to take me on for training as an unofficial apprentice. "I feel like the last time, we caught on to this thing and put the pieces together faster, so it was much easier to track. This time it's like we're one block over, and only catching glimpses of it between buildings."

"You're really hard to follow sometimes, Janzen."

"What I mean is -"

"Hard, not impossible. I get it. You think all of this seems random because we haven't connected the dots." I heard him get up, another grunt directed at someone nearby, asking them if they had a vehicle or knew anybody living in the neighborhood who had one that ran.

"Yeah, we've had a very unexpected piece that just popped up." A Wanderer was not only something to keep secret, I wasn't sure if the background he'd been built by even had an understanding of them. Right now I needed to get ready for the lake and brief Grove on what I thought we were facing. "I think whatever is going down at the lake is the endgame, and that whoever has been behind this shit is going to want to protect it."

"Makes sense, but I don't know man, it's thin."

"Anemic."

"Anorexic," The monk corrected.

"Don't be insensitive."

He opened his mouth to protest and stopped, sighed, and just surrendered with a chuckle.

"What should I tell the gang?" I could tell he was unsure if this warranted ringing the war bell, given it was guesswork attached to an unverified theory, but the Boy Scout in me and the criminal finally agreed on one thing; it would be dumb to be unprepared.

"Leave Gale with our people so we know that no matter what they'll be safe," As a man once afraid to ask for help, and timid when it came to taking command, even I was surprised in the confidence that permeated the order.

"Tell the rest of them to get ready for a fight."

***

"Is that my truck?"

"It's the only thing that could hold Johnny's speakers." I lied, still not sure where this yet-to-be-admitted resentment for the new truck had really come from.

The Bru-Maga and company halted at the sound of the rock-music pouring out of the vehicle, wafting to every nook and cranny of the lake. As if to punctuate the throat-clearing drum-solo before the climb to the songs' climax, Patrick hurled Julian out of the window with enough momentum to send the bastard into the ground hard and tumbling into a sprawling stop on the asphalt.

Holy Diver by Dio was clear as day, the soft-coaxing magic that lived in the music was empowering each of our allies. Helena was turning to tell me that I had to go, as the Bru-Maga let out a heinous scream that clashed with the aggressive soundtrack that Johnny had chosen to give us all hope. Grove had taken my arm and started to drag me back into the establishment so we could go through to the dock in the back and get to the boat.

Holy Diver - you been down too long in the midnight sea
Oh, what's becoming of me?
Ride the Tiger
You can see his stripes but you know he's clean
Oh, Don't you see what I mean?

Helena's nod was resolute, and before I could even call out to the Concrete Monk, the alleyway champion and the Master Artificer were walking down the stairway and into the clearing. It was almost poetic, there was a brilliance in their shared ballad, as Patrick actually quick-stepped right by a recovering Julian to both dodge his clumsy Mace swing and clash with an inbound pair of ghouls from the other direction while Helena managed to glide beneath the reach of the monk and intercept the Mace-swing with an angled deflection of her cane.

The same cane that whipped back as quick as it had come forward to manipulate the aim of the mace and bite Julian in the back of the head with a crack so sharp, I swore I heard the skin split before I saw the wound bleed. The blow had dislodged the sheath and showed the sword-cane for what it was, and as Helena squared herself up with the behemoth, I realized two things.

That even having nearly a foot in height on her and having bested me and Grove with relative ease, Julian suddenly looked terribly slight.

He was going to lose.

The truck was a lot easier to see, and between the sight of it and the music, I don't know if I could have been more motivated. It was the greatest band of misfits and well-meaning outcasts to ever live, all of them here to answer the call of community and found-family; to stand shoulder-to-shoulder against the insidious infection that had attempted for far too long to take everything from us. Nathan—looking completely petrified—was driving, and sitting beside him riding shotgun was Kaycee, outfitted for war and looking as fierce as Artemis herself.

Johnny B. was set up in the back, a pair of speakers flanking him, and a new, pristine guitar slung over with a strap as skilled fingers deftly worked the strings for everything they were worth. Its voice challenged the cry of the Bru-Maga, and instantly I could see a small stutter in the control she had on the assembled ghoul and vampire horde.

And standing in front of Johnny B., holding onto the steel railing on the back of the pick-up, was a surprise for the ages…. Jay, Kaycee's husband, the one-armed line cook who I'd known nothing about, was staring at the only currently un-addressed enemy combatant…the Stalker.

Nathan peeled the truck into a tire-screeching sideways stop, a screaming Johnny pinching the highest part of the song while lifting the gloss-blue Gibson nearly overhead as if trying to sacrificially offer the instrument to the rock gods the bard was so obviously channeling. Kaycee's emergence was smooth and explosive, that deceptive athleticism gave her the talent to actually hit the ground before the vehicle had completely stopped and never compromised her footing. In the same instant she seamlessly hoisted her staff and sent a snapping stream of lightning to challenge the screeching Bru-Maga.

The Half-elf was teeming with energy, and as I scanned her, I saw a matching pair of bracelets that reminded me of the collars we'd been seeing them use. Reverse engineering of the spellcraft was somehow allowing Kaycee to draw power from another source; as strong as she was, the way that spell hit the undead sorceress told me that it had the backing of a strength that even my formidable friend didn't have. As the lightning from her staff started to eat at the shielding cast by the vampire in a reeling attempt to protect herself, Kaycee opened a flat palm and conjured an oscillating series of glowing sigils into the air until they coalesced in the desired pattern and beckoned all the cold from the air, forming into a lethal shard of ice. The projectile went sailing forward and the enemy sorceress had to actually magically grab and drag one of her own foot soldiers in front of her to take the blow, else it might have robbed her of her life.

She was siphoning from the community she was protecting. They trusted her, and there would be no better custodian of that collective power. Grove gave me another yank, just as I watched the one-armed Jay jump supernaturally high and land in a superhero pose, caving in some of the asphalt he landed on, before straightening up to stand a dozen or so feet away from the slowly approaching Stalker.

"Oh come on, we've never even seen -"

"Janzen," Grove snapped, bringing me back to the seriousness of the moment. For a second, I realized that as great as this tide turning counter-punch was, all it meant was we were in a fight, and now everyone was laying their well-being on the line to see what we could do. The soldier, in a decidedly human moment, turned and gave one last look at his prized truck, before turning back to me.

"We've got to go."

I took one more look at the battlefield and watched Kaycee fighting with an undead sorceress, Patrick plowing into a gathering of ghouls and one of the two vampires I'd managed to identify, and Helena systematically taking apart her former student. With Grove demanding that we stay steadfast to the mission, I grimly nod, pivot, and clench my jaw as a means to keep me from joining the fray with all my friends…my family.

We move out briskly.

We tear across the broken glass floor, clearing one of the tables we'd turned over when we thought we might have to have our last stand—Alamo style, and break back out into the night through the back door. I manage to save Grove's ass by snagging the deaf soldier by the belt just in time to stop his forward momentum. The confusion as to why I grabbed him passed as quickly as the headless corpse that flew by.

Verrak was on, doing her best Sarah Conor from the Terminator franchise with a muscle shirt and tactical pants tucked into high-and-tight cinched boots. There was a black, ichorous substance smeared over her right hand, palm, and wrist, and taking a better look at the headless body, I realized it was the second vampire I'd caught sight of.

Almost comically, after our mutual pause and obligatory look around at one another, we all burst into a sprint down to the dock and piled into the last boat. Before Grove mourned the lack of a key I pushed him aside, away from the driver's station, and popped open the bottom panel to hot-wire the older model single-engine fishing boat.

Make no mistake about it, some of these new skills I picked up in jail were very helpful. Whenever I was burnt out on my studies of old-school sigil work, I opted for a few criminality 1-0-1 lessons with whatever nearby, chatty inmate was available. In a short time I'd become adept at lock picking, hot-wiring any pre-2005 car, and knew the basics of identity theft along with a plethora of other functional bad habits that I was excited to employ in my escapades.

Verrak snapped one line, Grove cut the other, and we were off.

When the first incident with Maria occurred, it took place close to a cliffside that looked over a portion of the lake that had a small island at its center. There was nothing too remarkable about the landscape, just a clearing, some foresting, a few surprisingly tall trees and a little rise onto a kind of plateau; but beside that, nothing really to write home about. The cultist's had actually run their rented yacht into this very landmass when we were fighting to free Maria from their rift tearing ritual. We'd stopped them from opening this port way into the Abyss, at a very high cost. We'd managed to thwart the ceremony but not before opening the doorway enough to start the rift. It wasn't in vain, because we did get it closed, but we still lost Maria that day.

Part of the Lake had actually been cordoned off, so we had to circle back by the restaurant and open parking lot battle-royal before pivoting to aim the craft toward the deeper end of the Lake and closer to the island. I managed to check over my shoulder in time to witness Kaycee whirling the staff overhead like a helicopter and sending out a myriad of bolts that arched high before careening down to crash into a dozen or so nearby enemies. Helena was not only beating Julian, but the gloved hand managed to bring another example of mastery to life in the form of a whip-shaped funnel of fire that was she used to bite any interloper that tried to get close to their duel, fending off a few more of the vermin undead that were in obedience to the Bru-Maga.

Jay was now dressed in some kind of magically conjured Nordic armor, its horned helm cutting a proud image of a lore I loved and knew very little about. The stump on his left side now sported an arm made of some kind of blue magic. Heels that had dug themselves in were literally cutting into the asphalt as the Stalker ran headlong into him, challenging the superiority of the Vikings stance, but not overcoming it as the warrior held-fast and upright until the momentum of the charge died and Jay could lock the head-down beast in a hold and literally lift it up, and over, in a bone-crushing suplex.

Grove, with the boat doing a few dozen knots in one direction before I wrenched it into a hard-bending turn in the opposite direction, managed to get off a pair of shots that found purchase in the side of the Stalker as it tried to recover. Spatterings of black blood explained the things laboring breath, and before it could determine that the shooting soldier was too far off to deal with, Jay had mimicked its own earlier move and came crashing into it with a head-down shoulder-charge.

From this distance it had to be a trick of the eyes, but I swore that the former one-armed line-cook was almost as big as the thing, and it looked as if every time Jay got a clean blow in on the Stalker he'd grown.

It wasn't long before we were too far away to affect the fight, and soon Verrak, Grove and I were all huddled around the wheel of the center-fed console boat.

Grove expertly flipped the gun and dutifully went to reload the lost rounds, as Verrak turned her left arm over to inspect a nasty gash and slash combination on her forearm. "Any idea what we should expect up here?" Watching a Stalker operate completely au naturale so to speak, was an almost uncomfortable reminder as to what Verrak really was underneath the well-tailored glamour. The fact her true nature was just beneath the crafted surface had a disconcerting impact, and the alien quality of her eyes reinforced this.

I thought back to the fact she'd visited me the most in jail, and in a way, walked a parallel path of growth with me. I held onto that and centered myself, and when our eyes met for the second time after my first uneasy glance it was a lot easier to hold them. "I don't know." Between the boat, and the fighting, signing as I spoke, after seeing her sign the question.

Grove and I didn't even need to finish our look before switching drivers, only waiting until he could sling the rifle on his back.

"The girl that'll be at the center of this—I need to get to her—and I need to be the one to talk to her. The rest? Anyone's guess."

"Traps?" Verrak asked, still having the wherewithal to sign her question while Grove focused on keeping us headed toward the island.

"Feels like the kitchen sink, to me."

Grove caught the confusion written over Verrak's face at the use of the idiom and nodded, even while expertly keeping us on course. The island was a visible shoreline now, and I could see three silhouettes starting to emerge from the loose foliage that had been obscuring them, to watch our approach.

"It's a last-ditch effort, using everything at her disposal. I'm not saying it isn't effective," I pointed at her gashed forearm and some of Grove's bruising, before vaguely highlighting my own rash of injuries. "But it feels like desperation." They each nod, before I give the island another look. There was a gathering of fog that felt too propitious to be coincidental, and the three silhouettes on the water actually waded into the water on our approach. The dark robing and low-cast hoods kept their features obscured, but the one in the center remained inhumanly still while the other two seemed to sway in creepy unison. Just behind them was a clearing and a rocky woodland climbing upward before cresting into a flat plateau.

And that's where I saw it, a sight I'd hoped never to have to look at again.

A stone tablet-table with a headstone at the back that was decorated with the familiar, insidious sigil work I'd seen carved into the abdomen of Maria on the day they tried to rip her open and pour her power into a bridge from our world to the Abyss. Beside it was a shorter, multicolored hair figure, and I immediately identified her as Cat, despite the distance and the last year and half's influence on her own growth.

There was some kind of illusionary figure beside her, and just above the table was a swirling green labyrinth of energy, interwoven with a black, living presence. I couldn't tell, but it looked as if Cat was either casting, or reading some kind of spell, and the growing energy forming into an obviously ominous portal was proof of that.

Grove punched the boat to go even faster, Verrak gave a growl as she crouched low, ready to cross the last hundred feet from us to the shore in a single bound. All I could do was stare stupidly at the ghastly phantasm beside the lost, orphaned girl. I immediately knew it to be Abigail, even if there was something softer and more human in the projection. I recognized the deception of her look and knew it was probably done to garner trust from this broken-hearted teenager. But more than that, there was something unsettlingly familiar in the image. I'd never thought of the Mistress as anything other than an undefined conglomeration of evil and awfulness, and even when I'd put together that she was more than a living nightmare, I think on some primal level it was still hard to imagine a version of her that didn't radiate with that fiendish intensity you were choke-throttled with whenever she looked at you.

As if hearing my thoughts, Abigail's ethereal image whipped her head my way and we locked eyes; her smile caused a physical reaction in me, a stammering of *no* from my mouth though too quiet for either of my compatriots to hear. I hated the effect she had over me. I went from finding myself emboldened by self-assurance, confident in the clarity of my thinking, and willing to reach out and ask for help when needed, to feeling insecure and unsure of myself with just one look.

"No!"

Something was wrong…she didn't just expect us here…she wanted me here—specifically.

The three figures in the water at the shoreline became even more visible, and the unified swaying was actually just the outer pair jostling against restraints tied not only their wrists but to each other as well; with the effect that when one pulled, the other lurched and when the other pulled the opposing one stumbled. A familiar, fiendish emblem came alive on the central figure's chest, and a flash of green encircled the collared throats of the flanking figures. I knew what this meant. Their energy and power were drained and drawn into the figure in the center, who then poured all of that power into one brutal pulse of unseen energy that was aimed directly at our boat.

The impact was devastating, the channeled power that had been enhanced by the siphoned life forces of the now dead servants hit the boat with such a full-frontal wall of energy that it actually dislodged me and Verrak instantly, and sent poor Grove rattling up and into the ceiling of the boat before the whole thing flipped over on itself and slammed into the lake upside down. I was thrown halfway to shore by the first arc, actually skipping like a pebble on the water. This was not something we'd expected, nor thought possible. Winning had created a subconscious kind of expectancy I suppose, even though I knew that right now time was not on our side.

The cold waters were numbing my limbs, and a swell of blackness had almost swallowed my thoughts. On some level I worried about drowning, but I couldn't get the thought to connect with motion, and in that lack of motion I felt myself start to sink both in the physical world, and in the depths of a mind that was beckoning me to rest.

In this half-conscious state I was aware of a beat growing weaker and fading, and on some level, I knew it was my heart—or at least my mind's interpretation of it.

This time there was no ghost sent by the embodiment of an ancient power. No hallucination born out of physical-testing action that would become a winning reality. Just the cold of Lake Erie, and the quiet of the black as I slipped further and further into it.

These people are my responsibility.
It was a spark. And in the dark I felt a pulse. Just beyond all this nothingness I heard a sound, a steady rhythm, and I mentally walked from that realization to the memory of Johnny. Suddenly, another boom cried over the landscape penetrating the water and it was as if that moment I held onto gave me a big, booming hello.

My eyes snapped open, but before I could pull my head out of the water somebody grabbed the back of my jacket in a vice-grip and pulled me up. Grove had a nasty gash over his left eye, and I knew without a doubt that it would leave about a four-inch scar. I also knew that it would look badass if we lived through this.

The boom I'd heard wasn't some symbolic, metaphysical thing either. I looked back at the restaurant area of the shore and saw an inferno reaching for the sky. It threw a spotlight on the action sprawling across the parking lot and up and down the front of the restaurant. I couldn't figure out what had exploded, and it was only when I looked at Grove that I realized what had blown up.

Grove was caught somewhere between exacerbated and heartbroken, just a tier below pissed and annoyed.

The explosion was his brand-new truck. The Bru-Maga sought to cut Johnny B off from the power source that was supplying our side with a bolstering effect well into the later rounds of this championship fight. Even I'd managed to hang onto a thread of it half-conscious and a few feet underwater.

I shook him free of the agonizing realization and we both quickly headed through the water to the shore as fast as we could. Unfortunately, we'd only gotten waist high out of it before we were face to face with the mage who'd smashed us and flipped our boat. For once it was nice to see that this wasn't some secret saboteur, or a long-trusted friend stabbing us in the back. I didn't recognize the wizard, but guessed from the thrumming energy reverberating in the air around him that he was teeming with energy from the sacrificial murder we'd just witnessed.

Rolled up sleeves showed similar craftwork to what I had seen on Alpha and Delta; I had even glimpsed a small bit of it on Julian when I'd seen the strength-enhancement symbol he'd tattooed on himself. The major difference between this one and those examples was that this man had not only carved them directly into his flesh, but they were fresh—looked like maybe an hour old.

Blood magic was a dark, dark type of magic and it was incredibly powerful. It should not be used for any reason, and if somebody was dumb enough to use it, they usually used it to imbue a power into an item or ratify an oath. Very rarely did somebody use it in an active type of magic, but the addition of blood magic to traditional spellwork made that spellwork a lot more formidable; and of course, the same would hold true of offensive magic and the like. Instinctively Grove and I reached out not to touch, but measure and then distance ourselves even with the disadvantage of being slowed down by the water. We'd practiced this in our own war-gaming; the idea being that with a caster the best chance of beating them was to give them a pair of targets instead of a single one. It was nice to see our training kick in, though my hope to close the distance to the shore was waning.

You don't rise to the occasion; you fall to your level of training. That muscle-memory had been one of our leading intangibles when it came to how Grove and I managed to escape a lot of the stuff we'd gotten ourselves tangled up with. The fact that we'd separated ourselves was probably pointless with a dozen feet of churning water and a hyper-focused, amped up spellcaster taking shots at us and keeping us from shore, but it made us two small targets instead of one bigger one.

Two targets split even further apart when the distraction of Verrak, in full Cura'Sha form, suddenly roared out of the southside tree line, moving in an injury-hobbled but still startlingly fast sprint toward the back of the mage. Unfortunately for her there was enough time for it to whirl around and send an open-handed gesture at the Stalker, bringing to life a surge of energy that lifted

Verrak up and sent her crashing brutally into the rock bed below the plateau.

Recovering quickly from the rear side ambush, the mage picked my most likely avenue of approach to square up with, catching me a dozen or so feet from reaching him as I was also using the distraction to try and close the distance to attack. Quick fingers worked with fast-lipped chanting, and the summoned spell sent bursting at me was in the form of red hued lighting.

The three marbles I'd stuffed into my pocket earlier were all I had left on me and so, more with instinct than mindfulness, I hurled the small orbs at the deadly energy before diving into the water. The marbles had a vortex defensive measure etched into them, basically an option to respond to challenging magic by emptying out their own in a kind of shield and absorbing the incoming power. The only thing was that this was a theory, I'd never actually tried to prove it in battle like this.

The marbles did their job, and unleashed a shielding blast, absorbing the ambient energy that should have caught purchase on me enough so that the leather jacket managed to actually shield me from the worst of it without causing me much harm.

I was closer to shore, but still in the water, and now at the soaked feet of this enemy mage, trying to keep from catching another wave in the face. A bruising set of fingers dug into my neck and lifted me up out of the water after my third attempt to get out after the searing blast had almost taken my head off. The crazed, brown eyes were outlined with that greenish hue, and I swore that while not exactly possessed, I could sense Abigail's influence steering him into this madness.

The mage snapped out of the madness long enough to realize he'd lost track of Grove, and right at that moment, I trapped the hand digging into my neck by collapsing both of my palms over it and planting my feet between his, holding and pulling the limb toward me as Grove came in on his blindside with a home-run worthy baseball swing of his ax aimed right at his exposed head. The dying battle cry from the mage was cut painfully short as the soldier cleaved his head clean off, both of us exhaustedly collapsing into the shallow water.

Grove had the scar-worthy split over his left eye that was steadily bleeding, and as we stood up and got out of the water I could see a piece of boat-shard embedded in his side. Make no mistake about it, this was the kind of injury that could kill you, and the only reason he hadn't bled out was probably because he was medically savvy enough to keep the object inside the wound.

The Sauron wanna-be we'd just decapitated had nearly choked the life out of me and I was using my first three gulps of air to just ward off the blackness that had threatened to leave me succumbing to unconsciousness. The raised plateau was still the center of the ceremony; the whirling tendrils of green now taking on a more defined shape—they were actually framing the living black behind them and attempting to solidify the conduit.

The rocky ascent was carpeted with wet, treacherous footing, and the prone and bloody form of Verrak sprawled across it. For whatever reason she'd converted back to human form, and while at first I thought it a little strange, I suddenly felt the pull from that portal and recognized that all types of magic were going to be thrown into a disturbance and would be stolen using these kinds of spells. Grove shakily shrugs the gun off and checks the soaked bandolier as we limp our way out of the water.

"How many rounds you got left?" I knew Grove wasn't ignoring me maliciously, and that when I signed for the second time it still didn't get him to stop counting; finally I jostled him and broke his strained concentration.

"How many?!"

"I don't know, sixteen, maybe seventeen..." Suddenly, the soldier saw why I was asking. From both ends of the island small hordes of ghouls had come together. Enough to account for every bullet and then some, and each of them had a greenish tint in their eyes; held into by some kind of influence that I suspected was Abigail herself.

I had confirmed this suspicion when I saw a human, uncomfortably familiar version of her, looking down at me with the same faint sheen in her eyes.

"Go!" I knew at that moment, leaping over Verrak's prone and unconscious body as I ran my ass off to get to the small hilltop clearing, that when Grove told me to go, it was the right call, and I didn't hesitate. Behind me, I heard shot after shot ring out as Grove slowly followed my ascent up the rocky bluff. I managed to get to a series of stone stairs and cleared them in a leap; this newfound athleticism and health made me thankful for the umpteenth time for the physical benefits of my stint behind bars. There were two pillar-like carvings that served as the entry to the clearing that the small figure and the astral projection were working at.

The plateau looked like a natural structure carved into something that served humankind, and even though it was now centuries beyond its original use, it was now easier to associate it with the essence of its earlier purpose. The two stone pillars opened into a large circular clearing of stone and moss, with bushes and trees encircling the whole of it. At the center was the stone tablet, and above it was the whirling, steadily growing darkness that the reaching green energy was shaping into something more stable and solid. The circular clearing had actual ringlets, and the ringlets were now faintly glimmering with sigil work I'd never seen before, but sensed was more ancient than anything I'd ever laid eyes on.

The hooded girl and the phantasm of Abigail were facing toward the large stone face cast of a boulder that stood perpendicular to the site. I counted four with the next shot I heard and couldn't resist the temptation to glance back. Verrak, that tough bird, was struggling to sit upright and cover her own wounded midsection while reloading bullets into the custom magazines Grove used.

Fighters to the end.

I turned back to the scene I came for and cleared my throat, realizing then that there was a sudden stormy quality to the atmosphere, and that suddenly a section of the blackness was still, and while the whirling green energy was attempting to pry and coax the living dark wider, a part of it had started to frame that one.

"Cat!" I screamed, shielding my eyes, as a flash of green momentarily blinded me. When I lowered my arm, I yelped in surprise to see Abigail nearly face-to-face with me, the sheer menace of her warped features was enough to inspire a dread I'd never known before. And just before I soiled myself and collapsed into a pool of nothing, I instantly realized something.

She was scaring me; she wasn't hurting me.

"Cat!" I bellowed, and on the second shout I thought of my old friend Johnny B. and just imagined the kind of desire and aim he used to direct the magic that lived in every octave he sang or spoke. I swallowed my crippling fatigue when I saw her shoulder twitch, and then I shouted her name for the third time, layering some love and empathy into my tone.

That stopped her cold, and even though the cowl she was wearing kept the majority of her face veiled, I watched her delicate jawline stiffen, turning as rigid as the stone beside her as she whipped her head back toward it. Abigail's disappointment at my ability to see through the fear-mongering of her illusion was suddenly renewed at the abject rejection from her choice host, this orphaned Wanderer she'd managed to somehow seduce while all of us were busy tending to our own bullshit.

If love wasn't going to reach her…maybe hate would….

"I don't know what's sadder, the fact that you let your grandmother die alone or that your loser father ended up having more of a spine than you ever will."

Wham.

I went flying back into one of the very pillars I'd passed on my way into this little area. I actually think the concussion of the energy impacting me knocked me out, and the blow to the back of my head woke me up. If love didn't work, hate was a hell of a way to invoke a reaction, but just as I was celebrating my newfound cleverness, I felt an invisible energy clutch my ankle and start dragging me toward the infuriated, pint-sized Wanderer, her face contoured in rage as the projection of Abigail sat smugly beside her. The gravel pretty much took half my shirt along with a good portion of my skin; road rash so agonizing I actually felt a moment of relief when she just tossed me into the boulder-face she was staring at when I first came up. Luckily, I caught that one with my hip and ass, and it was high enough that I had some time to brace my fall with my arms.

"Maybe he'd still be alive if you were any good at your job, Janzen!" Her shout was contorted with rage and echoed with magical energy. I had to literally shake my blood-soaked face to clear the haze from my vision enough to notice that Abigail was actually *mouthing* everything Cat was saying.

"Maybe my dad wouldn't be dead! Maybe none of this shit would have happened if you hadn't distracted Zachariah and actually let him figure out what she was actually trying to do." I was trying to catch up on a plot I was only half read in on with a head that wasn't fully working, and a clock going full press. From inference, I could tell that somehow this Abigail had spun a sympathetic story or had conducted some kind of tale about how opening this gateway was in everyone's best interest.

The Zachariah thing hurt; even worse because I'd never thought of it. I was halfway to my feet, depending on the very rockface I'd been sent on a collision course with a moment earlier, leaving an admirable homage to a macabre Jackson Pollock with my bloody handprints and smearing forehead on the stone.

"You don't know what it's like, Janzen. You have no fucking idea what it's like to be this alone, to feel like this big of a failure, to think everything you touch goes to dust and anything that survives turns to shit." Streaking tears poured down her face, and as the girl pleaded with me to challenge her, I felt this dark and powerful ire. This desire to remind this little shit that all of us go through struggles; I wanted to knock her own pain down and hold a mirror up to it, a mirror that showed how loved she'd been, a mirror that reflected the memory of parents and how losing something great meant that at least she once had it. This anger had the metallic taste of my blood and as I thought about how many bone-breaking beatdowns I'd already taken for this fucking brat I wondered what it would be like to serve her up a dose of humble pie and stack her pain next to the prolific pillar of misery which was my own sob story ...

I blinked.

Just as my mouth opened to spew this venom, I realized that as much as I wanted to lay that vile-wrought emotion at her feet as some kind of manipulation, I suddenly knew that the only reason there was any hope of shaping it was because it lived in me. Cat had turned completely to face me as if sensing I was on the precipice of spouting some long-endured abuse that she could then use to fuel her fury, but I paused, and suddenly saw why every one of these attempts had been so successful.

I saw how much of this fury lived inside of all of us.

I stood upright, and I could tell that the weird serenity that had walked over me was enough to alarm the projection of Abigail, even if she kept a cool face on. I looked over at Cat next and watched this young person who felt not only hurt, not only alone, but totally unheard. She was shouting into the void and even now the way she'd aimed her anger at me I could see the source of it and sympathize in a way that I hadn't been capable of before I'd not only found a family but lost so many of them.

"I don't Cat," I lifted my arms and just kept my palms up. Grove sent off another round. That was either the eighth or ninth. "...and I'm sure a lot of people have told you that they can. I know Penny is ill, she's worried sick about you by the way." I started there and found a kindling of hope when her grandmother's name elicited a small wince. Of course she followed that up with a warning glower, as if feeling the design of the comment. "I'm saying that on top of losing so much, you're losing the only person in your life that wants to hear about how bad it hurts." Suddenly, I lamented not bringing this girl into the fold sooner, and it dawned on me how easy it would have been to tell Kaycee, Verrak, hell even Grove about her.

Maybe we wouldn't be here now if I had, and that was on me, though now was not the time for regrets.

"I lost a lot of my people at once, not too long ago. It's actually how this whole thing started." I openly regarded the portal, and then the pint-sized conjurer who had (unbeknownst to me when I met her) been the second Wanderer in the city of Cleveland in nearly as many years—a thing that I could confidently say has never happened before. Cat was eyeing me suspiciously but nodded for me to continue. I couldn't help but notice Abigail hadn't interjected, and even while trying to stay fixated on the sincerity of my own story I distantly considered if playing the role of some kind of good guy to convince Cat to help her with this could have some disadvantages too. The dark queen did suck down an indignant snarl at the delay, making a point of drifting a little closer to the girl.

"I fell into a dark depression. I had people who wanted to reach out, people who loved me, but I ignored them and isolated myself. Even worse? I probably could have helped quite a few of them by sharing my experience and admitting how bad I was hurting, because a lot of them were too." I resisted the urge to bring up her grandmother again. I knew Penny would probably openly bemoan the lost time at being forced to leave her granddaughter, but that was the life. It would help them both process some of this if she opened up. I knew this from experience.

I also knew how big of an ask this was.

"I crawled into a bottle and started to do a lot of stupid selfish stuff. It was a real low point. I wasn't really worth knowing back then, and you couldn't rely on me for anything. It's hard to fathom how anybody tolerated me enough to get by my shitty sarcasm. That hurt side of me just hurled insults and spat venomous anger at whoever it was that brought them to the light of day. I don't know, I was a real toxic piece of work for a while there…and all because I had this hurt in me, this hurt that just suffocated the happiness out of me, this hurt that seemed to find a foothold in every part of my day. I couldn't get away from it, and because of that, it stole every bit of joy out of my life piece by piece."

"I miss them," I found myself admitting. "Even now after all these years. I'm still afraid to admit just how bad it hurts. How responsible I feel." At one time, a glaze would take over and I would wallow in the darkest part of those thoughts until I felt the impulse to do something terribly self-destructive. Luckily, a little bit of growth and the fact that I was already knee-deep in my death wish kept me from going too far.

I was able to answer the look in Cat's eyes with steadiness, almost finding some kind of companionable calm even in the thickest part of this pandemonium. Abigail cleared her throat, and after the small Wanderer had ignored her, she'd actually beckoned her by name; but the orphan couldn't bring herself to pry those curious eyes from my own: people like us recognize our own.

"How did it get better?" The softest narrowing touched the corner of her profile, the first shift in the bedrock of her current conviction. On another day I would probably play coy and ask how she knew it got better, but not because I would aim to avoid the question; I would be curious where her unquestionable faith that it got better came from. The truth is, it did, and she knew it.

For once, it was nice to have the answer.

"On a really bad day, I just thought about what some of the best people I knew would do, and kind of kept at it from there. It's a matter of progress, not perfection, and not every day is a winner." I half-tug my lake-soaked, crash torn, blood-stained shirt from my body as if to emphasize the point. My example broke her a touch more and the corner of her mouth turned as if on the verge of laughing at the wordless elaboration.

Above, the black stillness was moving again and the one section the green energy had started to keep safeguarded was regressing. Abigail followed my line of sight, and I could tell the distraction warranted some notice from the hyper-astute, street-smart kid.

"I think the worse you feel, the more this opens."

Cat got steely eyed, straightening a bit, and instead of retreating I pushed the point.

"You think anything fueled on the darkest parts of your feelings is what you want to be channeling?"

"You don't know me, Janzen, and quite frankly you already had your chance to help." The age of enamorment seemed to abate as swiftly as it came but I hung in there, knowing that sometimes aggression would just invite more aggression and that the footing I was on a moment prior wasn't lost, it just shifted a bit.

"I should have," I confessed, pausing her from turning away from me and back to the ceremony. "We had the network, even with me being in jail." That got her to balk for a bit, but I hastily waved it off. "Story for another day," The hope for another day was intentionally placed in front of her. "But ask your newfound fairy God-mother about it; if you end up nuking all of us, I'd be curious as to what story she spun." The jab got another glimmer of mischievousness from the girl, not that she entertained any more of the implication.

"I still suffer from some thoughtlessness and I'm a work in progress, but I meant what I said when we first met; I can help. I want to help." I managed to hobble a few steps closer, and after looking around a little, I settled on one of the shorter rocks around the circle's floor; half because this might be the only fight in which there were no more punches left to throw, and half because I was pretty sure I had a broken foot.

"You think maybe we can try and see if there's a place for you in our family before you go speed-opening a portal to some knock off version of hell?" Sometimes, you just had to tell the emperor they were naked. Abigail was probably confident she'd sold a good story; there was a part of her that understood she was preying on, and therefore relying on, the worst parts of people. Cat was precocious by intellect and sage by experience, so on some level the girl understood that this was beyond the pale of appropriate, and yet those lost in their grief don't know anything else.

I could tell that as much as it managed to get a proper, one breath bark of laughter out of her, the dawning of what she was about to do washed over her and suddenly, and with fresh sight, saw the truth of not only the ceremony, but the nature of this budding portal.

I heard another shot and knew that if that wasn't the last round it was fast approaching, and yet I couldn't let that impact what was happening here, and for some reason I took grounded solace that everyone on my team was willing to die for a cause such as this.

I was willing to die for it. It's why my calm was conveyed with such confidence, and I knew without a doubt that she could see the truth of it in my eyes. "You know this isn't right, Cat, and if you help me now, we can walk all this back. There's still time for another few days with Penny, and you've got my word that we can start to work on this outlet for you immediately. We have a place for you with all of us." I stopped short of calling it a home, and I could tell the conflicted teenager was about to break.

"You won't be alone in this."

Abigail had heard just about enough, and even though it caused every inch of me to scream I actually stood to impose myself between the warping projectile and the shellshocked, grieving girl. The familiar essence was melting away and there were glimpses and flashes of the Abyss Queen we'd first seen her as, this off-skin color with jet black hair and an inhuman, darkling quality.

"You would abandon your father, your father who died for you? Who died because of His failure?!"

An accusing finger jutted right in front of my eyes, and I resisted the impulse to flinch away from it, side-eyeing the digit and waiting, very purposely, for the worried girl who'd shuffled behind me to look. Very deliberately, and with great emphasis, I waved a hand over that finger and watched it pass through.

So did Cat.

"You can't hope to control what lives in you, *Catherine*, look at what it did to your mother." The pause was for effect, and the astral projection of the mistress standing just beneath the waning portal to the Abyss scowled threateningly at me.

"Look what it's doing to your grandmother."

I turned to the teenage Wanderer, sensing that the conflict was actually putting her in an emotional state of turmoil that went back to feeding the vortex-conduit trying to bring itself to life in a half-sphere over the space we occupied. The backdrop canopy of energy warped and wavered until it began to show a scene of Cat and her grandmother, and then another of her father, and finally one of their family going out. A dozen conversations and faux memories began to play out on all sides, drawing her into a further vat of emotional conflict; more and more I sensed that any chaotic, or negative emotion was going to help this thing grow, and it was growing out of her, the same way it had with Maria.

Abigail had duplicated herself as well, projecting them to the left and right, each spewing another memory, taunt, or ugly reminder that this end was inevitable and the only way that she could serve her family was by finally doing this dark deed. I didn't even know what was being promised, but I now understood the addiction to the abuse, the addiction to the powers commingled with her own; that the promise of the end of the pain had ultimately made that point moot.

I managed to kneel in front of Cat, taking her face in one hand and holding steady, repeating her name like a mantra over and over again until finally the teenager —who was probably only a decade or so younger than me yet seemed so incredibly childlike— opened her eyes enough to see me. She saw me through all this hurt, amidst this field of ruin and agony, at the center of the best hits at her worst fears that she could make—I saw her, knowing that it took a tremendous amount of courage for her to simply do that much.

And I rewarded her with as reassuring a smile as I could.

"This is going to hurt," I say slowly, pausing, "...but we can handle the hurt, can't we?"

Timid, but not unsure, the tragedies of the girl's life had proven enough to put her down but not knock her out.

"Look at me," and we locked eyes again. Slowly, I reach to the low part of my back with the hand not steadily holding her cheek. "Who is the best person you know?"

"My grandmother." The memory of her brought a touch of stability and I saw a spark of defiance ignite life in those tear-soaked eyes.

"Think of her. Think that you don't want to do this, and remember, she can't hurt you. Push it all out of your mind and hold on to Grandma and everything she is and would want you to be. Can you do that?" Somehow, she remembered the bat-dagger—I knew she did in the way her gaze dropped down to my back-seeking hand trying to quietly get a grip on its hilt.

When we locked eyes the third time, I watched her imperceptible nod for me to act and saw her steely nerves translate into a clenched jaw, each hand clutching tight on my wrist and forearm. Abigail was about to interject but screamed when she saw a flash of movement.

People are creatures of habit, and Abigail had once been a person.

The razor-sharp edge of the bat-dagger came up between us and cut a deep, scarring line in her stomach as she clutched and screamed through the agony. Below it, the sigil carved in her stomach that served as the anchoring conduit was ruptured. The design split and the new cut destroyed the purpose of the sigil thereby ending the funneling conduit between the wealth of power she had as a Wanderer and the bridge that was being built.

Abigail's shriek was crazed and ripped over the entire landscape; a pulse of power actually reaching out from the island, carrying over to the campsite and well into the city. The severing effect of the cut not only ended the bridge to the portal, it broke her control over the countless creatures she'd planted with some form of connection and control.

The whirling blackness trying to be mastered by the green energy imploded, and the black shot up and out before arching back down and crashing into the soil below. The blotchy, oily presence boiled when it hit the ground before soaking deeper into the soil—soil that was dying on contact. The green static burst from it and ultimately gathered itself shooting back into Cat—luckily after the slice to destroy the sigil I'd kept hold of her and was able to keep her upright as the power surged back into her and brought her back to consciousness. She gasped and gave me a shove to release her.

Both of us were drained, shocked, and scared, and more trauma bonded than any emotionally intelligent people who'd lived through their fair share of shit would care to be; and we were alive. I reached out to help her up before groaning and collapsing to a knee myself, causing her to laugh before groaning in pain.

"Don't make me laugh …"

"Don't do stupid shit and it won't seem so funny." I couldn't help it. I worked my jaw and surveyed the stone-tablet table with the sacrificial circle and the site of a scene which almost went a lot, lot worse and was amazed. I didn't dare think about her actual plan, or what would have been able to cross this threshold if she had gotten her way…

"Didn't you destroy a statue of Jim Brown in Cleveland?" She intoned skeptically, gingerly inspecting the new wound I'd given her with glancing at me with a side-eye. I apologetically wince before shrugging it off.

"Fair point." About the statue, and the fact I'd nearly had to cut her in half to help us save the day.

Suddenly, I remember and yell "Verrak," over the lip of the hill. I couldn't see over the slope, so I held my breath. "You guys dead?" I yelled, and waved over the Wanderer, not even trying to expend the energy to think about how much we would have to answer for in the face of all this. Once she was close enough, she helped me up, and we headed over to the top of the slope.

"No… but we can't move."

Once we got there, we found out why. Verrak had actually recovered some but still looked wretched, a stomach-turning opening was in her abdomen and her gashed arm was broken backwards. Grove meanwhile was covered in bile, with half a dozen dead ghouls and their dismembered limbs and heads all around him, trying to do everything in his power to keep his rampaging heart from exploding. We all looked like the second kill in an indie made horror film, which as any aficionado can tell you is the most gore-heavy of the genre, but we were alive.

Cat looked a little squeamish, which given the fact she was bathed in blood from head to toe was a little funny, as she nervously half waved at the Cura'Sha and the soldier. Verrak was obviously not a human given the grievous extent of her injuries and our blasé attitude about it, but if that didn't drive the point home, the abyss-black bleeding was a big clue.

"Cat, this is Grove, my partner at Full Circle Protection, and our good friend Verrak. Guys, this is Cat." I touted a little triumphantly, come to that, I was in fact introducing my closest friends to the person I'd every aim of taking on as my protege.

"She's gonna join our book club."

Grove gave a breathless thumbs up, making the gesture around the gore-covered rifle-ax that seemed infused to his trembling hand. Fighting after all we'd been through, and the boat crash, long hours, and the beatdown we'd gotten at the beginning was impressive enough; holding a whole hill from a demigod possessing ghouls that were assaulting from all sides was awesome squared.

"Hey Cat," When the steady cadence of breathing helped him enough to speak, Grove offered the first olive branch, "...let me know when you want in the group chat we use to bitch about Janzen, it's very cathartic." Just then, we heard another boat off in the distance pull out from the restaurant and saw it make its way over to our island.

"We make our own memes." Grove quipped. It was perfectly conversational, and the levity of our collective chuckle was the first moment of camaraderie between the lot of us; relative strangers forced together by capricious fate and crazy circumstances. Verrak used the moment to give us to a front row seat of her snapping that broken leg back into place, which gave us our second moment of camaraderie as we groaned and gagged in response to the grotesque sight.

Using my jacket and Grove's know-how, we crafted a makeshift sling, and the four of us managed to make it down the treacherous rocky footing to the shoreline. All it took was a little leaning on each other, something we were getting really good at.

We waited at the shore for our inbound friends, relieved to find that everyone had made it through the fight, and for once we hadn't lost anyone. We knew that wasn't usually the case, and likely wouldn't be again, so gratitude was the theme of the day. Kaycee led the charge to our crew of beaten Gilligan Island rejects, Helena was able to heal the worst of our wounds though she had to be sparing with how much she'd exhausted herself. On the dock we found Jay with a restrained Julian, whom Helena assured me would be taken care of by their own judicial system.

The Concrete Monk was nowhere to be found, and I learned he'd vanished after the fighting subsided. Apparently not long after the pulse, all the creatures tied in with the Abyss seemed to get a sense that their Mistress' influence had been severed. Whether willing servitude or subjugation, it was over now, and they had no reason to stay.

Once again, a Stalker vanished in the throes of the chaos. We had a really bad track record when it came to Stalkers, but then again, they were as tricky and slippery as they were vicious and capable. I was sure it wouldn't be the last time we'd heard from those particular creatures. Johnny B. was nice enough to hand over the keys to Grove's destroyed truck with the kind of mocking reverence that I would have strived to emulate but never could quite duplicate; even giving them a half-salute as if knowing the soldier would characterize the vehicle as a lost friend—even if the rest of us wouldn't.

And for once as I turned to look over Lake Erie, I felt a deep abiding calm, and the absence of that undercurrent of dread that had accompanied me every time I'd been here since we'd lost Maria. I breathed the first sigh of relief I'd felt since I started this unexpected journey.

***

EPILOGUE

Six Weeks Later

"Janzen Robinson," I heard someone call out from behind me. That's not good.

It's never good when somebody uses your full name like that, as if you somehow don't know it.

But the English lilt that it was carried on gave me cause for hope, and as I turned to regard where it came from, I was pleasantly surprised to see the Master Artificer and my most recent advocate, Helena Muranti, standing a few feet away with a cane in one hand and a fresh cup of coffee in the other. I say recent advocates because after the latest Lake Erie debacle, and second time destroying a pretty storied Shoreside bar and eatery, we were probably running out of our nine lives. Luckily, Iandor had contacts and money galore and with some of that influence and money aimed at our own local municipality and chamber of commerce, we were able to get out of this debacle without any prison time.

She was dressed in a pair of black slacks and a white shirt, with a camel blazer thrown casually over her shoulders. The brim of her hat was broad, and complimented the large square framed sunglasses she topped the look with. The stark silver hair was still her signature, and as she strode closer to me, I was even more pleasantly surprised to see that the coffee was apparently for me.

"For me…I didn't get you anything" I quipped, taking the drink, and turning it around to read the order printed on the cup.

I was pleasantly surprised to find it was precisely what I would order whenever the rare occasion that I sprung for a coffee came around.

Five sugars, three creamers, and whatever else you had to add to make it taste less coffee-like.

"If it keeps you from drinking that battery acid commonly known as energy drinks, I will foot the bill for the rest of your tutelage."

I paused the sip I was about to take then and there and pinned her with a questioning side-eyed glance at that declaration. Straight to the point, it would seem. "Hold," I signal for her in unison to the request, putting a single finger up and leaving her where I found her to walk over to the construction worker I'd been talking to. His name was Tony, a botanist of all things, and in our network; somebody who was now a regular in my introductory course. He worked with sewers and man covers, and today he was going to be taking me on an impromptu tour. After a quick conversation, I told him it would have to wait for another time. We joked a bit and before jumping into his car, he pointed at my new sedan, gave me a thumbs up and waved bye.

"Tutelage?" I echoed skeptically, this time managing to get a sip of coffee down. We'd been through it together and survived, and that changed a lot about how you saw a person. Even if I didn't like her, I would always have a deep and abiding respect for her, though she's actually pretty difficult not to like. Helena had been a great emissary for the Institute and had made some real headway with the other sects of power that dictate those worlds.

After we cleared the local police from the incident, there was an official investigation by whatever department in her own organization took care of that sort of thing. Me and my team were about as agreeable and cooperative as you'd expect, and by the end of it there was not only no wrongdoing found, they had officially commended us with some weirdly named award, and gave us a decree of gratitude.

The Iandor Institute was apparently a more connected and networked agency than I'd have guessed, and for now I was just glad to see it all behind us. I eyeballed the car I'd parked across the street, motioning for the Master Artificer to follow and glimpsed the beanie wearing teenager sitting shotgun, idly playing on a switch while waiting for me. Cat had healed up well, and they had been working with her grandmother on a trust so that she had some kind of estate when her inevitable and untimely death came to pass. For now Grandma was holding on, and though weakening, was still very present of mind.

"I'd heard you'd taken her in."

I liked Helena, and appreciated what the Iandor institute had done, but Zachariah was very particular when speaking about them. With everything that had happened, there were some reservations I couldn't just abruptly let go of. In a way we'd been arm and arm in a battle as two different armies, but now the war was over, and she was in an organization that seemed to have spent the last four weeks deciding whether or not it was going to punish or reward me.

"What do you mean, tutelage?"

Helena straightened a little, drinking in my reticence and sympathizing with it in a way that reminded me of just how much I enjoyed the personality I saw beneath the perpetual reserve. I had to repeatedly remind myself that this was somebody Zachariah had trusted. "Part of the arrangement is that we will have a presence in Cleveland in a heavily official capacity. I just knew that you'd not only have problems with that, but would inevitably run afoul, amok, or whatever with it."

Helena actually steered me to a nearby hot-dog vendor and ordered three of their signature dogs. It was some combination of relish, condiments, and a footlong dog topped off with homemade potato chips and some kind of off-brand root beer. Basically, the dream meal of any kid ...

Or me.

I got a mouthful in, and for a moment almost completely abandoned my guarded mind state to just experience how delicious this was. I told the vendor to make the third one to go before stepping far enough back to take us out of earshot. I even turned so that Helena and I could speak more privately and took another addictive bite of mashed-meat bliss; figuring I had another four bites before she got to her point.

I kept as neutral a look as I could manage in response to what she said, while that heavenly hot dog was having a Jimmy Buffet song celebration in my mouth.

"So in order to mitigate against that potential disaster, I have opted instead to train you until you're qualified enough to pass the certification curriculum at the institute."

That was surprising. I'd seen Helena work, and truthfully even I knew not to be a brat about being offered training by her, but the fact this was in such an official capacity surprised me. I paused my rampant inhaling of the hot dog on the third bite to try to get more of the truth out of her.

"Why do you need me to say yes so bad?"

An approving, demure smile cut off whatever her scripted response was going to be, and I could tell there was a flash of something else behind her controlled expression. "Because this placement is going to happen regardless of what you want Janzen, and my station within Iandor is currently in a vulnerable place. Zachariah and his theory about Cleveland were popular during his banishment. They could never quite turn him into the pariah they wished and given that he ended up being right about this place, it has called our governing body into question about some of their decisions, methodology, and tenets. I had an option to play along with their narrative and not be made a scapegoat, and instead..." The trailing sentence died on her lips, and I could tell she was trying to weigh out what was and wasn't important to tell me. I couldn't help but notice her head was turned toward my car, and though the black faced sunglasses didn't give any kind of insight as to where her eyes went, I was sure she was watching my protege, Cat.

"I was able to keep them from coming down on you and yours for all that's happened by using the last of my clout to advocate for your placement here, in a capacity as agent. I bet my career on it actually."

That got my attention, and my dumbfoundedness gave her the opportunity to elaborate.

"Nobody wanted to be my apprentice anyway, not after Julian, so don't flatter yourself." That correction was to soften some of the exposure she felt, but I knew the poignancy of what she said hadn't been understated. I could just tell. "If you do not pass the certification test in a year's time they will remove my status as a Commander, and they will revisit all the investigations they just closed here without my moderation."

The hot dog vendor tried his best to help me save face, signaling soundlessly for me to wipe my face. Eventually Helena abandoned the solemn tone of the conversation and snatched a wad of napkins herself to wipe the offending smear off the side of my mouth. The break in seriousness was needed, and as much as the much more polished Artificer tried to fight it, after an exacerbated shake of her head she even began to laugh a little.

"Well," I shove the wrapped dog into a bag. "I wouldn't be one to look a gift horse in the mouth, and as we both know, I need all the help I can get, so actually this sounds great." I watched a trickle of relief take some of the tension out of her shoulders, so I try to temper expectations without taking momentum. "Of course, playing Barney Fife doesn't really seem like my cup of tea, but if this is what we've got to do to keep the wheels turning... alrighty-then."

I gaze off a little, shrugging before tossing the last bite down the hatch and offering her the third hotdog we'd ordered.

"I got you two, I figured Grove was with you."

"He's filing the insurance claim for his truck."

Helena smiled and then sighed, as if debating whether or not there was anything else to speak about.

"We'll make it work. You want to come by to say hi?"

"I'll bring dinner for the three of us before the first lesson." A sly rejoinder shifted her studious look at the car and Cat and back to me. "If you're going to be training her against my explicit orders and request, as well as Iandor's, I might as well lean into it."

The cane-rasped twice on the asphalt, stopping me from stepping away before my own parting comment.

"Yeah," I laugh, scooping up the hot dog she'd ordered for Grove, and hustling over to a nearby homeless woman. Kneeling over to ask after her if she'd like some lunch, she gladly accepted. "I guess that makes her kind of your Grand-pupil, right?"

"Watch it." The Silver-fox' eyes flashed, a touch of mirth swimming at that remark. "Tuesday, six o'clock."

"Full Circle?" I yell, stepping backward on the crosswalk and walking over to my car across the street.

"Perfect. See you then." I launch a thumbs up skyward and hold it there as I turn around eyes straight ahead.

I felt bad since I probably had more than a little part in destroying Groves' truck, so I'd pitched in to get us a newer sedan that made tooling around town a little more tolerable—at least for me anyway. I wasn't surprised to see that Cat was using one of her first crafted items to eavesdrop on us. She pulled a flat, oval piece from her ear and removed the top of the cup in the door. After analyzing a few of the Styrofoam cup sketches I left on my table, she'd been able to make one of those travel cups into an interesting listening device enchantment that she'd used to tune in on more than a few conversations that weren't hers to hear.

The impressive part wasn't the ingenuity or even the magical engineering, it was that she'd been able to duplicate the magic effectively in just one try, and the only point of reference she'd had for the thing was a few loose sketches with fragmented summations and explanations. Cat was a Wanderer, which meant she had a ton of pure power that was hard to quantify, and even more than that, she was a natural of the highest order.

"She's going to teach you?" There was a raw, unbridled openness to her searching glance that bounced between me and the departing Iandor Agent.

"Seems like it."

"And she's good?" It was a clinical inquisitiveness, and while some might be a little uneasy around such a thing, I'd told Cat that not only could she trust me with her voracious curiosity, I would teach her how to balance that drive and interest with everything else life had to offer—to the best of my ability anyway.

"Best I've ever seen." It was an easy follow-up, and the kind the growth-obsessed wonderling would approve of. Plus, it had the distinct advantage of being the truth.

"Ready little Shiva?"

I ask, while simultaneously handing over the thoroughly wrapped hot dog. Luckily, her sensibility was less petite teenage female and more famished, tried-and-true street kid, so dietary restrictions weren't really her scene. With one more glance leading back to the departing Englishwoman, my newly minted apprentice silently nodded while pulling out the vendor-approved lunch and digging in.

"For any and everything," She answered expectedly, a scripted back and forth we'd started at the beginning of training.

"For any and everything." I repeatedly happily while merging into traffic.

*For More News About Lawrence Davis,
Signup For Our Newsletter:*

http://wbp.bz/newsletter

Word-of-mouth is critical to an author's long-term success. If you appreciated this book please leave a review on the Amazon sales page:

http://wbp.bz/dol

GET THE OTHER BOOKS IN THE SERIES

Janzen Robinson must confront a life he left behind when an ancient creature is summoned into the world.
http://wbp.bz/bfma

No longer torn between two worlds, Janzen Robinson dives headfirst into the magical underworld hidden in Cleveland.
http://wbp.bz/doj

More Sci-Fi and Fantasy from WildBlue Press

5-star, science fiction-techno thriller story filled with twists and turns, excitement, action, adventure and a . . . thought-provoking storyline." —Artisan Book Reviews
http://wbp.bz/happenstancea

The return of an alien craft sends the planet careening toward WWIII in this action-packed sci-fi thriller by the author of *Happenstance*.
http://wbp.bz/tribulationsa

THE JAMES BYRON HUGGINS COLLECTION

In **Dark Visions**, a legendary homicide detective forced into retirement when he lost his eyesight in the line of duty, is compelled to find whomever or whatever killed his grandson

In **The Reckoning**, the murder of his mentor and the theft of an ancient manuscript entices a deadly special ops warrior out of solitude.

In **Cain**, legendary CIA hitman is given a second chance at revenge when a top-secret project code-named Genocide One brings him back to life—more dangerous than ever.

In **Leviathan**, an illegal experiment turned a once-innocent creature into a terrorizing biblical Leviathan, and scientists must hold the line and keep it underground or risk total annihilation.

In **Hunter**, the American military's greatest tracker must locate and hunt a savage beast loose in the artic circle.

In **Crux**, a machine designed to explore the galaxy opens a gateway to an evil universe, and a team must battle to destroy the deadly creatures unleashed.

Get them all at http://JBHugginsBooks

www.ingramcontent.com/pod-product-compliance
Lightning Source LLC
LaVergne TN
LVHW012038070526
838202LV00056B/5529